JUST JOHNSON

The London Delivery

Timothy Schmand

Jitney Books

#MADEINDADE #MIAMISOMETIMES!?

For M, B & J

CHAPTER 1

Miami, 1995

Al told Johnson not to worry about the hotel room. She'd get that covered as a business expense. Their food and entertainment, too, were on her. All he had to pay for was his flight to London and his bar bill. She laughed after she said "bar bill."

Johnson closed *The Miami Herald's* color comics and sat up on the couch. Sunday, just after 11 a.m. He wore a red polo shirt and the blue-green Bermuda shorts Al called the most embarrassing piece of clothing she'd ever seen. The house smelled of coffee and toasted bagels. Sports talk radio droned in the background, stewing Dolphins fans for a one o'clock game against the Patriots. "What's so funny?" he asked.

Al stood barefoot at the end of the couch, dressed in maroon sweatpants and a gray Brown University t-shirt. She shook her head and covered her mouth with her left hand.

Sometimes when Al covered her mouth like that, Johnson wanted to race into the bedroom and fuck. Sometimes, it just pissed him off. That time he got pissed. "Are you saying I drink too much?"

"No," she said, and giggled.

"Then why don't you tell me what's so damn funny?"

"I just realized that what you'll pay and what I'll pay could be about the same."

"And that's funny?"

"To me it is," she said.

Johnson shook his head. Al was strange that way. She found

things Johnson said or did funny -- things that didn't seem funny even when he thought about them afterwards. Maybe humorous, but not funny. Not that funny. Not doubled over on the couch, snorting through your nose funny. He didn't care what they'd smoked. The shit just wasn't that funny.

"You know," he told her, "someday you're going to laugh at me at the wrong time and you're going to find your ass and all your shit on the back of a Gomez Moving Truck, heading to Miami Fucking Beach, or Kendall..."

"Or goddamn North Miami Beach," Al chimed in, speaking his own words back to him.

"You think I'm kidding?"

Al shook her head and covered her mouth with her left hand.

"Hey," Johnson said, "you want to fuck or what?"

"How much?" Johnson asked, lying on his back naked, long-ing for a smoke and wishing he hadn't made such a big deal about quitting. He'd lost a good friend when he quit smoking. A cigarette after sex completed the act. Smoke rings popping to-ward the ceiling, the French inhale curling up his nostrils post-poned his return to the real world. Johnson never drank alone as long as a cigarette smoldered in the ashtray beside him. They accompanied him on long distance drives and to ringing phones in the middle of the night. Cigarettes stood by him on rainy days when Johnson believed all he had left was a cup of coffee, a steamy window and a bucket of self-pity.

Al stirred beside him, rolled out of bed and stood naked be-fore the full-length mirror on the back of their bedroom door. She licked a finger and smoothed an eyebrow. "How much what?"

Johnson looked up from her ass. Their eyes met in the mirror. "How much to fly to London? And give me an estimate on my bar bill."

She turned and faced Johnson. Al stood five foot four and had a thin, leggy body. Her breasts were asymmetrical, the left more rounded than the right. That fascinated Johnson. When he commented on it, Al told him that he'd read too much *Play-boy*, "Perfectly round orbs are an adolescent dream." She wore her hair shoulder length and changed its color monthly. Johnson had seen it wheat straw yellow, cherry soda red and dark chocolate brown. Al claimed she dyed it to match her moods. That day it was light brown, streaked to blonde. The darker triangle in her crotch exposed her true hair color -- a lackluster brown. Johnson's eyes lit on the small scar to the right of Al's navel. She'd told him she got it in a fall from monkey bars when she was seven. There was a broken Coke bottle involved and not as much blood as you'd think. "It's my only flaw," she told him, laughing. The scar was frown shaped and cherry-colored; it felt like a piece of hard candy under Johnson's tongue.

"About $500 for the airfare," she said, "and another five for your amusements."

"A thousand dollars!"

"We're not talking about a trip to Cleveland. There's an ocean of water between Miami, Florida and London, England."

Jesus, a thousand? "It's not the distance." A thousand!

"Johnson, the air fare is five hundred dollars. I'm just guessing on your bar bill."

"The bar bill is fine," he said. "That's to be expected, but the plane fare. Jesus."

Al closed her eyes. Her chest heaved -- breasts jiggled. She laughed, left hand raised covering her mouth.

See, he thought, what's so damn funny?

CHAPTER 2

The next morning, as Al dressed for work, Johnson lay in bed planning.

One thousand dollars. One grand. Ten large. One long.

Johnson knew plenty of ways to get his hands on a thousand dollars in the three weeks before Al's trip to London. He could get a gun and go into business. Tourists. Jesus, Brazilian tourists! Up here buying twos and threes of everything to take back home. Man, they had money. You get a Brazilian tourist in downtown Miami, stick a gun in his ear and what do you get? Six -- seven long. You could take a real trip to London on something like that. Or convenience stores. Three, maybe four, convenience stores and he'd have it.

Johnson imagined himself pulling the stocking mask over his head as he burst through the front door of a QuickDixie Mart on LeJeune. Pistol pointed toward the ceiling, he'd pump two rounds into the acoustic tile overhead just to get the clerk's attention. A Black kid with two gold teeth and Gerry written on his name tag cries, "Don't shoot," raises his hands and ducks behind the counter. "Don't worry," Johnson says. Gerry reappears, smiling, as he levels a sawed off shot gun.

"Hey, this ain't about that," Johnson tries to tell him. "I just want the..." The gun's muzzle flashes once, twice. Johnson is lifted from his feet and hurled back through the plate glass window. He hears and sees his own death. The bullets. The blood.

"Oh, god," Johnson moaned. "I don't want to die."

"You say something?" Al asked, coming into the bedroom dressed in a blue business suit, sipping a cup of coffee.

"No," he said.

"Well, what do you think? Are you going to London?"

"I'm working on it."

"Yeah, I can see that."

"Listen, I'm not like you," he said. "I got to think through the stuff I do."

She nodded. Sipped her coffee. "Good luck."

"Thanks," he said.

"Tell the Fat Man hello for me," she said, her voice needling.

"Shut up," Johnson said. "You don't even know him."

"Right," Al said.

"You always think you're right."

"Only when I am," she said.

"You're going to be late," he said.

"Tell the Fat Man hello."

"Fuck you," he said.

"Can't. I'll be late."

There were inevitables in Johnson's life. There was never just one drink. He could quit smoking as long as he didn't really want another cigarette. And when he needed money there was only one thing to do. It didn't matter how many different ways he thought to get it: the cheap hustle, the rich scam, robbery, burglary, kidnapping, extortion or even, god forbid, working. When Johnson needed money, he called the Fat Man. When the Fat Man needed something done, he called Johnson.

In his circle of associates, Johnson was known as the Fat Man's boy. When the man wanted to go out, he called Johnson to drive him. If a respected business associate died and the Fat Man couldn't attend the services, Johnson put on a suit bought for him by the Fat Man and extended the Fat Man's condolences to the family. If a politician had a fund raiser, the Fat Man sent Johnson and an envelope. If something needed to be whispered in a guy's ear -- a warning, a piece of advice, a wish for good luck -- it was Johnson who took the man's hand and leaned in close enough to see the blackheads on the back of his neck.

Johnson had connected with the Fat Man twelve years earlier through a bartender at the Ocean Wreck. The Wreck was Johnson's regular joint. In the bottom of the Shirley Hotel, on Atlantic and Fourth in Miami Beach, the Ocean Wreck was built in 1949 to resemble a tramp freighter destroyed in a big whimsical hurricane. The club opened during the revolving bar craze in America and the designer installed a hydraulic system that rocked the bar back and forth as if at sea. Brilliant -- except customers got seasick and found it difficult to drink and vomit at the same time. By the time Johnson washed up at the Wreck, all that remained from the club's past glories were booths shaped like shattered lifeboats, dusty cargo nets on the walls, and the bar itself, shaped like a freighter. The hydraulic system had blown a hose in 1967 and the freighter listed badly to port. Drinks, propelled by gravity, regularly slid off the bar.

"I know a guy," the Wreck's daytime bartender, Jose 'Pepe' Renaldo, told Johnson, "who's looking for a guy like you."

Johnson shook a cigarette from his pack and lit it. "Really," he said.

At the time, 1983, Johnson drove trucks from a Miami warehouse to a parking lot just south of Atlanta. He'd leave the keys in the ignition, take a cab to the airport, and fly back to Miami. He liked to drive, and the job paid better money than Johnson had ever hoped to make. But a couple weeks earlier, the feds had stopped one of the other drivers on I-75. The back of the truck was full of cocaine. The driver, a guy Johnson sort of knew, disappeared while out on bail. Johnson knew two things: the driver's body would never be found, and he needed another job.

"What kind of work?" he asked.

"I don't know," Pepe said. "But he's looking for a guy like you."

"What the fuck does that mean?"

"It means you should call him. He's offered five large to anybody who can deliver the guy he's looking for."

"Large?"

Pepe nodded. "And he's good for it." Pepe reached into his shirt pocket and snapped a business card across the bar.

Johnson looked at the card. It read *'Stephen Teitelbaum,*

Friend.' There was a telephone number beneath the man's name. Johnson laughed. "That's pretty funny, Pep. You had me going."

"It's not a joke."

"Right."

"Johnson, the guy's offering five hundred dollars to whoever finds him the right guy. You could be him." Pepe tapped the card. "Do you know who this guy is?"

"A friend," Johnson said. He laughed at his own joke.

"You may be the dumbest fucking Anglo I know. Why do I tell you shit?"

"Because I'm the only person dumb enough to listen?"

"Fuck you, asshole. Here's the deal, okay? When Teitelbaum was just a kid. He's going to school up in the Bronx. High School, mind you. He's got an uncle on the Beach. One of the old mamzers from Lansky's crowd. They're always looking for smart guys to bring into the business, so the old mamzer says, 'You want to see smart? My sister's nephew, Stevie. There's smart.' They bring the kid down. Introduce him around and he's smart. Smart the way you don't know smart. But he doesn't want the business. Says he wants an education. The mamzers don't care. They like the kid. They treat him like a grandson. So he goes to the University of Miami, and gets kicked out."

"I'm impressed," Johnson said. "Boy, getting kicked out of U.M. Did he play football, too?"

Pepe waved his hands. "Wait, will you... He fixed an election, sold copies of exams, ran a sports book. They couldn't prove anything, but they say he got the football team to shave some points. The college president himself, personally, asked Stevie to leave the school. And you know what he said?"

Johnson shook his head. "Can't imagine."

Pepe lit a cigarette. "This is class. The kid says, 'I like it here, but I don't want to be any place I'm not wanted.' That's class, Johnson. He's still a big supporter of the school. Gives them money all the time. They say he can do things with numbers...things I don't understand. The guy's large. He's connected. Wired. He's somebody you want as a friend."

7

"Yeah, he seems to know it, too."

"I'll even give you the quarter. Just call and remember to tell him who sent you."

"I'll do that," Johnson said, and held out his hand.

"What's that for?"

"The quarter. You just said you'd give me the quarter. I'm not spending my money for your jokes."

"Man, you are absolutely the dumbest Anglo."

"Yeah, right and you're the smartest fucking Cuban I ever met. You want me to call, give me the quarter."

Pepe opened the cash register and flipped a quarter to Johnson. Johnson missed it and it rolled under a bar stool. "Jesus Christ," Johnson said, as he bent after the coin.

He dropped it into the pay phone beside the men's room door and dialed the number. After the second ring, a high-pitched, screechy voice asked, "Need a friend?"

"I need a job," Johnson said.

"A job?" the voice asked.

"Yeah," Johnson said. "A guy named Pepe Renaldo said you were looking for somebody. He said I should call."

"I see," the voice said. "Do you have a name?"

"Johnson."

"Johnson," the man repeated. "Is that all?"

There was more, but Johnson wasn't going to tell this guy. "Just Johnson," he said.

"Mm hmm. Well, Just Johnson, can you be to Star Island in twenty minutes?"

Star Island? Shit, Johnson thought. Guard gates. Mansions. Shit. "Yeah," he said. "Yeah. I'm on South Beach, I can be there...I can be there in ten minutes."

"No. Twenty minutes. Tell the guard you're a friend of Steve Teitelbaum. Past the gate, turn right. My house is the fifth one down on the right. Do you understand?"

"Yeah. I'm a friend of Steve Teitelbaum. Turn right at the gate. Fifth house on the right."

"That's good, my friend. Twenty minutes." The man hung up

the phone.

Twenty minutes later Johnson's black 1982 Ford Crown Victoria sat, engine cooling, on the cobblestone driveway of a gold-colored mansion. Johnson stood beneath the house's Moorish arch studying a massive wooden door. An ornate brass doorknob marked its center. Johnson tucked his t-shirt into his jeans, scuffed his black loafers against the back of his calves and wished he'd worn socks. That morning he hadn't thought he was going for a job interview. That morning he hadn't thought he was going to be on Star Island. He expected to spend the day with Pep, drinking beer and scaring tourists. Johnson took a breath, pushed his fingers through his hair and pressed the doorbell. He waited. After a moment, he pressed it again, then gently rapped the door with his knuckles. Nothing. He looked for signs of life and didn't see any around. Fucking Pepe had gotten him. It's a joke, he thought. Fucking Pepe. He was going to kill that motherfucker. Fucker. He punched the door with his fist.

"It's open," a voice cried.

Johnson straightened up and stared at the door. Okay, he thought, here we go.

He turned the knob and pushed the door open. A smell drifted from the house -- fried food and something. Fried food and what the hell was that smell? Sweat? Something sweet? Johnson stepped through a small entryway into a grand reception room. Bed sheets, yellowed by the sun, draped the windows. A staircase directly in front of him curved up toward a second floor, its wooden treads covered by a fine layer of dust. The room to his left stood empty. The sunlight filtered through the bed sheets cast the room in a sickly yellow light. Dust particles drifted in the air. Jesus, Johnson thought, what the fuck is this?

"Here," shouted the screechy voice from the phone. "Here. I'm in here."

Johnson pushed the door closed behind him. "It's Johnson," he said, his voice echoing in the empty rooms.

"Yes, I know. I'm expecting you. What are you doing standing around in the hall? Come in here. I'm in here."

Johnson moved toward the sound of the voice. To his right, through an arch, he spied a huge lump of a man sitting on the edge of a hospital bed. He had a head the size of a basketball, short-cropped hair and bug eyeglasses. He wore a light blue jump suit, belted at the waist. Beside him, on a bedside table, Krispy Kreme donut boxes climbed toward the ceiling. The man beckoned Johnson toward him with his right hand, then reached into a box with his left, lifted out a glazed cruller and dropped the entire donut into his mouth.

Johnson walked slowly toward the man. An oversized green recliner stood next to the bed. A brown cloth couch sat beside the recliner. Rows of televisions on gray metal warehouse shelving covered the wall opposite the furniture. Johnson stopped counting the televisions at twenty and there had to be twice that number. The sets were of different makes, models, sizes, and colors. Each presented a different version of the world: a news show, a sitcom, game shows, talking heads, a car commercial, a basketball game, a black and white newsreel, an old movie in Technicolor. Johnson saw a woman with a man's cock in her mouth. The man grimaced. The woman pulled back and stroked the cock. Sperm squirted onto her face.

"What are you watching? Quickly. Quickly," the man screeched.

"The sex," Johnson said.

"That's good. You're honest."

Johnson looked at the man. "What?"

He waved his hands. "You haven't lied to me yet, so you're honest."

Johnson laughed at the idea.

"Have a donut, sit on the couch and tell me about yourself, Johnson. It is Johnson, isn't it?"

"Yes sir," he said, "Just Johnson." Johnson crossed the room and as he approached Stephen Teitelbaum, Friend, he realized the smell was coming from this very fat man. A sweet cloying aroma, it smelled like flowered soap and mildew. Johnson lifted a cruller from the open Krispy Kreme box between two fingers.

It was stale and dry. "Thank you," he said.

The man waved. "Tell me."

Johnson sat down on the couch and told Stephen Teitelbaum he was thirty. He had been driving trucks for some people, but there wasn't really a future in that. And, because he was getting older, he needed something more stable. Something with a future. Johnson said he was reliable. Trustworthy. He knew how to do jobs. And Pepe Renaldo, the bartender at the Ocean Wreck, had told him to call.

"I see," the man said. "So you drove trucks. Good, I need a driver. Have you ever been arrested?"

"Nope."

"Nope?"

"Nope. Not much to say. Never been inside."

"Inside? You say that like you might have been."

"Friends," Johnson said. "People I've worked with. They call it that."

The man nodded. "So, who do you work for?"

"A guy named Harvey."

"Harvey? You drive trucks for a guy named Harvey?"

"Yeah."

"How much does Harvey pay?"

Johnson collected $1,000 plus expenses for every trip. Sometimes he did two trips in a week. "He pays pretty good."

Stephen Teitelbaum nodded. "What's in the trucks?"

"I wouldn't know."

The man laughed. "You probably wouldn't."

Johnson smiled. They had an agreement.

"Johnson, my friend, why should I hire you?"

"I'm the only one here."

"Very good," Stephen Teitelbaum said. He took another cruller from the box, tilted his head back and dropped it into his mouth. He ground the donut between his teeth as he spoke. "Now, Johnson, let me demonstrate the value of friends." Teitelbaum smiled. "My friends tell me that your name is Marion Johnson. Your mother named you after her favorite actor, Marion Morrison, known to the public as Mr. John Wayne. You hate the name Marion Johnson, hence 'Just Johnson.' She lives in Hollywood, Florida on Van Buren. You see her twice a month. You live alone at the Betsy Ross Hotel, and you're the only resident with a phone in his room. Your friend Harvey is Harvey Singer. He works for an organization based in Cali, Colombia. He paid you a thousand dollars a trip, plus expenses. I'm afraid Harvey is being followed by the government. His friends in Cali know this and don't like their people talking to the *Federales*. I believe he will disappear soon, and there's nothing you nor I can do about that. If you decide to work for me and treat me as a friend, you will not have to worry about the vagaries of life in Miami. I am offering you my friendship and a job. Are you interested?"

"Jesus," Johnson said. "How did you find that out? In twenty minutes?"

"Friends," the Fat Man said. "Where would we be without them?"

CHAPTER 3

After Al left for work, Johnson grabbed *The Miami Herald* and a cup of coffee and hung out on his back porch for two hours until he knew the Fat Man was up and taking business calls. The line was busy the first time he tried the number. The second time, the Fat Man answered. "Need a friend?" he chirped.

"It's Johnson," Johnson said into the receiver, listening to the chewing on the other end of the line. During the time he'd worked for the Fat Man he'd seen him eat anything within reach. He picked his nose and ate it, his skin, his hair. He rolled paper and cloth into tiny balls and tossed them in his mouth. Johnson had seen him chew a shoelace like licorice, consume the entire front page of the Sunday New York Times, and anything left on a plate, his or someone else's -- a soggy piece of bread crust, the stem from a pickle, a sliver of gristle.

"Johnson," the Fat Man squealed. "How's my friend, Johnson?"

"Good, sir, " Johnson said. "I was wondering if you have any time for me today? I have a problem I'd like to talk over with you."

"Johnson, Johnson. Have I ever not had time for you? If ever a day should exist where I don't have time for a man who makes my life as good as you, I should die on that day rather than take another breath."

"What time, sir?"

"Anytime Johnson, anytime. But between two forty-five and three o'clock this afternoon would be the best time for you to get my uninterrupted attention."

"Two forty-five, sir?"

"Precisely."

Different concepts of time existed throughout Miami -- Cuban Time, Chicago Time, Israeli Time, Jamaican Time, New York Time, Trini Time, Haitian Time, Nica Time -- where the length of the minute expanded and contracted with the barometric pressure. But the Fat Man only acknowledged Eastern Standard Time. You could be late for your mother's funeral, you could be late for your own, your girlfriend's period could be late, but you couldn't be late to see the Fat Man.

At two-forty, Johnson stopped his car beside the guard house at the entrance to Star Island. It had rained off and on that day. The air conditioner on Johnson's 13-year-old Crown Victoria had broken two weeks earlier. He meant to get it fixed, but something about taking a thousand dollar hit on a car with over 120,000 miles just didn't seem right. Air conditioning should be free in south Florida, he thought. You couldn't live without it. Fuckers. Thousand bucks. That wasn't right.

During the rainstorm, he'd ridden with the windows closed for as long as possible. But the windshields, front and back, misted over. A gray fog hung in the car. He wound down his window and rode with his head out in the rain. Puddle splash from trucks and cars drenched his left shoulder. Rain soaked his face and dripped down the front of his shirt. The two dozen donuts in the Krispy Kreme boxes on the seat beside him stayed dry.

Johnson looked up at the guard, a Black guy with short-cropped hair and, even in the rain, oversized mirrored sunglasses. Johnson saw himself in their reflection and was reminded of a wet dog.

The guard smiled. "Sir, may I help you?"

"You're new," Johnson said. "I've never seen you before."

"That makes two of us, sir. I've never seen you before either."

The guy said 'eye-ther' for 'ee-ther'. Johnson liked that. He said "eyether" under his breath, and wondered if he'd remember to say it that way next time with Al. "I work for the man who lives at 2472 Star Isle Drive. Stephen Teitelbaum. Maybe you know him? He's expecting me in about five minutes, and he doesn't like it when I'm late."

"I see," the guard, said. "Do you have any proof, identification- ...something?"

"No," Johnson said. The digits on the car's radio flipped to 2:42. "All I've got is me and two boxes of donuts for Mr. Teitel- baum."

The guard nodded and stood a little taller. "I can't let you in, sir."

"How long you been here?"

"First day."

"Okay, so they didn't tell you. But you should know, anyone who comes to this gate and says he's a friend of Stephen Teitel- baum you let in. Period. You can call him now, and I know you have to, but you'd be better off just letting me pass."

The guard licked his lips. "Standard operating procedures."

"Yeah, I know," Johnson said.

The guard stepped back into his house, flipped through a notebook, and picked up the phone. He dialed a number, then spoke into the receiver. The guard jerked the phone from his ear. He moved his mouth as if trying to speak, but all he did was nod. Johnson wished the man wasn't wearing sunglasses. He wanted to see how bad the Fat Man had scared him.

The guard turned back to Johnson. The traffic arm rose in the air.

Johnson shrugged.

As Johnson pulled up before the Fat Man's house four men in business suits, opening umbrellas, stepped off the porch and hustled through the rain to two cars parked side-by-side in the driveway. Johnson recognized the Mayor of Miami, a City Commissioner and their two aides. They peered quizzically at Johnson over the roofs of their cars. He knew what they were wondering. Was the driver of that Crown Vic stopped at the curb a reporter with *The Herald*? A federal agent? *The Herald* called the Fat Man "a King Maker," and "...a back-room mastermind."

Federal grand jury reports linked him to numerous organized crime operations and called him "the inheritor of a criminal enterprise dating back to the earliest days of Prohibition."

Johnson parked on the street in front of the house and waved as he climbed out of his car. "Mr. Mayor," he shouted. "Commissioner."

"Johnson," they both cried and waved back.

Their car alarms beeped. Doors opened and slammed shut. Engines fired and they were gone.

Johnson reached back into his car, grabbed the boxes of donuts, and jogged through the rain to the Fat Man's front door. He banged on the door and tried to shake the water out of his hair.

"Johnson, what a surprise," the Fat Man shrieked before he'd pulled the door open. "My good friend, Johnson. So nice to see you. Come in. Come in. Why, you're all wet." The Fat Man shook his head. "Johnson, that's the way you'll take cold. Even in this warm climate, hypothermia is not an impossibility. The average human body temperature is 98 degrees, but should it fall seven to ten degrees, you black out. That is entirely possible. There have been studies. But what am I saying? Come in Johnson, come in. Here, what's this you're carrying? Donuts! Donuts! Are these for me? Oh, Johnson. Come in. Come in."

Johnson stepped into the foyer and handed the donuts to the Fat Man. "I know you like them, sir," Johnson said.

"You are a rare commodity, Johnson," The Fat Man said leading him into the living room and the wall of televisions. "A true friend. Thank you."

Johnson stared at the televisions as he waited for the Fat Man to take his chair. In the years since Johnson first visited the house, the Fat Man had made a major investment in his home entertainment system. Though yellowed sheets still hung over the windows and layers of dust covered the grand staircase, the Fat Man had spent tens of thousands to purchase a satellite system and a bank of televisions that completely covered one wall. Some days all of the sixty-three sets would be tuned to the same station, though the sound would be off. On others, each set would be tuned to a different station. The entire operation worked off a complicated remote-control system that only the Fat Man understood. He'd once told Johnson he had the world at his fingertips.

That afternoon, as Johnson dripped rain water onto the Fat Man's floor, the TVs presented a world where Elmer Fudd shot at Bugs Bunny, a soap opera man begged a soap opera woman not to leave him, CNN showed clips of floods in Oklahoma, a Japanese news program carried footage of a hula hoop contest, an African talk show host interviewed a bush doctor, and a blonde and a brunette French kissed in the middle of the afternoon.

The Fat Man settled into his recliner and propped the boxes of donuts onto his stomach. "Sit, Johnson, sit," he said.

Johnson dropped onto the couch.

"What are you watching?" The Fat Man asked.

"The women kissing," Johnson said, pointing.

"That, my friend Johnson, is one of the many things I like about you. Honestly predictable. Rare qualities today. I believe the last time you were here, you also watched some pornographic display."

Johnson didn't know if that was a compliment or not. He said, "Thank you," because that's what he always told the Fat Man. "And you, sir, what are you watching?"

The Fat Man laughed, shrieking like a woman. "Johnson, Johnson, only you would be brave or stupid enough to ask me such a question." The lounger trembled under the Fat Man's weight as he laughed again. "Would you like a donut?" he asked peeling open the first box's lid.

Johnson stood up, took a glazed cruller from the box, and sat back down.

"I assume there is a purpose to this visit, other than the warm friendship and high personal regard we have for each other," the Fat Man said. He slid a whole donut into his mouth.

"Yes sir," Johnson said, swallowing his second bite of donut. "There is."

The Fat Man held another donut above his mouth. "That being?"

"My girlfriend wants me to go to London with her."

The Fat Man spoke through the donut in his mouth. "London. A wonderful city, you should enjoy the visit. I've long admired British Royalty. I know they've taken quite a fall these last few years, but you've got to admire the organization. Did you know the Queen gets a piece of all the action going on over there? Amazing. You buy gas; she gets a piece. You buy a drink; she gets a piece. You take a leak; she gets a piece. Now, that's organization. That's smart. I can't think of an organization, without the heaviest muscle, that could pull that off. And what can she threaten with? The Cold Spring Guards? She's got no muscle, but she's got them believing some cockamamie story about divine right. Amazing." The Fat Man eased another donut into his mouth.

"Well," Johnson said. "I need to get a thousand dollars together for the trip and I was wondering... "

The Fat Man shrieked, "You're not here for a loan."

The shriek scared Johnson. He leapt up. "No. No, sir. I would never jeopardize our friendship by asking you to loan me money."

"That's good, Johnson," the Fat Man said. "If I loaned you money, you'd owe it to me. You are not the type of man I want in my debt. If you couldn't pay, god forbid, you have nothing of value -- not even your life. I don't know what I could hold as collateral." Another donut dropped into the maw.

Johnson shifted his weight from foot to foot. "I would never ask you for a loan, sir, but I know you are well known and liked throughout the world. That you have friends outside the Beach, outside the country, worldwide. I was wondering if there was any little bit of business I might do for you in London. Visit old friends, collect debts, deliver an important package. I don't know, sir. I could be helpful."

"Helpful for a thousand dollars?"

"That's the base price, sir. More would be better."

"The greater the value, the higher the risk," the Fat Man said, peering over his glasses, holding Johnson in his gaze.

"I wouldn't need much more than eleven hundred."

The Fat Man said, "I'll give it some thought."

"Thank you, sir." Johnson began easing himself back onto the couch.

The Fat Man dropped another donut into his mouth. "I wish you could stay longer," he said. "But I'm sure you have places to go."

"Thank you for your time, sir," Johnson said, reversing up to stand.

"Johnson, if a time should ever come when a man doesn't have time for his friends..."

"Don't get up, sir. I can find my own way out."

Johnson recognized a dust-off when he received one. The Fat Man had as much as told him he had no use for his services, at least not worth a thousand dollars.

Shit, fuck, shit, he thought, turning the key on the Crown Vic. His clothes were wet. The seat was wet. His whole fucking life was wet. He sucked up to that fat piece of shit. He bought donuts. He called the man 'sir'. If he was smart, which he knew he wasn't, it could be him sitting all day in front of those god-damn televisions. He turned off the Star Island causeway and onto the MacArthur. It could be him that people called 'sir.'

But no. He had to be stupid. He had to be dumb. Maybe he could get the money from his mother. A thousand dollars? She probably had it. Aw, hell, she definitely had it. But the asking? The asking really sucked. What could he do? What could he do? He could print up Cuban cigar labels, buy some cheap cigars and sell them to the hotels along Ocean Drive. He could buy a lottery ticket. He could sell his car. Sell the house, take a second mort-gage, or he could tell Al that he just couldn't go to England with her. That's the only thing he saw to do. Just tell her.

"Al," he'd say when she got in from work. "I can't go. Okay? I don't have the money, and I can't figure out how to get it." Maybe, if he said it pitifully enough, she'd offer to pay for him.

He began working on looking low.

Johnson lived by the Method. He never studied with Lee Strasberg nor heard the name Constantin Stanislavski but when he had to sell an idea or seek pity from an acquaintance, he went deep within himself to evoke the correct emotion. Johnson knew to look low, he had to be low. By the time he pulled up in front of his house, Johnson felt the flu coming on. Feeling low worked great. He felt like shit. When he got into the house and saw himself in the mirror, he got concerned. He looked even worse than he felt. He was reaching for a thermometer when the phone rang.

"Yeah," Johnson sighed into the receiver.

"Johnson," the Fat Man squealed. "Johnson, my good friend, I found something that needs doing. It's worth nine hundred dollars to me."

Johnson, deep into his Method, knew he was going to die soon. It no longer mattered what the Fat Man thought. "The price went up to two thousand," he said.

The Fat Man gulped for air. "You're not serious?"

"Afraid so," Johnson said. "Airline tickets and all."

"You're a thief. An absolute thief. You make a man a proposition, then you jack up the price when you think you've got him on the ropes."

"It's not that," Johnson said. "I've just discovered that I am very sick."

"Cancer?" the Fat Man shrieked.

"It really doesn't matter what it is," Johnson said. Speaking had become such a chore. Why bother?

"You looked fine when I saw you just now."

"Yeah, well, these things get you and it's over like that..." Johnson snapped his fingers -- and realized how brief life truly was.

"You were wet when you got here. I warned you," the Fat Man said.

"Yeah, you warned me. I'm sure somebody warned Lincoln."

"What do the doctors say?" the Fat Man asked, his voice consoling.

"Doctors, what the fuck do they know?"

"Too true, Johnson. Too true."

Johnson looked around for a place to sit down. He suddenly felt very weak -- no, weary. He felt very weary. He carried not only the weight of his life, but now the weight of his death. God, God, God, he thought, capitalizing the word for the first time in years. Right after he got off the phone, he'd see a priest. Give a good confession, list it all -- god was he sorry. No, God was he sorry.

"Will you have the strength to make the trip?" the Fat Man asked.

"No one knows for sure, but I know I'm going to try. Not for me, but for my girlfriend, Al."

"Your girlfriend's name is Al?

"Yeah, well, no," Johnson stammered. "Her name's Alexandra, I just call her Al."

"You know," the Fat Man said, speaking in a low voice, "I was married once."

"What?" Johnson said, feigning surprise. Everyone knew the Fat Man had been married once. It lasted, depending on who you believed, either forty-eight or seventy-two hours. His wife was in the chorus at the Landlubber. She ran off with a jewel thief named O'Toole and died a year later of a heroin overdose. Some thought the Fat Man had her killed.

"Mmm hmm," the Fat Man said. "Ginger Margolese. A beautiful girl. A fun kid. She danced for a living. She died young."

"I'm sorry to hear that," Johnson said. "I had no idea."

"Grief is a private expression, Johnson."

"It always is."

The Fat Man sighed. "The news is bad now, but who knows, you might survive this."

"My chances aren't good," Johnson said.

"I'm sorry, my friend," the Fat Man said. "But nonetheless, you came in here and asked for one long. I'm offering you nine large. Are you interested?"

"Of course I'm interested, but the one long was before I got sick. Now we're looking at two."

"Johnson, I share your grief and wish you weren't..."

"Going to die."

"Right," the Fat Man said. "But I'm not in the insurance business. I'm in the business business. I can't go back to my people and renegotiate because the runner's ill. How would that look?"

"Sir," Johnson said, "with all due respect, you're talking to a man who has doesn't have much time left." The emotion built in Johnson's chest. "You guys with long horizons, you can plan and joke and mess around, but I don't have that kind of time. I can see the end. It's staring right at me. If you want to play hardball with a dying man, well..."

"Okay," the Fat Man said, "one long and not a penny more."

"You'd play tough with a man on death's door. Seventeen large. It's a good price and you know it."

"Twelve because you've been a good friend."

"This could be the last time I travel anywhere with my girlfriend, I'd like to show her a nice time, fifteen."

"Done," the Fat Man shrieked. "Done. Done. Done."

"Thank you, sir," Johnson said.

He settled the phone into its cradle, walked over and dropped down onto the couch. He stretched out and stared at his reflection on the screen of Al's big TV. He thought he was starting to look a little better. Actually, he was feeling much better.

Later that afternoon, he felt well enough to run out, buy a bottle of champagne, shower, and dress in an old smoking jacket. His imagination running wild, his cock hard, Johnson stood in the middle of the living room as Al walked in from work.

Al glanced at him when she came through the door. "And, what have you been doing all day?"

"Just waiting for you, baby."

"I bet. Whenever you dress like this it's to tell me something's gone wrong, or you've gone wrong or some Colombians want to kill you, or your..."

"It's nothing like that this time."

"Yeah, so what is it this time if it's nothing like that?"

"I met with the Fat Man today. He's giving me the money for the London trip." Johnson watched Al's face to see her response.

She frowned.

"Hey," Johnson said, "What's that all about?"

"The Fat Man? The Fat Man is giving you the money for the trip? Does he have you carrying somebody's head out of the country? Or will you be hustling one of his sleazy politicos around?"

"I don't know what he wants me to do. All I know is that he's going to pay me fifteen large for it."

"And that's all that matters. He's paying you, what did you say, 'fifteen large'? What the hell is that in English?"

"That is English," Johnson said.

"How much is it in dollars?"

"Fifteen hundred dollars." Johnson snapped out the words crisply as new dollar bills.

"And for fifteen large," sarcasm rich in the air, "for fifteen large," Al asked, "what does the Fat Man get from you? Murder? Extortion? Vote buying?"

"No, of course not. I don't do that stuff. Besides, you can get somebody killed for two large, why would the Fat Man go long with me? I'm not a killer."

"I'm so happy to hear that, Johnson. So what are you? For fifteen large," she smiled at him, "for fifteen large what can I get from you, Mr. Johnson?"

"Loyalty." Johnson knew what he was selling. He always wondered why people just gave it away.

"Loyalty." Al shook her head. "Are you telling me that any shmoe who comes along with fifteen large can buy your loyalty?"

"Why, you think that's too cheap?"

Al growled deep in her throat. "What if somebody wanted to buy your loyalty from me?"

Johnson's eyebrows popped up in surprise. It wasn't a question he'd considered. "Well, I'd need more than fifteen, that's for sure."

"You'd sell it?"

Johnson knew he'd screwed up, but he wasn't sure why. Everybody had a price. He knew that much. Some people's were higher, some lower, but everything and everybody, at least everybody he knew, could be bought. They were bought all the time. It might be money or sex or power, but he didn't know anyone who could not be bought.

Johnson tried to laugh. "Jesus, you should see the look on your face. You can't be kidded at all, can you?"

"Don't tell me you were kidding, Johnson. I know you better than that. You actually believe that, don't you?"

"What do you want me to say? That I don't believe people can be bought? That they're basically good? Forget it, Al."

"I see," she said.

He watched her thinking. It scared him.

"You know my friends tell me..." She stopped. "No. No," Al said, and waved a hand as if pushing something away. "I'm not doing this."

Johnson finished the thought for her. 'You know,' he imagined her friends saying, 'he's such an asshole. You could do better. He's kind of old, isn't he? What does he do for a living, anyway? Does he always drink so much? Maybe I'd like him if I just got to know him. Why do you go with him? He's a man, · after all.'

"Al," he said. "I'm sorry that we disagree about this stuff."

"Yeah, me too." she said.   She turned and walked into the bathroom, slamming the door behind her. He knew she was in the bathroom flossing. That's what she did whenever she closed the door.

Johnson stared at the closed bathroom door, then put the champagne in the refrigerator and popped open a beer.

CHAPTER 4

The following morning Johnson lay staring at the clock radio as Al prepared for work. She walked out the door without speaking to him, not even nudging him to say goodbye. Al held her anger like a stone in her fist.

Johnson rolled out of bed, showered, dressed, and called the Fat Man. The man told Johnson to be at his house at eleven-thirty.

Johnson drove over to the beach, parked the Crown Vic and walked up and down Ocean Drive wasting time before the meeting. He often went to Ocean Drive to think. Not because of the ocean, which you could barely see from the street, but because of the buildings and himself. Johnson had lived on Ocean Drive when he first moved to Miami Beach, at the Betsy Ross, north end of the street. He moved in on the tail end of the seventies, when South Beach was home to the old, the addled and the dispossessed. Rents were cheap. A Pulmanette on Ocean Drive – a closet-sized room with a bath, bed and Lilliputian kitchen appliances – $30 per week. One hundred twenty per month included a wheezing and rattling air conditioner, a black and white television in the lobby, people so old they didn't cast shadows, lunatics who forgot to take their medication, a group of transvestites, and Johnson. He worked hard back then -- cleaning up scraps at construction sites, washing dishes, bussing tables.

In 1981, a regular at the Wreck introduced him to Harvey Singer. The guy's name was Casey. He had a rich father in Rhode Island, a buck-a-day coke habit and a dark green lizard he carried around in his shirt pocket.

"See that guy in the booth over there? Name's Singer," Casey said, "needs drivers. You interested?"

Johnson had a job bussing tables at the Easy Rest retirement home south of Fifth Street on Miami Beach. Since 1980, after the Mariel boatlift, the neighborhood surrounding the home had descended into a nightmare version of cops and robbers. Johnson worked a five-day week, Wednesday through Sunday, six to six, bussing tables and mopping piss-stained floors. Someone always left their dentures on a plate. He didn't mind pushing left over corned beef, mashed potatoes and peas off plates with his bare hands, but the sight of false teeth made him gag. It took his two days off for the aroma of oil soap and piss to clear his nostrils, only to return the moment he walked back through the Easy Rest doors.

And the neighborhood. Jesus. Depending on the day he was, by turn, an innocent bystander, a witness, or a victim. He'd come around a corner on three occasions to find dead bodies cooling in the street; he'd watched a short, muscle-knotted man wearing a Dolphins t-shirt, white shorts and no shoes wave a pistol in the air and car-jack a family of Canadian tourists, leaving them weeping on the street; and, finally, two Marielitos came up and, without a word, pushed him to the ground, took all the money from his pockets, maybe seven dollars, and strolled off into the neighborhood as if Johnson was a walking talking ATM. Johnson stared after them, knowing they would kill him for seven dollars, so for the moment it felt like a win.

The green lizard eyed Johnson from Casey's pocket.

"Interested?" Johnson said. "Fuck yeah. I'm interested."

"Come on." Casey led Johnson across the bar to one of the lifeboat-shaped booths. A guy in a New York Yankees cap, a loud Hawaiian shirt and dark sunglasses looked up.

"Harvey," Casey said, "This is Johnson. Says he could use a job."

Singer dragged hard on his cigarette, sucking half down with a single draw. "Thanks, Casey," he said, through a cloud of smoke. Then to Johnson, "You drive, kid?"

"Yeah," Johnson said. "I can drive."

Singer slid a key-ring toward Johnson. "Car's out front. It's the blue Crown Vic."

"Yeah?"

"Drive to Deerfield Beach. Go to a phone near the water and beep me at this number. Wait for a call back." Singer slid a scrap of paper across the table.

"That's it?"

"I think so," Singer said.

Johnson had never been in a Crown Victoria before. When he opened the door and slid into the front seat, he felt as if the car had been made for him. The windshields, back and front, were open and wide. The seats as comfortable as a recliner. The steering wheel at the perfect height. It didn't bother him that the car reeked of cigarettes and English Leather after-shave. He stuck the key in the ignition; the engine turned easily. The radio was on, set to a pop music station. Johnson powered down the windows and adjusted the rear view. He dropped it into drive. Tires squealed as he pulled from the curb.

Crossing the Julia Tuttle Causeway, at the top of the bridge's western span, it occurred to Johnson that he should be a driver. A driver. That's what he could do. He liked to drive. He was good at it. It's what I should do, he thought. He knew there was more to being a driver than just driving. You had to take responsibility for your car. You had to accept it as a tool, a tool that allowed you to do your job. That's when he checked the gauges and discovered the gas tank on empty.

Singer didn't tell him anything about gas or about money. He could turn around, go back to the Wreck. Or he could put some gas in. He had five bucks in his pocket, but five bucks wouldn't get him to Deerfield. Johnson tried to act like he had no other money. He tried to forget about the ten-dollar bill, tucked under the Dr. Scholl's in-sole deodorizer in his left shoe. His emergency ten. If he met a babe in a bar and was short the necessary funding to get her to go home with him. If someone approached him with a sure thing that a ten would get him a piece of. If there was a tiny joint of Cambodian black dope, which he'd smoked once and seen Jesus. Mad money, sad money, money that freed him from his life if only for a moment.

The ten dollars was for emergencies and Johnson recognized he was in the midst of one. He hadn't been off Miami Beach in three months. Three months surrounded by the near dead and those he wished were. The smell of the old people drifted out of the sky like dandruff. The crazies smelled too, thorazine and mellaril sweat, the deep orange tans, the crazy wide-eyed stares. He would spend the ten so that he could drive this beautiful car to Deerfield. He could make it back. He could make it back and more. It was practically a vacation. He had the day off, a car and he was free. Away from the crazies, away from the Wreck, away from the strange circle of things his life had become. Spend the ten. Fuck it.

The Sunoco station on Biscayne Boulevard was like visiting his life. He had not pumped gas there or taken the cash or swept up around the pumps, but he could have. As he stepped out of the Crown Vic, he realized he was not that guy behind the bullet proof glass, or the other with a spray bottle wiping down the pumps, he was a man with a Crown Victoria. Johnson didn't own a car, but he pumped gas like a man who did. His plan called for five in the tank and ten in his wallet. Ten, just in case. He pumped to five, missed the dollar on the spot and ended up putting $5.03 into the tank. He took off his shoe at the cashier's window and peeled back the Dr. Scholl's. The guy behind the window looked beyond bored with the whole procedure.

Back in the car, up onto I-95 North. Wind raced through the car as Johnson cranked the radio. Life was good. Life was beautiful.

At Deerfield Beach, on A-1-A, Johnson pulled up beside a phone booth overlooking the water. The beach was quiet. A few people strolled the shoreline in the distance. Small ripples splashed against the shore. He dialed the beeper number and waited. Dialed the phone booth's number and hung up the phone. What a beautiful spot, he thought. This was not Miami

Beach. This was not humping bits of food and teeth to the trash. This was freedom. The phone rang. The shrill bell shocked Johnson. He jumped, then reached into the phone booth. "Hello," he said.

"Where are you?" Singer asked.

"Deerfield. Along A-1-A. At a phone booth."

"Good," Singer said. "Come on back."

"Back where?"

"Where you left me."

"Sure," Johnson said. "Be right there."

He drove back wondering how a man could give him car keys just like that and expect him to come back. What if he'd just driven off? Run away? Sold it? Junked it? Cracked it up? Didn't know how to drive?

There were answers to those questions. Maybe Johnson just looked like a guy who wouldn't steal a car. Maybe somebody had vouched for him. Maybe the deal was most men wouldn't do anything like that. Maybe there had been an implicit threat in the conversation between him and Singer that he didn't notice. What could he say or do? He did what the man told him. Even used his own money. Was he being stupid? That question often troubled Johnson. If he was being stupid posing the question wouldn't help. It was like trying to figure out when he was too fucked up. He knew when he wasn't quite too fucked up, but by the time he was completely fucked up, he was past the point of knowing.

Driving over the causeway onto Miami Beach, Johnson had a sense of his old life beginning again. It hung in the pit of his stomach. That guy, Singer, was probably just playing him. Just messing. That was it. Goddamn. Well, the trip was fun. Someday, he'd get a car. He'd drive to that spot in Deerfield and remember what a beautiful day it had been. Maybe he could even take the bus up. No, he decided. You had to arrive in Deerfield by car. Anything else would be bullshit.

He pulled into a parking spot down the street from the Wreck, turned off the engine; had to turn it back on to power up the windows. The tank was about where it had been when he left. He wondered if Singer would reimburse him for the gas. He wasn't sure if he'd ask. Maybe. It depended.

Singer sat exactly where Johnson had left him. There were two ashtrays full of cigarette butts and one more near full on the table before him. Singer lit another cigarette.

"Here are your keys," Johnson said, sliding them across the table.

Singer drew deeply on the cigarette. Johnson imagined him sucking down the entire smoke in one drag. "Fuck, those aren't my keys," Singer said. He snatched the key ring off the table and threw it under the booth. "Car's stolen. Tell me about your trip."

"What?" Johnson said. "What did you say?"

"The car's hot. The fuck? You think I'm going to let you drive my car? The fuck do I look like?"

"What if I got stopped?" Johnson whined.

"You'd go to jail. And, know what, kid? Some cop stops you while you're working for me -- you're going to fucking jail. End of story. Still interested?"

"Shit," Johnson said. "I gotta sit down." He slid into the booth. "Jesus."

"Look, kid. There are hundreds of thousands, fuck millions, of cars on the road at any time. If you're good and lucky you'll never get stopped. You want a job, or what?"

"All I do is drive, right?"

"Yep," Singer said. "Just fucking drive."

"Okay," Johnson said.

"Tell me about your trip."

Johnson took a deep breath, "Not much to tell. I had to put gas in your...excuse me, the car."

"How much?"

Johnson didn't want to lie. "Fifteen and change."

"Did you get a receipt?"

"No." Shit, Johnson thought, I fucked up.

"Good. Never get a receipt. We pay expenses, but we know what the costs should be. No receipts. No paper trail. If you stay overnight in a motel, stay near the interstate. Pay cash. Don't party. Don't pick up women or men. Don't bring people to your room, don't associate with anybody. You're a driver. A professional. We expect you to act that way."

"How's the pay?"

Singer smiled. Smoke drifted out between his teeth. "This is the best fucking job you ever imagined."

"All I do is drive, right?"

"Right."

"When?"

"Whenever we say. You got a phone?"

"No," Johnson said. "There's one in the lobby where I live."

"Get one in your room. Get a beeper, too."

Johnson laughed. "I can't afford a phone. Or a beeper."

Singer pulled a wad of bills from his pocket. He counted out a number and handed them to Johnson. "There's a thousand dollars there. Go to the Bell Telephone office on Fifth and Drexel. Ask for Mario. Tell him I sent you. He'll get your phone installed. You can get a beeper two blocks further down Fourth Street. Get a haircut. Buy some new clothes. Jeans, cotton shirts, nothing fancy. Drivers either wear sneakers or cowboy boots -- those half-boots. Get a pair -- I don't care which, one or the other. And remember this. You got the job because you're a plain looking Anglo. No one would remember your face. No one would care. Don't do anything to mess that up."

Johnson wasn't sure how he felt about that. But it got him a job. Maybe a good job. "I won't."

"What's your name?"

"Johnson," he said.

"Johnson? What Johnson, or Johnson what?"

"Nothing, Just Johnson."

"I see, Just Johnson. Beep me when you get your phone."

"I will." Johnson sat for a moment staring at the man who'd just given him a thousand dollars, who had him drive a stolen car and who smoked with a ferocity that defied life, death, tobacco, cancer. "You'll hear from me," Johnson said.

31

"I know, kid." Singer took a drag from his cigarette and stubbed it out in the pile before him. "Oh, yeah. The people I work for get very angry when their employees make a mistake. If I screwed up by choosing you there will be consequences. And, Just Johnson, don't think this is a threat, but if you fuck me, I'll kill you."

Johnson was tempted to hand back the thousand. Nobody had ever threatened to kill him. At least nobody Johnson believed. It'd be stupid to fuck with this guy. "It'd be stupid to fuck with you," Johnson said.

"I'm glad you realize that."

"You know what I do? Like my job?"

Singer shook his head. "Like I give a fuck."

Johnson didn't care that Singer didn't give a fuck. "I'm a busboy. Twenty-six fucking years old and I'm bussing fucking tables for the nearly dead. You're offering me a chance to make some real money, and like I'm going to fuck that up."

"Hey, hey," Singer said, holding his hands up. "Like I said, I don't give a fuck. You fuck me," he leaned closer and whispered in Johnson's ear, "you fuck me and I'll kill you." He leaned away from Johnson. "I just want to be clear on that."

Johnson nodded. "We're clear."

"Good. Beep me when you get a phone."

At the Bell Telephone office, Johnson was just another mope in line, another person begging to have service restored, a break on their bill, a lonely person looking for company or a crazy demanding the phone company stop tapping their private thoughts, until he asked for Mario. The clerk looked up at him for the first time.

"And you are?" the woman asked.

"Johnson," he said, "A guy named Singer sent me."

"One moment." The woman left the window and returned with an older Latin man. "Yes?" he said. His accent made the word, "Jes?"

"Harvey Singer said I should see you about a phone."

The man nodded, his eyes blinking shut. "Where do you live?"

"The Betsy Ross, Fifteenth and Ocean."

"Room number?"

"Three-two-three."

"Two hundred dollars."

"What?"

"Give me two hundred dollars. Go home and wait. The installer will be there in one hour."

"Two hundred dollars? That's a lot of money."

"Two hundred dollars, *mi amigo, es nada.* Nothing. If you don't think so -- go stand in line," he gestured with his head toward the line snaking through the office. "Stand in line for an hour and try and explain how you'd like phone service, how you'll pay for it and you want it installed, where? The Betsy Ross Hotel? Oh, I'm sorry, sir. We don't provide residential service to the Betsy Ross Hotel. Maybe we could put a pay phone outside your door. Maybe we could. Maybe we. Maybe. No maybe's, just two hundred dollars, *amigo,* it's nothing."

Johnson handed him the money, more than a month's rent. Eight trips to the grocery store, a pound of second-rate pot. An ounce of very good stuff. Vacation money, if he wanted to take a bus to Key West, drink in the bars, sleep on the street. Two hundred dollars, gone. Like that. Fingers snapped in his mind. He'd started the day with a $20 bill tucked in his shoe and the day wasn't half over. He'd gotten a new job, ordered a phone for his apartment and coughed up two hundred bucks as if it were two. Two hundred bucks, he thought, walking back to the Betsy Ross. Two hundred bucks, gone. He snapped his fingers. Just like that. Gone. Amazing.

He told Harold, the old man at the front desk, that he was expecting company.

"I'm no fucking butler," he replied.

"I know, Harold, I'm just letting you know."

"And I'm just letting you know, I'm no fucking butler."

Johnson was not depressed by the sight of his room. The gray sheets twisted about his bed. The faded, nicotine-stained paint on the walls. The once stylish furniture, rattan and wood and silk brocade, painted and chipped and painted and chipped again. The dresser marred by nail polish, spilled whiskey, and cigarettes missing the ashtray. His refrigerator groaned in a cooling cycle. Water dripped in the sink. Rust stains scored the drains in the sinks and the tub. Water ran in the toilet. Clothes scattered about the floor, none clean, some beyond help. He ran some water into the sink, cooling it down before filling a fingerprint-smeared glass. He lifted the glass to his lips and heard tapping to his left. He glanced toward the window. A Black man wearing a white hard hat smiled at him. Johnson dropped the glass in the sink. It shattered.

The man mouthed, "Open the window." Someone knocked at the door.

"Bell Telephone," a man shouted.

Johnson froze. The guy at the window mouthed, "Open the window." The other rapped at the door.

Fuck it, Johnson thought. He stepped to the window, undid the latch and pushed it open. The man rapped at the door again. Johnson walked to the door and pulled it open. Another man in a white hard hat entered the room and crossed to the window. "You didn't tell Mario what kind of phone you wanted, so I brought a black one."

"Black is good," Johnson said.

"Good." Then to the man in the window, "Alfred, pass me the line."

The guy threaded a length of telephone line through the window. The guy in the apartment stretched the wire across the room. Then he returned to the window and began stapling the wire to the window frame. "You're about to become very popular, buddy."

"Who?" Johnson asked.

"You. As soon as the phone rings the first time your neighbors are going to know -- you got a phone. I seen it before. Very popular."

The guy at the window nodded. "Yep, very popular. And judging by the looks of your neighbors, these are not the kind of people I would want to be popular with."

The guy connecting the phone was on his knee stripping plastic coating off the wire. "Where do you want it?"

"Want what?"

"Where do you want the phone? Next to the bed, on top of the fridge, next to the shitter? Where?"

"The bed."

The phone guys were gone as quickly as they arrived. The new black phone sat on the table beside Johnson's bed. The installer had written Johnson's new telephone number on a piece of paper between the buttons. Johnson picked up the receiver and punched in Singer's beeper number. He waited, punched in his own and hung up the phone.

Johnson hadn't lived in a place with a phone in four years. Four years without a phone and now, just like that, he had one. He'd call his mother, give her the number. She wouldn't believe his good luck. Who knew what she'd say. He looked at the clothes scattered about his room. The old furniture. Things would shape up, now. He was sure. This gig with Singer. He wouldn't fuck it up. He wouldn't ever have to scrape dentures clean and return them to old people who'd rather gum their food anyway.

The phone rang. Johnson put the receiver to his ear. "Hello," he said.

"It's time to go to work," Singer said. "I'll be in front of your building in three minutes."

In the Betsy Ross Hotel, Johnson became 'the guy with the phone.' People called and left messages for his neighbors.

His phone rang. He'd answer it. "Yeah."

"Are you the guy with the phone?" a man asked.

"That's me," Johnson would say.

"Tell that asshole in two-thirty-two that if he fucks with Charlie again, I'm going to break both his legs and stick a pipe up his ass."

"I'll let him know," Johnson would say.

"You do that."

During his time as at the Betsy Ross with the phone, Johnson called the police eight times, fire rescue three and the suicide hot-line exactly once. He took messages from brothers in search of sisters and wives who sought their husbands. He knew when someone's parents died and when it was time for someone to pack up and move on.

Now, standing on the corner of Ocean Drive and Fourteenth Street, in the shadow cast by the Betsy Ross Hotel, Johnson believed he had packed up and moved on at just the right time. When he'd moved to the beach you could roll a bowling ball down the middle of Ocean Drive at 9 p.m. on a Friday and hit nothing. Now, at 4:30 a.m. on a Tuesday, you couldn't swing your arms without hitting a model or a model wannabe, or some agent or hipster who called the neighborhood SoBe and chased across the lower end of Miami Beach in search of some ongoing and shifting celebration.

Johnson knew what had happened to him. He'd gotten lucky. Just like the hotels, which were really flea bags that somebody painted and called Deco. Both he and the hotels were like cheap whores in the right light -- the Miami light. That Miami light had been kind to the buildings and the Miami light had been kind to him. The cheap hustle, the wise move, the right connection. The Fat Man. The Fat Man saved his ass. He paid less than the truck driving gig, but it was steady. Johnson moved off the beach. Bought a house. Met Al. He'd gotten lucky. There was no arguing with that.

But what was he going to do about Al? What did she want from him, anyway? Not to talk to the Fat Man? Not to take his money? Lie to her? Johnson didn't care what women wanted, just what Al wanted. He might not be able to give it to her, but he believed he'd be better off if he knew. And what was that loyalty shit all about? Johnson knew he had only a few things to sell. Not his brains or his looks. He could drive, speak English and enough Spanish to get him in trouble. Plenty could do that and more. He was nothing with numbers. Hated heavy lifting. What else did he have? Loyalty. Trust. Jesus, he thought, what's the big fucking deal? It's just my job.

CHAPTER 5

All the Fat Man's televisions were off when Johnson walked into the room. He'd never seen that before. Never. A man about five-six stood beside the Fat Man. Clean shaven, with a small hard face, the man stood at attention: hands at his sides, eyes straight ahead. His wire-brush short gray hair stood on end as if he had been frightened by something. He wore a starched, white guayabera over gray flannel slacks. His gold wristwatch looked old and expensive.

Johnson said, "Hello, sir," to the Fat Man.

"Alfredo Mondongo," the Fat Man screeched, "this is the friend I've been telling you about."

Alfredo Mondongo thrust his hand at Johnson. "Alfredo Mondongo," he said.

"Mucho gusto, *Señor*. Me llamo Johnson."

"Johnson?" The man smiled at the Fat Man. "The most important document in the world and you bring me a man with just one name."

The Fat Man laughed. "My friend. You asked for a good man, not for someone with a beautiful name."

Mondongo nodded. "You're right. You're right." He turned back to Johnson. "So you're going to London. Do you know the city?"

Johnson shook his head. "No, sir," he said. "This will be my first visit."

The man nodded. "London is marvelous. It reminds me of Havana in many ways. Truly a capital. Not like this stinking shit pot Miami."

The Fat Man stood looking over Mondongo's shoulder at the blank television screens.

"I don't know," Johnson said. "I like Miami."

Mondongo snorted. "And a pig likes mud. You, my friend, don't know any better."

"What the fuck do you mean by that?"

The Fat Man shrieked with laughter. "You're so funny, Johnson." He laughed again. "You're so funny. Did I tell you, by the way, that Mondongo fought with Fidel Castro and Che Guevara in the Cuban Revolution?"

Mondongo's grimace softened and he turned his head to the side, striking a pose very much like a statue.

"But as soon as he realized they were communists, he broke with them and worked for their downfall. My friend knew very early on who the communists were. He was the first member of the revolutionary movement to know what Fidel had up his sleeve."

Mondongo puffed up like a rooster. He waved a finger in the air. "When Fidel came down out of the mountains, who do you think cleared the way for him? Oh, Fidel. How I knew you then. How I know you now. I sleep, eat and drink the downfall of Fidel. And it's coming. I can hear it, feel it, taste it, smell it." Mondongo held his hands in front of himself and motioned toward himself. "Come in Fidel, come in my little puppy."

The Fat Man stood straighter and put a hand over his heart. "The work I do for Mr. Mondongo is not about money, Johnson," he said. "It is the future. It is the human race."

"That is exactly right, my friend. We are all, every person on the planet, from Havana. Havana is the mother of all cities. Havana is heaven on earth and," he waved his finger in the air, "Havana shall be ours again."

Johnson began to wonder if the Fat Man was fucking with him. This guy Mondongo? What the fuck kind of name was Mondongo anyway? He knew a lot of Latinos, never met one named Mondongo. And this 'we're all from Havana' bullshit. What the fuck was that all about?

"Sir," he said, addressing the Fat Man. "What is it that you and *Señor* Mondongo want me to do?"

"The easiest and the hardest thing anyone has ever asked you to do," Mondongo said. "I want you to deliver a letter from history. History will speak to Fidel from my pages. Fidel will...will." Mondongo's face reddened, his hand quivered. His entire body quaked.

Johnson wondered if the man was having a stroke.

"...will understand how history will judge him. He will see that he has created poison all around him. His cruelty has never been exceeded -- not by Stalin, not by Hitler. His brutality makes the Genghis Khan an innocent child. Their names will be forgotten, as if written in dust. But Fidel will be remembered by the world forever for the cruelty he inflicted on the Cuban people." Small dots of spit flecked Mondongo's lips. He shook and quivered.

Johnson had seen people talking like Mondongo when he lived at the Betsy Ross. He knew them by their Thorazine tans and always crossed to the other side of the street. They were crazy that was plain enough. But in the Fat Man's house there was something about this man, Mondongo, that cancelled the possibility of insanity. Something? The answer arrived like a bolt. MONEY. Only money allowed people to act crazy and not get locked up.

Mondongo stepped next to Johnson. His cologne sweetened the air. The man draped his left arm across Johnson's hip and raised his right hand into air, fingers spread, palm open toward the ceiling. Johnson's gaze followed the man's hand.

"You are the future, Johnson. But to be so you must step back. Will you take your place in history, Johnson?" Mondongo asked, his eyes shining with tears.

Johnson wasn't sure he wanted to get involved with this crazy man. Maybe this wasn't the job for him. He tried to step from the man's grasp. Mondongo tightened his fingers on Johnson's hip.

"I don't know," he said. "This sounds pretty big. Maybe you

better..."

Mondongo cut him off. "If it's the money, I'll double it." He turned to the Fat Man. "Our original price was five thousand. I'll make it ten. One cannot be cheap when purchasing a place in history."

"What?" Johnson shouted. The Fat Man had fucked him.

The Fat Man squealed with delight. "Yes, Mr. Mondongo. I am sure that for that amount, even if Johnson won't do it, I'll find somebody."

Mondongo hugged Johnson closer. "You'll find nobody," he said. "I've looked into his eyes. *I know him.* Johnson is my man. Either he does it, or I go to another organization."

The Fat Man looked to Johnson. "Well," he squeaked. "I can't speak for the man. But I am sure for ONE HALF of your generous offer, he'd be more than happy to do this for you."

Johnson grinned and nodded his head. "Yeah. Sure. For ONE HALF of your generous offer and that spot in history. Gosh, it'd be hard to say no."

"You're sure," Mondongo demanded. "There must be no backing out."

"*Señor*, for ONE HALF of your generous offer, you have my word and my loyalty."

Tears welled in Mondongo's eyes. He leapt at Johnson and hugged him, burying his face in his neck. "Thank you, *Señor* Johnson. Thank you," he cried. The man's breath raised goose bumps on Johnson's arms.

The Fat Man nodded and smiled at Johnson, showing him double thumbs up.

Yeah, Johnson thought, fuck you. Try to hustle me for nine large when this guy's going five long. Yeah. Fuck you.

Mondongo released Johnson and turned toward the Fat Man. "And you, *Señor*. You have always showed yourself a friend of the Cuban people in our time of wandering. We have much in common, your people and mine. You have your exile and wandering and we have had ours. You had your Holocaust and now we are living through ours. But you, my friend, have always shown

yourself to be a true friend and an honest man. Thank you.
Thank you." Mondongo grabbed the Fat Man's hand.

No one <u>ever</u> touched the Fat Man. Ever. He struggled to free
his hand from Mondongo, who seemed to mistake the gesture
as a clumsy attempt at a hug. Mondongo clung to the hand and
tried to reach around the Fat Man's bulk with his free hand. The
Fat Man shrieked and whined, trying to free himself from Mondongo. As he backed away, his feet tangled and the Fat Man fell
over on his back, pulling Mondongo down on top of him.

"Jesus H. Fucking Christ," the Fat Man shrieked. "Get him off.
Get him off."

The Fat Man kicked and paddled like a turtle on its back. Mondongo slid off the Fat Man's girth. He lay beside him on the rug,
an arm across the Fat Man's neck, singing the big man's praises
and pointing out the numerous parallels between the Jewish and
Cuban experience.

"Johnson! Johnson, get him the fuck off of me."

Johnson watched for a moment. He bent down and tapped
Mondongo on the shoulder. "*Señor* Mondongo. *Señor*, Mr. Teitelbaum doesn't like anyone to touch him. Sir." Mondongo turned
his head and looked up into Johnson's eyes. "Que?"

"Don't touch the man," Johnson said. "He hates to be touched
by anyone. Isn't that right, sir?"

The Fat Man had broken down into sobs that swept out of his
chest like gusts off the ocean. "Yes, yes," he sobbed. "Don't touch.
Don't touch."

Mondongo nodded and scrambled to his feet.

"Do you need a hand up, sir?" Johnson asked.

The Fat Man shook his head. "Don't touch. Don't touch."

"Fine, sir," Johnson replied. "Will you be okay if we leave you
there?"

The Fat Man nodded. "Don't touch. Don't touch."

"Okay, sir," he said. "I'll just be leaving now."

The Fat Man nodded, sobbing.

"Good day, my friend," Mondongo said.

"Yes. Yes." the Fat Man sighed.

CHAPTER 6

Five thousand dollars.

Johnson had a victory and cause for celebration. He honked and waved at the security guard as he drove off Star Island, then laughed at the puzzled look on the guard's face. Five thousand dollars, five thousand dollars, five thousand dollars. Johnson imagined the money -- five thousand one-dollar bills raining from the sky, fifty hundreds stuffed into a bulging envelope, five thousands sliding easily into his wallet. Was there a five-thousand-dollar bill? He'd have to ask Al. She knew shit like that.

Five thousand dollars. Five grand. Fifty large. Five long. Five easy. Five, five, five. He could take a thousand for London. That left four home. Hell, he could take two to London and have a great time. Okay, take two to London, leave three back. He could trade in his car and get one with AC. Maybe he'd just get his AC fixed. He could pay his mother back some of the money she'd loaned him twenty years ago. He could invest it. Give it to some import-export guys, let it work for him. Maybe Al would explain the stock market to him again. He could try that. Johnson looked at his reflection in the rear-view mirror and laughed. Invest? Jesus.

Two weeks after he'd begun the job with Teitelbaum, Johnson drove the man in his 1962 avocado green Lincoln Continental to a business appointment up in Ft. Lauderdale. They stopped at a 7-11. Johnson bought a quart of chocolate marshmallow ice cream and a bag of white plastic spoons. As he piloted the car through Golden Beach, Johnson knew he had made the right move going with Teitelbaum. It was a good gig. Sure, the fucking car drove like a boat, the guy was fat as shit and there was the smell, but he was getting used to that.

"Johnson," the Fat Man squeaked, while spooning ice cream from the container. "What did you do with the money you made from Harvey Singer?"

Johnson glanced at the man in the rear-view mirror and grinned. "Had a blast, sir." And he had. There were no drugs he couldn't buy, no toys, drinks or meals he couldn't afford. He sighed at the wonder of it all. "An absolute blast, sir."

"Spend, spend, spend," the Fat Man sighed. "Johnson, I thought you were smarter than that."

"Smarter than what?"

"You're in your prime earning years. You won't be able to make what you're making forever. You'll get old, slow down. You need to build equity. To be comfortable in your retirement."

Retirement? Johnson didn't believe he'd live long enough to be old. He couldn't imagine it. "I won't reach sixty-five for another thirty years or so."

"That's right," the Fat Man said. "You begin planning now and when you're old, you'll have an income."

"Okay, sir," Johnson said, humoring the Fat Man. "How do I do that?"

"I'll have my accountant call you. He is particularly adept at dealing with people like you."

"What do you mean by that?"

The Fat Man laughed. "Don't get upset, Johnson. I meant people who earn money outside the general economy. People who someday may have to explain themselves to the government. People like you and me."

Johnson looked at the Fat Man in the rear-view mirror. He wanted to ask him what an accountant could do for him. But the man had his face deep in the ice cream container, and Johnson didn't want to interrupt him. Instead he wondered how, all of a sudden, the Fat Man and he had become 'people like you and me.'

Johnson lived at the Betsy Ross Hotel. The Fat Man lived on

Star Island -- the Bee Gees were his neighbors for Christ's sake. Johnson's neighbors had prison tattoos. They were boys who believed they were girls, and Cubans who spoke to African gods. The Fat Man had an eighteen-room mansion (even if he only used two of the rooms) six phone lines, forty-three televisions and an industrial size refrigerator. Johnson lived in a Pulman-ette with a bathroom, a bed and a phone. The Fat Man weighed 490, dry and naked. Johnson felt heavy at 160. Yeah, he could see all the similarities.

The Fat Man belched. "Johnson, my friend, if you see a place where we might find some chips. Please."

"Of course, sir."

"My accountant will call. Do what he says, Johnson. A good accountant can keep you from needing a good attorney."

"I will, sir." Johnson pulled the car into a QuickDixie. "Anything other than chips, sir?"

"Beef Jerky or Slim Jims, if they have them. For the meeting."

"Right, sir."

Johnson's phone rang the following Friday, while he lay across his bed watching *The Night Before Day,* a soap opera he'd loved since childhood. He reached over and pulled the receiver to his ear. "Yeah?"

"Mr. Johnson," said a sing-songy voice.

Anyone who called him Mister was trying to sell him something. "He's out right now," Johnson said.

"Tell him Dinesh Ramgoolam called. Mr. Teitelbaum's accountant."

"Yeah, this is me," he said, and listened to the confusion on the other end of the line. "My name is Johnson, just Johnson. Anyone calls and asks for Mr. Johnson, it makes me nervous."

"I see," the man said.

"What did you say your name was?"

"Dinesh Ramgoolam."

"Dinesh? What kind of name is that?"

"Indian," the man said.

"I knew a guy who claimed to be Iroquois. Jimmy. Know

him?"

"Indian from India."

"A dot head?" It was out before he could stop it. "I didn't mean anything by that," he said, grimacing.

"Yes, Mr. Johnson, a dot head," the voice said. "Mr. Teitelbaum has asked me to meet with you to discuss your finances. When would you be available?"

"Pretty much anytime," Johnson said.

"How would 11 a.m. tomorrow be?"

"Tomorrow's fine," Johnson said.

Eleven o'clock the following day Johnson drove through the narrow lanes of Storage R Us, a burnt orange-colored complex of one-story warehouses just west of Miami International Airport. Airplanes on runway approach flew seventy feet above him. The ground trembled beneath the Crown Vic. He stopped in front of bay E-11, parked next to a new green Toyota Camry and rapped at the frame door beside a garage door. A security camera leered at him.

A voice squawked from a loudspeaker, "Come in."

A plane thundered overhead.

The door opened with a sigh that Johnson associated with vacuum sealed jars. He stepped from the hot asphalt parking lot into a cool, almost chilly office and pulled the door closed. The wall in front of him and those to his left and right side had been painted white and were completely bare. The interior of the garage door was burnt orange and looked hot to the touch. Before him sat a broad wooden desk with a computer off to one side. An automatic coffee maker sputtered on a low table in the corner. A small, dark-skinned man stood behind the desk. He seemed young. The word 'pixie' came to Johnson's mind.

The man walked around to the front of his desk and extended a hand to Johnson.

"Mr. Johnson, a pleasure. Dinesh Ramgoolam."

"Just Johnson," Johnson said, taking the man's hand.

"Please have a seat. Coffee?"

"No," Johnson said.

"Fine," Ramgoolam said. "Please sit down." The building shook and quaked -- a jet engine roared overhead. Dinesh shrugged. "After a while you don't notice them anymore."

"Notice what?" Johnson asked, smiling.

"Very good, Mr. Johnson."

As he dropped into his seat and Johnson noticed a strange looking statue on Ramgoolam's desk -- an elephant with a human body, swinging something in the air.

"Ah, you've noticed my Ganesh," Dinesh Ramgoolam said. "Don't even think about it, it's just some silly dot head thing."

"Hey," Johnson said. "I didn't mean anything by that. It just slipped out."

"I'm not here to judge you, Mr. Johnson. I'm here as an accountant. Now, please, tell me about yourself."

Johnson started out as delicately as possible. "As you know, I work for Mr. Teitelbaum and sometimes his associates."

"And that's all you do?"

"It's mostly what I do."

"Where do you live?"

"The Betsy Ross. A hotel on Ocean and Fifteenth."

Ramgoolam nodded. "Bank accounts? Safety deposit boxes? Investments?"

Johnson shook his head.

"Records, receipts, pay stubs?"

"I'm pretty much in a cash business."

"Can you tell me how much money you made last week?"

Johnson thought for a moment. The Fat Man gave him five hundred. He'd earned an additional two because he had some free time on his hands and somebody needed a car moved. "I don't know," he said. "I made some."

"Some? What is some?"

"You know -- some."

"No, I don't. Is some a dollar? Two dollars? What? A hundred?"

"More than a hundred," Johnson said.

"More than a hundred. And less than?"

"Less than four thousand."

"How much less than four thousand?"

"Don't you see?" Johnson said. "I don't want to tell you."

"Yes, that's absolutely clear. But don't you see that I need to know?"

"For what?'

Ramgoolam shook his head and gestured toward the statue of Ganesh. "I honor you, and you send me fools."

"Hey," Johnson said. "I'm not a fool."

"Mr. Teitelbaum tells me that you worked for an organization headquartered in Colombia. That organization, through its local representative Harvey Singer, paid you a thousand dollars a trip to drive their product north. You made two trips a week, and they paid your expenses, too. By my calculations you made, potentially, one hundred thousand dollars last year."

Johnson thought about it. It seemed right. "Yeah."

Dinesh Ramgoolam nodded. "What did you do with your money, Mr. Johnson?"

"I ate, drank, bought a nice car. Paid cash. Eighty-two Crown Vic, fully dressed. It's out front."

"But what did you do with your extra money? Or did you spend it all?"

Nobody had ever asked Johnson what he did with his money. It wasn't anybody's business. "No, I didn't spend it all. That's too much money to spend."

"I agree. But what did you do with it?"

"I hid it," Johnson said. And that's what he did. He hid it in a Maxwell House coffee can in his mother's garage in Hollywood.

"In your mattress?"

"No." Johnson was surprised the guy would think of such a stupid location. "That's a stupid place."

"In a coffee can somewhere?"

Johnson blushed. "No, that would be pretty stupid too."

"I agree," Dinesh Ramgoolam said. He inhaled deeply and leaned back in his chair. "Mr. Johnson, when was the last time you paid income tax?"

"Three, maybe four years ago. No. Five years ago. Nineteen seventy-eight. Is that a problem?"

"Potentially. Mr. Johnson, how familiar are you with the economics of your situation?"

Johnson wondered if the guy was bullshitting him. "I don't know anything about economics."

"Mr. Johnson, I have spent a lifetime studying the dynamics of the gray economy, the area you and Mr. Teitelbaum inhabit, economically speaking. You, Mr. Johnson, operate at the lower levels of the gray economy. You're not too smart. You take risk for reward, but you, and believe me Mr. Johnson I know this, are not moving up the ladder into the higher echelon. No one is ever going to give you a percentage of a deal because of who you are. You'll be paid for what you do and that's it."

"Yeah," Johnson said. "I do work and they pay me. So?"

Dinesh Ramgoolam grimaced. "Another man might laugh at your foolishness, Mr. Johnson. I can't, I'm afraid. I find nothing funny about your ignorance."

"What the hell are you saying?"

"I'm saying, Mr. Johnson, that you made over one hundred thousand dollars last year, tax free, and you kept what you couldn't spend in a coffee can."

"I didn't say that."

"Not in so many words. Your position in the gray economy is threatened as we speak. Miami will not always be the wide-open market that it is now and, Mr. Johnson, just like all those steel and auto workers in the Rust Belt, you, my friend, will find yourself taking lower paying jobs and doing more for less. But you have not proven to me yet how stupid you are. Mr. Teitelbaum sent you over here for me to advise you. But first I need to know, how much money is in the coffee can?"

Johnson stared at Dinesh Ramgoolam and wondered whether he should tell him.

"Mr. Johnson, don't think so hard, you'll get a headache. Just tell me how much. I can assure you that I wouldn't begin to know how to get my hands on your cash."

"Thirty-two thousand." There. He'd said it.

Dinesh Ramgoolam nodded. "That's good, Mr. Johnson. That's quite good."

Johnson felt like a kid in school. "Thank you," he said.

Dinesh Ramgoolam nodded. "Will you be home tomorrow?"

"No, I'm working."

"Thursday? Will you be home Thursday?"

"Yeah, Thursday. I'm off Thursday."

"Good. Thursday, an associate of mine, Peggy Brown, will pick you up in front of the Betsy Ross at nine a.m. She shouldn't be kept waiting."

"What's she coming for?"

"Mr. Johnson, you are going house hunting. Welcome to the world of home ownership, Mr. Johnson. Good luck."

CHAPTER 7

The exhilaration of his victory had diminished by the time Johnson pulled the car into his driveway. The five thousand dollars was no longer a surprise, but a fact. He had it, or at least the Fat Man's word of it. He slid the gear shift to park and stepped out of the car. The sun shone bright enough to make him squint through his sunglasses. Johnson surveyed the neighborhood. A mourning dove cooed in his neighbor's yard. A mail truck's brakes squealed to a stop at the corner mailbox. He looked up into the coconut palm growing from his front lawn. His ideal afternoon, the one he had planned as he walked from the Fat Man's house, was being challenged by his conscience. His yard needed mowing; all the green shit growing around his house needed to be hacked back. He sighed, disgusted with himself.

In the old days, before he bought the house, Johnson could have smoked a joint, driven over to the Wreck and drunk beer all afternoon. Jesus, what had happened? But Johnson knew what happened. Dinesh Ramgoolam had him buy the house. It was creepy at first, moving from a room at the Betsy Ross to a house. All Johnson owned at the time were his clothes, the Crown Vic, a baseball bat, and a black rotary dial phone. No furniture. No pots and pans, not even a coffee maker. The house had a kitchen for Christ's sakes, with a sink and a stove. Jesus. It had a washing machine and dryer.

And a back yard. Man, that fucking yard. Even with the Fat Man's promise of five long there was still the yard. Nothing stopped the yard and there was only one thing Johnson could do about it. He went into the house, changed into his work shorts, grabbed his machete and plunged into the yard to attack the green.

He knew the names of some of the less sinister plants he battled -- Christmas palms, royal palms, coconuts, bananas. But there were others whose names he did not know -- vines that crept 200 feet across the yard in an afternoon; thorn bushes that rose up out of the ground on haunches; surly spiked plants that multiplied in the night like mushrooms. Johnson hacked and chopped the green through the afternoon and early evening, beating back its progress. He dragged vines and branches to the curb. Tossed coconuts and palm fronds onto the pile.

Just after Johnson had purchased the house he'd noticed a sound, a thin searing hiss. He believed it was traffic noise from US 1, ten blocks east. Then one night, as he stumbled from the car to the house, he fell on his lawn and lay listening to his heart pound. It was a still night, after a day of rain and sun. Moisture from the grass-soaked Johnson's clothes. A mosquito buzzed his ear and he heard the hissing sound again. In the dark, with the shadows of blades of grass towering over him, Johnson realized the hissing noise was the sound of plants growing -- the sound of everything green in Miami stretching and straining toward the sky. Johnson giggled at the idea, then passed out. During the night he dreamt of Miami's future. Vines strangled office buildings, trees sprouted from the roofs of houses, brush and shrubs consumed the roads. In the dream Johnson saw green blanketing all of Miami, from the ocean to the Everglades.

The next morning, as he squinted against the risen sun, a snuffing and hissing sound broke through his emerging hangover. Sniffing and hissing -- poking and prodding his body. Panic struck -- the green had won during the night! It was probing his body, trying to capture him in its vines and encase him in its tendrils. Johnson yelped and rolled into a sitting position. His neighbor's collie, Lady, barked and raced away down the block. Johnson looked after the dog, then down at himself. Grass stained and wet with dew, he wished could vomit and get it over with. But with it all -- the throbbing headache, the dry mouth and aching stomach -- he heard the searing hiss, the sound of green things growing.

Johnson knew the sound predicted Miami's future. People got bored and gave up, but not the plants. Eventually no one would have the strength to beat back the green and it would win. It was inevitable. But while Johnson was alive and able, the green would not win.

Johnson stood at the curb, admiring the pile of palm fronds and grass clippings. He had won that day. The green's victory was postponed.

Johnson stood under the shower, rinsing off the battle, when Al came in from work. He didn't hear her drop her purse or flip through the mail. Johnson turned off the shower just as the TV came on. He heard the newscaster's voice and Al's sigh as she lay down on the couch.

Every day after work Al came into the house, flipped through the mail, turned on the TV, then crashed on the couch. She napped for fifteen minutes -- called it charging her batteries. It amazed Johnson at first. She'd lie on the couch for fifteen, maybe seventeen minutes, then pop up like a jack-in-the-box, refreshed and ready to go.

"How do you do that?" Johnson asked once.

"Do what? Sleep?" Al smiled at him. "First, I close my eyes."

"No," Johnson said. "Not sleep, but that fifteen-minute thing. How'd you learn that?"

Al shrugged her shoulders. "Beats me."

Johnson walked into the living room, drying his crotch with a towel while watching Al sleep. The newscaster joked stupidly with the weatherman. Johnson turned to the screen. When he turned back Al's eyes were open.

"You were in the shower when I came in," she said.

Johnson nodded. "I was out back trying to control the yard."

"It'll be nice when the weather cools down, huh?"

"It'll be easier. But nicer is high summer, when everything's as green and lush as it gets."

"Yeah, I remember you saying that. Still," she said. "I'd like it if it got a little cooler."

Johnson shrugged. "There's nothing wrong with cooler, that's for sure." They were making up. "Do we have plans tonight?"

"Dinner. Maybe go to Heaven's Gate for a drink."

"It's only Tuesday."

"What? You don't like to watch naked women on Tuesdays?"

"No, I do, but usually..." Johnson stopped himself. "Dinner and Heaven's Gate," he said. "Just you and I, or do you want me to call someone?"

"Just you and me," she corrected.

"Right," Johnson said. "You and me."

Johnson didn't know how he and Al had gotten together. Two years earlier, on a Thursday in March, he'd started drinking at his home in south Dade, then gone out. He remembered the first couple stops, but not much after that. Somehow he ended up home again. The next morning Johnson found a naked woman beside him in his bed. She slept with her back to him. Johnson didn't recognize her back. He got up and crept around to see if he recognized her front. He didn't. But she didn't have a beard or six eyes, either. She looked pretty good to Johnson, even a little young. He congratulated himself, but for what he wasn't sure. He didn't remember if they'd fucked or not. There were no spent condoms on the floor, which was generally a sign. He made coffee, brought in the morning paper, and showered. Johnson drank half the pot of coffee before the woman appeared.

"Bathroom?" she asked, standing naked at the entrance to his living room.

He looked up from the newspaper. "Down the hall to your left," Johnson said, pointing.

The woman disappeared.

Johnson heard urine splashing the water and a loud fart. He smiled. The toilet flushed, water ran in the sink. She reappeared wearing his robe. It was too big for her. She looked even younger.

"Do I know you?" she asked.

"I don't think so," Johnson said.

"Oh man, that's good," she replied. "Did you ever think you had forgotten a whole part of your life? Like you had married, moved to the suburbs, had children, your husband sold real estate, you played tennis at the Jewish Center, then one morning you woke up and just didn't remember it."

"No," Johnson said, smiling, "That never happened to me."

"Wow," she said. "It just happened to me."

"Well, don't worry about it."

"Hmmm," she said. "What year is it?"

"I think it's 1993," Johnson said.

"Damn, that's a relief."

"Yeah, I guess it is," Johnson replied. "You don't really believe that could happen, do you?"

"It happened to my mother," the woman said. "When I was eleven, she walked into our kitchen, looked at my brothers and me and said, 'Who are you?'

"We laughed. My brother Jeremy said, 'We're your kids.'

"My mother shook her head. 'I don't have any children. I'm too young to have children.'

"Mom,' Jeremy said, pointing at me, 'This is Alexandra, that's Michael and I'm Jeremy. We're your kids.'

"My mother looked worried. 'No, I don't think so,' she said. She looked around the kitchen, as if she'd never seen the room before. Her eyes stopped on the clock above the stove. 'I don't know who you kids are, but I'm going to be late for class if I don't go now.'

"I started crying. Michael crawled down under the kitchen table. Jeremy was older, he told me to shut up. 'Mom,' he said. 'Your name is Joyce Cohen, you're married to Gerald Cohen. You have a bachelor's degree in Sociology. Your parents live in Chicago. We live in...'

"I don't know who you are, little boy, but my name is Stern, Joyce Stern. I know a boy named Gerald Cohen. But I'd never marry him. I want to live a little before I get married. I want to see the world. I don't want to wake up when I'm forty and wonder where my life has gone."

"Jesus Christ," Johnson said. "Did that really happen?"

"Yeah," she shrugged. "That first time, my father got home just as she was walking out the door. He got her into a car and they went to see a doctor. She came home and slept for a long time after that. They gave her drugs. She'd be fine. Then we'd be in a mall or a supermarket and she'd look at me and say, 'Do I know you, little girl?' At first it scared me, but you can get used to anything."

Johnson nodded his head. His mother suddenly seemed more sane and normal than he'd ever imagined. "Must have been pretty tough on you kids."

"Naw," she said. "You'd be surprised what you can get used to. My dad had it tough. He'd take her places and she'd snap. She'd leave him at a restaurant and take a cab, who knows where."

"Where is she now?"

"Dead."

"I'm sorry," Johnson said.

"Don't be. The medication shortened her life, which," she shrugged, "is kind of OK. Could you imagine her at sixty claiming to be a student in college? Jeremy has children now. Imagine how confusing she'd be for them."

Johnson nodded, but the story had put him adrift. What do you say to a woman who has just told you a story like that? There was nothing he could think of that would make any of it better or go away. He could tell her his mother's pat line, well, all things work out in the end. But he knew that meant nothing, which was why, he suspected, she repeated it so often. Johnson didn't want to say something hollow. He wanted to say something with meaning, something important.

"You want to shower?" he asked. "We could go for breakfast."

The woman nodded. "Yeah," she said. "I'd like a shower and breakfast, and who would I have to blow to get a cup of that coffee?"

"No one," Johnson said, laughing.

"Cool," she replied.

Johnson had known plenty of women, but none quite like this Alexandra. In the Breakfast Nook, she flirted with their waitress. Said things like, "nice tits" when a woman walked by. "Not a bad ass either," she'd said, cocking her eyebrow.

"You're pretty funny," Johnson said.

"Why is that?"

"Well, the whole nice tits and ass thing. The women I know don't talk that way."

"They have narrow, limited minds," Alex said.

"Narrow, limited minds?"

"Yeah," she said. The waitress brought their food. Alex looked up at her, "Thanks, honey," she said, and plowed into a plate of bacon, sausage, eggs over easy, and dry wheat toast. "Look, women are the most attractive creatures on earth."

Damn, she's a lesbian, Johnson thought. He spooned some sugar into his coffee and decided it didn't matter. He liked her.

"But," she continued, dipping the edge of a triangle of toast into a runny egg yolk, "they don't have cocks. I mean, really. I've strapped one on, powered it home. But let's get real, here. Precisely." She laughed at her own joke. "I like it real. Now don't get me wrong, some of my best friends are," she giggled again. "You see what I'm saying. I'm sure you feel the same way about other guys."

Johnson shook his head. "Honestly," he said, "I don't see much attractive about other guys. I mean, when I lived on the beach I'd see a guy that was attractive, but the thing that made him most attractive was he looked like a woman. So, if that's what gets me, why go for the facsimile when I can, generally, have the real thing?"

"Variety?"

"Yeah, maybe," Johnson said. "But all things considered, I'm fine just the way things are."

"And how are things?" Alex asked. "How are things with you?"

Johnson pushed his eggs around his plate. "I guess things are pretty good with me. A few years back I had a job that paid well enough to put a big down payment on the house. My monthly nut is low enough that I rarely have to scramble. I suppose I could drink less, fuck more. I don't know. Things are good."

"How old are you?" she asked.

Johnson wanted to say that it wasn't how old you were, but how old you felt. His problem was that he felt exactly as old as he was, thirty-nine. Then he nearly said, 'I don't think age matters.' But if he thought that why not just say it. "Thirty-nine," he said, then took a sip of coffee.

"That's so cool," Alex said. "Thirty-nine. Wow, thirty-nine. I bet you know all kinds of neat shit. About life and everything."

Johnson tried to imagine what he knew about life. He knew when things were going really well, look out, they're going to get fucked up. And if you think things can't get any worse think again. He knew the government wasn't as smart as they said in the newspapers and that really powerful people treated you okay. He knew that buying a house was a good idea, that owing money to friends was not. He knew that if a friend went to prison you didn't go and visit his wife, but it was good to send something nice at Christmas. Johnson smiled at Alex. "Yeah, I know some things, but I don't know how old you are."

"Twenty-five," she said. "A quarter century."

Johnson laughed. "Twenty-five ain't shit. Now, thirty-nine. Thirty-nine's where things start to go bad. Ten years after thirty-nine you're almost fifty. At twenty-five you still got at least another ten good years of pure fucking off. You're fine."

She nodded and smiled. "I knew I'd like older men."

"I'm an older man?" Johnson said.

"Yeah, but don't worry, you're on the cusp."

"What?"

"You're fourteen years older than me, right?"

Johnson nodded. "Right, so?"

"Let's see. Say you're fourteen. What does it mean if you've got a crush on a girl who's one year old? Which, I must point out, is the reality of our ages."

"I wouldn't."

"Of course not," she said. "That would be strange, wouldn't it?"

Johnson nodded. "Very strange." He didn't even like thinking about it.

"Okay. Say you're twenty-four and I'm ten. What about that?'

"No fucking way."

"Right," she said. "Now, you're thirty-nine and I'm twenty-five. What do you think about that?"

Johnson liked her. She seemed smart. "No problem with that."

She nodded. "It's the percentage thing. You know how people think that you never catch up to anybody who's older than you. They were born first. They get older. You get older, but you never catch up. Well, you never catch up in one measurement, but you creep ever closer in another. If we measured our lives as a percentage of each others' we'd all be growing closer together."

Johnson was confused. What the fuck was she talking about? "What are you? Some sort of mathematician or something?"

"Percentages are arithmetic," Alex said. "Simple. No math."

"Okay," Johnson nodded. "So what is it you do? Teach college or something?"

Her entire demeanor changed, her face became serious, she sat up straighter in the booth. "I'm a marketing consultant," she said.

Johnson was so fascinated by the change in her attitude that he didn't hear the words. "What?"

"Marketing," she said. "I'm a marketing consultant."

Johnson nodded his head and tried to look like he knew what she meant. "What does that mean, marketing consultant?"

"I develop plans for companies to position their products in the marketplace. I advise them on product development and suggest ways they might better meet the demands of consumers. I help convince them to sell things that you probably want to buy, but don't know it. Then I convince you to buy what they sell."

"Oh, so you're like in advertising."

"Advertising is a strategy of marketing, but marketing is much bigger than that. Advertising is an attempt to direct your capital toward a specific belief or purchase. Marketing directs investors, manufacturers, distributors, retailers, consumers toward a single goal -- the movement of resources."

Johnson shook his head. He heard the words, but they didn't have any meaning to him.

Alex waved at the waitress. "Honey," she said. "Can I borrow your pen?"

The waitress brought over a tiny golf pencil. "You can keep that one," she said.

"I will," Alex said. "I will."

Alex pushed her plate aside and turned over the place mat. She drew a circle on the paper. "Inside this circle is the economy."

"Which economy?"

"It doesn't really matter," she said. "There's only one economy, so let's just say it's the economy. The world-wide economy."

"Okay," Johnson said, wondering what Dinesh Ramgoolam would say to that.

"The deal with the economy is this -- it's all there. Just like thermo-dynamics," she said. "Wealth can be neither created nor destroyed. Sure, it changes shape. Mutates. Sometimes the rich become less rich, the poor less poor. But wealth, resources -- they're always there. Even if we haven't found them yet, they're still there."

Johnson nodded his head, but only to keep her plunging forward. He'd learned over time that if he kept someone talking long enough, eventually he'd discover something that made sense to him. He could comment, then, and not sound like a complete asshole.

Alex started making little dots all over the circle. "These," she said, "represent consumers, or potential consumers, though I've been thinking lately that there is no such thing as a potential consumer, there are just consumers, period. Sometimes I think I'm splitting hairs on that one." She looked into Johnson's eyes.

"I'm losing you." She made a face at him, seeming to indicate apology.

"No, no," Johnson said. "I'm with you. Really."

"Are you sure?"

"Yeah, yeah, go on."

"Well, the consumer thing is only part of it. I'll skip it. The thing you need to notice..." She began connecting all the dots with lines.

Johnson loved connect-the-dot puzzles when he was a kid. He wondered if her drawing would be a picture when she finished.

"The lines represent the possible routes of wealth, you know -- capital, money. As a marketer it's my goal to keep that wealth flowing. Create opportunities for people to use their wealth, no matter how much or how little they've accumulated. Let's face it, after you've taken care of your basic food, clothing and shelter, everything else is a marketing opportunity."

Johnson nodded his head, but he still didn't get it. "Can I take a look at the drawing?"

She slid the paper across the table to him. "Sure, but it only means something to me. It's the way I represent the idea in my mind. It probably won't mean much to you."

"I know," Johnson said, "I just want to look at it." He held the place mat up, twisting it side to side. He looked hard but couldn't find a picture. He didn't know what he hoped to find -- a picture of a tree, a rabbit, maybe a kite on a string, but there was nothing there. "You're right," he said. "I don't see it."

"But you get the idea. I get people to spend their money."

"Yeah, I get that. I guess."

"Good," she said. "So what do you do?"

"I'm a driver."

"Cars, trucks, what?"

"Yeah," Johnson said. "Cars, trucks, whatever."

"Do you work for a company?"

"Let's get the check and get out of here."

She walked beside him through the restaurant's parking lot.

"Hey, I'm sorry if I said something wrong in there."

Johnson looked back over his shoulder. "Don't worry about it."

"No really," she said. "I'm sorry."

"Listen, don't worry."

"Well, it's not like you work for the mob."

Johnson wondered how to respond to that. 'Yes it is. It's just like I work for the mob.' Or, 'The idea of the mob is silly. Actually there are many mobs. I work for just one of them.' Or, 'Shit no, hell. I don't really know who I work for.' Or, 'You know there's an awful lot of ways to make money in Miami.' After considering all the possible responses he gave the standard. "I'm a bonded courier and a licensed chauffeur. I have a very limited clientele. I'm on twenty-four-hour call. I move things and people around."

"There's probably more to it than you're telling me," Alex said.

"Not really. I could try and make it sound sexier, but I'm a driver."

"Is that what you wanted to be?"

Johnson turned and looked at this strange woman. "What do you mean?"

"When you were a kid and thought about what you wanted to be, as an adult, was driving it?"

He couldn't tell whether she was being serious or not. Maybe she was messing with him. All that stuff about the economy and marketing bullshit, maybe she was just fucking with him to see how long it would take him to notice. "No," he said, finally, "I didn't always want to be a driver."

"What did you want to be?"

She was definitely fucking with him. Johnson stopped and looked at her. "Listen," he said. "Maybe where you come from, what you wanted to be as a kid has something to do with what you are as an adult. But not me and not most of the people I know."

She smiled. "I wanted to be a ballet dancer." She flapped her arms, slowly, and leapt around the parking lot. "But it didn't work out."

Johnson laughed. "That's pretty funny."

"What is?"

"Nothing," he said. "Why didn't you?"

Alex stopped and put her hands on her hips. "I can't dance."

"I'm sorry," Johnson said.

"Don't be. If I were a dancer, my career would be close to over by now, and I'd have to figure out something else to do."

Johnson nodded. "I didn't know that about dancers."

"If you're a dancer, life really sucks."

"Hmm," Johnson said.

"So, what did you want to be when you were a kid?"

"A priest," Johnson said. It was out before he could think not to say it, and the idea struck him as both sad and funny. He hadn't remembered himself as a child in decades, and Johnson blushed as he recollected his religious fervor. Baptizing dogs and cats, trying to give his life to Jesus. Dressing in black so he looked like a little priest. Praying to god. Praying to saints. He felt tears in his eyes at his silliness. He wanted to get a look at himself to see if there were any traces of the boy in the man he had become.

"A priest?" Alex said. "I don't think I know any priests," she said. "Why didn't you become one?"

"I don't know," Johnson said. "Guess I couldn't dance."

"That's a real problem," Alex said.

Johnson nodded. "I discovered sex."

"From what I hear they don't care about priests and sex anymore."

"Yeah, they do," Johnson said.

"So you became a driver?"

"Uh huh."

"Can I ask a real stupid question?"

"Sure," Johnson said. "Those are my favorite kind."

"Do you know how we met?"

"Yeah, sure. I was sitting in my living room, drinking coffee and reading the paper. You came out of the bedroom and asked where the bathroom was."

"No," she said. "Before that."

"There was no before that."

She nodded her head. "Do you often meet women that way?"

"You're the first."

"Have we fucked yet?"

"Not in this life."

"Would you like to?"

"I think it would be fun," Johnson said.

"Fun?" she said. "Sex should be fun."

Johnson recognized the Fat Man's promise of $5,000 and Al's change of mood as good omens. Al kissed him on the cheek before she went to shower, and said, "Decide where we should eat tonight."

"Raffie's," he said without thinking. "I'll buy."

"Have a good day, did we?" Al asked.

Johnson smiled, then shrugged. "A day."

They took her Lexus. Johnson drove.

Each time they ate at Raffie's, Al told Johnson she loved the place. "They do such exciting things with food here."

"Yeah, they cook it," Johnson said.

"They do more than that. They create."

Their waiter, Marcell, a short stocky man with a shaved head and a blond Fu Manchu mustache, delivered their martinis and explained the daily special as if it were a secret he had kept just for them. "This evening, the chef has taken advantage of sunflower season and created a delightful sunflower pollen-based reduction, which, after simmering in a crushed pepper and banana-based tomato mash, is served over a bed of fresh mango pasta and topped with Jamaican watercress, flown in fresh today."

"That sounds great," Al said. "I'll have it."

"I'll have spaghetti with tomato sauce and sausages," Johnson said. "And bring a bottle of wine. Red. Medium priced."

When the bottle arrived, he told Al that spaghetti was food and pasta was marketing.

"You've been hanging out with me too long," she said.

"But that's right isn't it? The spaghetti, pasta thing."

Al nodded. "Yeah, it's one of those things that you have to admire. It changes everything about the food. Say spaghetti, you see a heavy-set Italian woman sweating over a stove, stirring a pot of red sauce. Say pasta and you see thin WASPs, dressed in white, sipping chardonnay over glass bowls of linguini and clams. Not a stain in sight. It's beautiful. And so radical. Spaghetti? What name recognition. They gambled on pasta. A ballsy move."

"It's still spaghetti," Johnson said.

"On the plate it's spaghetti. In the mind it's pasta. Good marketing, like good sex, takes place in the mind, Johnson. You know that."

They ate quietly, talking more about Al's day than his. She was doing the preliminary work for her London client. Researching market trends, the competition, and price breaks. "You know," she said, "I'm doing those things you can find on-line and on paper. I'm trying to figure out what everybody else is doing to develop a competitive advantage."

Johnson nodded. "So what are they selling? Did you tell me and I forgot?"

"Vacation resorts in South Africa," Al said, smiling her 'oops' smile. "Maybe I didn't. South Africa is really a fascinating country. Since Mandela, I mean."

"So, vacation resorts... Like Club Med?"

"Right," Al said. "I've been researching the hell out of that bunch."

"Having fun?"

"Yeah, I'm having fun. I like what I do. But you need to know, I'm going to be very busy when we're in London," she said. "For you it's a vacation, but for me it'll be work."

Johnson nodded. He'd be working too, at least until the letter was delivered. But shit, what was that? Deliver a letter. Nothing.

The parking valets at Heaven's Gate were busy for a Tuesday

night. Johnson stopped Al's Lexus beneath the canopy leading to the club's entrance and handed the keys to a brown-haired kid with pimples on both cheeks. "No scratches," Johnson said. "And don't fuck with the radio."

The kid's eyes grew larger. His white uniform shirt was grease stained and too big -- his black trousers were cinched into gathers by a brown belt. His name tag read, "Benny Taggart."

Al wrapped Johnson's arm with her hands. "Don't let him scare you," she said. "It's my car. No scratches, but you can fuck with the radio."

"No fucking with the radio," Johnson repeated.

"Maybe somebody else should park your car, mister," the kid said. "I'm new here."

"Go ahead. Park the car. Fuck with the radio," Al said. "I don't care."

The kid looked from Johnson to Al and back again.

"Get the fuck out of here," Johnson said. "You're killing me."

After the kid left, Al asked, "Why do you have to fuck with them?"

"What do you mean?" he asked.

"The kid. Why do you fuck with the kids?"

"Somebody needs to. Do you want them thinking life is easy, or some other Mister Rogers bullshit like that? Don't worry. I'll take care of the little fucker if he brings your car back in one piece."

For Johnson, walking into Heaven's Gate was like entering someone else's dream. From valet parking, down a canopied walkway and through a mirrored glass door, the feel of the club's bass thumped the air. When the door opened the music blew out with the smell of cigarettes and air freshener, a false cherry aroma that Johnson had discovered, through his excursions with Al, was the choice at most sex establishments. They all smelled never quite clean; the cloying sweetness masked something that no amount of scrubbing would remove.

The doorman, Eddie Mount Morris, a Jamaican Chinese Rastafari, stood close to seven feet tall and had arms as big as Johnson's legs. Ropes of dreadlocks framed his face and hung past his waist. He wore a thick gold ring on his right thumb and dark sunglasses day and night. If he lowered those shades to look at you over the rims, nothing about your future was guaranteed. Eddie was mellow, except when he wasn't. Annoy him at your own risk. Harass a dancer and face consequences you didn't think possible. Eddie sold Johnson hydroponically grown dope from an apartment building in North Miami Beach. The dope had a skunky aroma and a very somber high. Eddie called it the Emperor's Herb, "...for when you want to be thinking," he said. It had become Johnson's smoke of choice. It brought him a quiet, thoughtful high, requiring no words or action – while delivering an acute awareness of all around him.

Eddie nodded at Al and waved her into the club.

Johnson stopped before the man, put his fists together in front of his chest and bowed slightly. "Respect," he said.

"Respect," Eddie said, returning the salute.

Johnson handed him the five dollar cover charge. "The little ones? Missus Mount Morris? Things good?"

"All's right with me and mine. And you Johnson, my blood?" he said. "You, your stash? Everything good?"

"All is fine, Eddie," Johnson answered.

"My respect, my blood."

Heaven's Gate's walls and ceiling had been painted flat black. Lights, fixed and moving, shot around the club's interior. As Johnson's eyes adjusted, he saw a woman's ass shaking to the music, breasts jiggling, pubic hairs trimmed into the shape of a heart. Men sat alone or in groups holding fists of money. Bills slid from their hands to women's garters. Greenbacks fluttered through the air. Groups of boys, stag parties, bachelor parties, one drunker than the next, rolled their tongues at the dancers, pumped their hips toward the stage. Businessmen partied with out-of-town clients. Tourists who'd come to see Heaven discovered it was a loud, dark, smoke-filled room full of naked women.

The bouncers moved around the room like ninjas, dressed in

black trousers, sneakers and turtlenecks. They were large men who treated Johnson with a pimp's indifference. No matter how much time he spent in the club, he was not one of them. His relationship with Al made him suspect. They knew secrets, or what were supposed to be secrets. But according to Al, the bouncers didn't know shit.

Johnson's favorite at the club was a bartender named Lucy -- a woman his age, an ex-biker chick. Goosey Lucy to friends. Miss Lucy to Johnson. Fine tattoos and indigo ink scribblings covered her forearms and biceps. She wore her hair in a brush cut. Her face had been ravaged by something, Johnson never figured out what -- acne, a biker's knife, acid? There had been an attempted repair -- botched plastic surgery of the sort practiced off-shore. Lucy was not Johnson's favorite because she was a crusty old babe with wry attitude or some tough grandmother ready with a wise remark and a clean handkerchief. She was neither of those things. Lucy's attitude bypassed mean and stopped just past nasty. Her cruel remarks were not meant to wound, but scar permanently. Johnson understood her anger, sensed her jealousy. She was old and damaged, surrounded by the young and beautiful. Her life carried the world's reality to Heaven Gate's fantasy. If by some twist he ended up in similar circumstances, Johnson knew he would be bitter too.

"Miss Lucy," Johnson shouted as he passed the bar. She glanced up from the beer cooler, scowling. Johnson winked. She flipped him off.

The dancers blew kisses and waved to Al as she and Johnson wove their way through the crowd to a table. Johnson hadn't been much for nude bars before meeting Al. He'd been a few times but couldn't get used to the idea that you weren't allowed to touch the women. He had seen what happened if you did. For the most part he liked his face the way it was. But going to a strip club with Al was like going to an amusement park with a rich uncle. She knew all the dancers and they knew her. They came over to the table to say hello. Some stopped by the house, brought their kids, their boyfriends or girlfriends. They showed

Al their new tits, the trim they put on their pubic hairs, their piercings and tattoos.

The dancers, Johnson discovered, were regular people with nicer bodies. They had drinking problems, drug problems, children and marriages. Johnson's favorite dancer, a small redhead named Joanie Fitzpatrick, had moved on to New York, which (depending on who you listened to) was either a great move or a very stupid one.

Al shouted, "Go Nancy...Go Nancy," to a young Black woman on stage. She had the cheeks of her ass shaking in rhythm to the music. A drunken man in a business suit staggered up behind and reached out to touch. Two bouncers appeared out of the darkness and the businessman disappeared between them.

A dancer named JoJo, wearing knee high socks, a plaid skirt and a white blouse unbuttoned to her navel, stopped by their table, nodded to Johnson and said, "Alex, did you hear? Tony and Suzie got married last night."

"No shit," Al said. "Good for them."

"Yeah, even if it don't last at least they got it out of their systems," she said. "I'm in the barrel next. You guys hanging?"

Al looked at Johnson. "Yeah, we'll be here."

"See yah."

"What do you think of her?" Al asked him.

"I don't know," Johnson said. "That whole Catholic uniform thing is a little too strange even for me."

"I didn't mean that. That's just a costume. I mean without it."

"Oh," Johnson laughed. "She's great, but you know, that outfit. I'd keep seeing her in it, and I'd probably freak out."

"Yeah, that's right, Johnson. You have such delicate sensibilities."

"Are we getting into it again? Cause I don't need it. You asked me what I thought, and I told you. Period."

"You know," Al said, "for somebody who works for the people you do, you certainly have an odd sense about what's appropriate."

Johnson sought out JoJo in the darkened room. She had shed

69

her white blouse and wore just the plaid skirt, bunched up at her hips. She danced before a group of men, running one hand over her crotch and the other through her hair. She pouted her lips and shook her head. "Yeah, yeah, okay," Johnson said. "If you want to bring her along, go ahead."

"Unbelievable."

"What?"

"What? What?" she said mimicking him. "You're really something, you know that? Really something."

"What's that supposed to mean?"

"Shut up and drink your beer."

"You asked me what I thought, goddamn it. I told you, but if you want to hit on her, bring her by the house, that's fine with me."

"And what are you going to do?"

"Be nice," he said. "I'll be nice."

"Listen, Johnson," she said. "Your life isn't so tough. You know how many other guys are sitting home right now with wives and kids wishing they were where you are? Wishing they lived your life?"

"Don't believe it," Johnson said. "Just don't believe that for a minute. Even if they thought they wanted to live this way, they wouldn't."

"What are you telling me?"

"Nothing about us. Nothing about me, but about other guys. Other guys might like it once or twice to have a couple of women."

"Or to have a couple of women have them."

"Right." Johnson nodded. "But most guys don't want to complicate things with women. They want it easy. So they can put their lives on auto-pilot. Just cruise."

"And your life Johnson? Is your life on auto pilot?"

"No, I don't believe it is."

"That's good," she said. Al looked at her watch. "You know one week from today we'll be on the plane to London."

Johnson took a sip of his beer. "Jesus, that'll be a long flight, won't it?"

Al nodded her head. "We'll fly through the night. You might sleep."

Johnson nodded his head and glanced around the bar. JoJo had finished her dance and was working the crowd. Men stuck money into her garter, kissed her hand. One man fell to his knees and begged her for something. Johnson couldn't hear what. She laughed and waved the man away. Behind the bar, Lucy shook her finger in the face of one of the dancers. She was a new kid. Johnson figured her for about 17 with fake identification. There were tears on the kid's cheeks.

Dressed again as a parochial school girl, JoJo approached, grinning. "Did you enjoy my set?" she asked.

Al held her index finger in front of her lips. She nodded, one eye closed and pointed a finger at JoJo. "Beautiful," she said. "Absolutely beautiful. Isn't that right, Johnson?

Johnson nodded his head. "Beautiful," he said. "Absolutely."

Al put her hand on Johnson's arm. "I'll get this one," she said, lifting a five dollar bill out of the breast pocket of her blouse. She smoothed it between her fingers, then lifted the garter away from JoJo's leg and slid the bill in amongst the others. Her fingernails rode the dancer's thigh to her knee. "Johnson and I were wondering if you had plans later?"

JoJo placed her hand against Al's. "I don't have plans," she said, "but later is four a.m."

Johnson saw what attracted Al to JoJo. She had small pert breasts, a young ass and a direct way of talking that Al had brought home before. He wondered how women spotted each other. Women who liked women and didn't mind men. Or, maybe, women who liked men and women. Or women who liked men and didn't mind women. But Al spotted them and she was spotted back. Johnson had seen it all. Butch chicks who followed him into men's rooms and ask if he wanted to fight for Al. Al's old girl friends who stumbled up to their table -- sometimes drunk, sometimes sober -- and railed against Al's sudden interest in men. She'd told Johnson that she'd just changed her mind.

A person, she claimed, had a right to do that, you know. Yeah, Johnson agreed, knowing if you could change your mind once, you could change it back.

And at first he didn't mind. At first, Al was too young. She came from somewhere else, not a place Johnson had been to. They had fun. Johnson had had fun before. It started and it ended, like he was sure Al would. But as time passed and he grew more attached to Al, the thought of her changing her mind woke him in the middle of the night, leaving him to stare into the darkness that he imagined his future would be without Al.

She was good for him. He told her once, only half joking, "You know, you're old enough to fuck and still young enough to believe in something."

"What is that supposed to mean?" she asked.

Johnson didn't want to get into it. He said, "Fuck if I know."

But he knew. He paid attention. Al lit candles and sang in Hebrew on Jewish holidays. She gave money to charity. Not dimes or quarters to wineheads on the street, even Johnson did that, but she sat down and wrote checks. She once told Johnson that you could change things for the better. Johnson knew you couldn't change anything that mattered, but he didn't tell Al for fear she might agree with him. She knew *we* needed to do something about Bosnia, Rwanda, Chechnya. And she had ideas.

"Here's one," she said, handing Johnson a child-proof jar of aspirins. "A catalog of things that are not child-proof."

"Yeah, that's right," Johnson said. He pulled the cap off with his teeth and handed her the bottle.

"The potential market is huge," she said. Al dumped three aspirins into her hand, tossed them back and chewed as she spoke. The pills crunched like candy. "Okay. It's kind of a yuppie thing, like the left-handed catalog, but just think about it. You've got all the people who don't have kids and all the people who have grown up kids. That's a huge market."

"Yeah," Johnson said. "And you've got all those people who want their kids to grow up in the real world and don't believe in that child-proof crap."

Al laughed, covering her mouth with her left hand.

"What's so funny?" he asked.

Johnson didn't mind when Al laughed at him, people had done worse. There wasn't much about Al that bothered him, except her TV. Johnson hated her television.

Al's TV, a big screen Sony Trinitron, moved into Johnson's house the same day she did. When the guys from Gomez Moving carried it into the TV-less living room, Johnson shouted, "Jesus, Al, what the fuck is that?"

"My TV," she said.

"Yeah, I see that," he said. "I never saw it before. You just get it?"

"No, I've had it for a while, but it was too big for my apartment. I kept it in storage."

"Well, it's almost too big for the world, don't you think?"

"Don't be silly. It fits fine."

"I don't think I like it."

"My grandmother gave it to me. It's a family heirloom."

"A TV can't be an heirloom."

"Why not?"

"For something to be an heirloom," Johnson said, "it needs to be old and useless."

"Well, maybe for you," she said. "But for me, anything my grandmother gives me is an heirloom."

"A bag of apples?"

"What?"

"A bag of apples," Johnson repeated. "If your grandmother gave you a bag of apples would they be an heirloom?"

"Yes, they would," she said. "And I would eat them."

Johnson stood between Al and the three guys holding the TV. One of the guys, the one who spoke English, smiled at him and shrugged. Johnson figured they saw a lot of fights on moving day. He knew people got tired and scared when things changed, and hauling all your stuff from one place to another, Jesus, what could be worse? Johnson looked from Al (she'd crossed her arms over her chest) to the three guys. Nicaraguans -- must be, he thought. They've got the shit jobs now. *"Nicaraguense?"* he asked. They all nodded, but only the one who spoke English smiled. Aw, fuck it, he thought, this was not an argument he could win. He waved his hand. "Put it over there," he said.

"No, no," Al said. "Not there, over here."

Johnson watched the movers place the heirloom in the corner and convinced himself that he might get used it. How bad could it be? He didn't have to turn it on.

It wasn't the idea of TV that bothered him. He didn't mind watching football in a bar. But this one, the one in his house, was huge. The screen measured more than a yard square. When off, it fish-eyed back everything in the living room. The cold gray screen distorted shapes and erased all sense of depth. The heirloom reduced Johnson's living room to a cartoon. It made his things, and by extension his life, seem paltry. He'd turn it on to erase his own image from the screen, only to discover that the heirloom presented the entire world as a cartoon. The Serbs were road runners, the UN coyotes; Dole, Gingrich and Helms became Curly, Larry and Moe; the Clinton Administration seemed a cross between Gilligan's Island and the Beverly Hillbillies. Johnson believed life was more complicated.

One Wednesday night, while Al and he tasted 'the best naturalgrown reefer available north of Bogota,' Johnson decided it was time to talk about the heirloom. He told Al the story of the plaster head of Jesus that hung in his first girlfriend's living room. "Her parents were real Catholics," he said. "But back then everyone was."

Al, holding in the hit from the joint, croaked, "Speak for yourself."

Johnson ignored her. "Everywhere you went in that room," he said, "Jesus's eyes followed. You couldn't do anything without him watching. I'd be on top of her, on the couch, trying to feel her tits. I'd look up and Jesus would be staring at me. The TV is like that. Everywhere we go in this place, it's watching. You think you're watching it, but it's watching you. It's stolen my fun," he said. "Let's get rid of it." Johnson reached for the joint and took a deep hit.

"Did she have nice tits?" Al asked.

"What?" Johnson asked not getting her point.

"Did your girlfriend have nice tits?"

"I'm not talking about tits," he said, exhaling. "I'm talking about TV."

"Well, I'm talking about tits. Did she have nice tits?"

"She had tits. At twelve or thirteen, any tits are nice."

"So Jesus watched you fondle those nice tits?"

"Not Jesus," he started to say.

Al laughed.

"What's so funny?" he asked.

She rolled off the couch and lay on the floor clutching her stomach. "It's the pot," she gasped.

The music in the club stopped for a moment and began again. Al rubbed his knee, the way she did when he drifted and she wanted his attention. "Where are you?" she asked.

"Right here," Johnson said.

She smiled, nodded and turned back to the dancer. "Sorry, JoJo, but we're civilians and it's only Tuesday. I have places to be in the morning. But here," Al pulled her card out, like Johnson had seen so many times before. "Call me. We'll have dinner and maybe a little fun."

Johnson waited until JoJo was out of earshot before he thanked Al.

"You're welcome," she said. "But I do have to get up in the morning."

"I know," he said. "But thank you, anyway."

"Johnson, you're killing me. I'm not changing my mind."

He nodded. "Yeah, yeah."

"We have a deal. I don't go back on deals."

Johnson looked around Heaven's Gate. JoJo climbed up on a table and began to dance for group of men in business suits. The new dancer on stage had Christmas red hair and a boa constrictor wrapped around her neck. She didn't really dance, just stepped from side to side, holding the snake in place.

"I'm pretty beat," he said. "You ready to go?"

CHAPTER 8

"Classic? Classic my ass," Johnson would say when people admired the Fat Man's 1962, avocado green Lincoln Continental. "It gets two miles to the gallon...drives like a fucking barge. There's no parking spot big enough. It's got suicide doors. You think they're called 'suicide' cause they worked? Classic? Know what classic means? Classic means your mechanic can afford a wife, a bunch of kids and some strange on the side. Classic means you get the drizzle shits when tires squeal behind you. Classic means every time you stop for gas, some motor-head is going to start yammering about valve tolerance, manifolds or fucking transmission linkages. Fuck classic. Buy a Crown Victoria -- a Crown Vic. That's a car. Brand new? They're a fucking dream."

The Fat Man didn't buy a new Crown Vic or any other car. The Lincoln worked for him. Half the front seat had been removed, and the suicide doors opened out, like the double doors at the back of a hearse, providing Teitelbaum enough space to heave his ample bulk into the rear seat. The engine, eight cylinders of Cold War overkill, climbed from zero to sixty in ten seconds while lugging the Fat Man's 499 pounds. It rode as smoothly as a recliner and, in the 1990s, the green Lincoln wheeled through Miami Beach like an apparition -- a reminder of a time past.

It had been conferred on the Fat Man by the old mamzers, men who, in the forties, fifties and sixties, had interests in Miami Beach -- book making, prostitution, loan sharking. The Lincoln had history. Meyer Lansky sat in the back seat and bitched, again, about getting fucked by Israel. Izzy Cohen assured a CIA agent that he shouldn't worry so much: whacking Fidel would be easier than taking out the trash. Frank Sinatra, Dean Martin and Sammy Davis, Jr. had ridden in the car. Martin, drunk again, rode in the trunk. One of Jack's women rode in the car from Joe's Stone Crab up to the Kennedy compound in Palm Beach. On the way up, the take-out order dripped stone crab juice on the seat. On the way back, she dripped Presidential cum. And *The Four Guys* met in that car for the first time, but no one mentions them anymore.

Two Krispy Kreme donut boxes, one empty, lay on the back seat beside the Fat Man as Johnson navigated the Lincoln up Washington Avenue to meet Mondongo at Katz's Deli, Teitelbaum's favorite restaurant on South Beach. Through mouthfuls of donut, the man's high-pitched humming filled the car like the chirping of young birds. Johnson had a hangover. The Fat Man's humming annoyed him; he recognized the murmur as a sign of nervousness. He watched the Fat Man in the rear-view mirror. His glasses, oversized frames perched on his oversized head, glinted in the sunlight and prevented Johnson from seeing his eyes. He wore a powder blue jump suit, zippered and belted. Its collar disappeared under a roll of fat that flared out from the Fat Man's neck.

"Are you okay today, sir?" Johnson asked.

The Fat Man laughed, a high piercing giggle. "Why, Johnson, I'm fine," he said, his squeaky voice rising higher and squeakier.

"That's good," Johnson said. "It's just sometimes. You know?"

"You know what, Johnson?"

"You know, like, when we're going someplace that makes you nervous, you hum. Like today."

"Examples, Johnson, give me examples."

"The doctors. Whenever you go to the doctors."

"The doctors don't count. I am nervous then. Aren't you nervous when you go to the doctors?"

"I don't go to doctors."

"Yes, you do."

"No," Johnson said. "I don't go to doctors."

"Last month. You told me you went for a pain in the middle of your chest."

"I did," Johnson said, "but I only go when I have to. It's not like I go regularly."

"Then say, I don't regularly go to the doctor, but I do go."

"Okay, I don't go regularly. I don't have check-ups." Johnson wondered if he should. Maybe they'd catch whatever was going to kill him. No. He knew his life was going to kill him. That was the real bitch.

"When else?" the Fat Man chirped.

"When else what, sir?"

"When else do you think I'm nervous?"

"The mamzers. Whenever we go visit one of the mamzers."

"They're smart men, Johnson. A little fear can be a good thing with them."

"Okay," Johnson said. "So, you are nervous."

"You know what I do."

"You have friends, sir."

"Well, Johnson, do me a favor. Be a friend. Shut up."

"Yes, sir," he replied.

Katz's Deli had a take-out counter and eight tables with four chairs each, scattered about the narrow room. Eight-by-ten publicity stills of Kirk Douglas, Dino, Sammy, Jerry Lewis, and others who'd visited the deli circled the restaurant. The place smelled of new kosher pickling and old people's clothes. Fluorescent lights buzzed over-head; an Afro-French patois crept from the cook's tinny radio, tuned all-day to a Haitian Creole talk station.

One day, as he demolished his fourth brisket on rye, the Fat Man had told Johnson that when the old mamzers paid his way down to Miami, they brought him to straight to Katz's Deli. He said they fed him blintzes and talked business. "I was a kid, Johnson. Seventeen. These were men who knew things...Who'd seen things. And they talked to me like I was one of them." The Fat Man closed his eyes for a moment. "You know, Johnson," he said wistfully, "If these walls could talk, most of the mamzers would be doing life upstate."

Johnson parked the '62 Lincoln in the deli's loading zone, then ran around to open the Fat Man's door. A Miami Beach cop would sooner shoot the mayor's dog than ticket the Lincoln. Teitelbaum heaved his body from the car and marched into the deli, his great bulk quaking and shivering as he approached Mondongo, who sat with his back to the wall at the "business table" in the restaurant's far end. "Blintzes," the Fat Man cried. "I need a triple order."

Sophie, a waitress with the face of a woman who had bad feet, raced up, holding his plate of blintzes aloft. She was dressed in pink sneakers, white support hose, and a pink waitress uniform with a blue apron. Red and yellow rubber bands circled her wrists. She carried a pencil behind each ear. Her coiffed hair was the color of Miller High Life beer and the texture of spun fiberglass.

The Fat Man sat down using two chairs, one for each butt cheek.

Sophie slid the plate of blintzes in front of him. "How are you, Stephen?" she asked.

The Fat Man dipped a blintz in sour cream and dropped it whole into his mouth.

"Much better, now, Sophie. Much better. Thank you. And you, dear. How are you?"

"Don't ask," she replied.

"Sophie, can I get some coffee?" Johnson asked, still trying to scatter the hangover moths fluttering in his head.

"And you, honey?" she said to Mondongo.

"Nothing," he replied.

"You must have something," the Fat Man insisted. "A man must always have something in front of him when he sits at a table with me."

"Water," Mondongo said. "No ice."

The Fat Man laughed. "My friend, you are so much yourself."

"We are both ourselves," Mondongo observed solemnly.

The Fat Man gestured at Mondongo. "Did you hear that, Johnson?"

"Yes, sir," Johnson said, wishing for some aspirin.

Sophie placed a coffee mug in front of Johnson. A glass of water before Mondongo.

Teitelbaum continued. "A pearl. A gem. Mondongo, you are a spokesman for your people."

Mondongo sat up in his chair and lifted the glass in the Fat Man's direction. "I drink to you."

The Fat Man returned the salute with a blintz and dropped it whole into his mouth. "You're too kind, Mondongo. Too kind," he said, chewing. "Shall we do a little business?"

Mondongo opened a black leather portfolio and placed a business-sized envelope on the table. He looked at the Fat Man, then leaned closer to Johnson. Mondongo whispered, "I know that you are dying to know the contents of this package, *Señor*." He tapped the envelope. "But you must let history take its course. You are not a great man, do not concern yourself with these issues. Your mind is not capable. You will deliver the pages that change history, but your name shall not be recorded. Know that to the future you are nothing."

"I'll keep that in mind," Johnson said.

Mondongo pushed the envelope to him. "Deliver it as soon as possible to a man at the Cuban Embassy in London. His name is Antonio Gomez. There may be a reply. There may not."

Johnson nodded and lifted the envelope between two fingers. It was made of plain white paper of not particularly good quality. No address had been written across its front. He guessed, by its heft, it held two pages, three at the most. "Right," he said, looking Mondongo in the eyes. "It goes directly to Antonio Gomez. You're sure he's there?"

"He's there."

"Do I hand it directly to him? Or..."

Mondongo turned to the Fat Man. "Must he make this so complicated?"

"Johnson?" the Fat Man asked.

"Sir," Johnson said, "I want to know if I can hand this letter to someone at the embassy other than Gomez."

"Mondongo?" the Fat Man asked, shifting his gaze.

"Hand it to Gomez and no one else," Mondongo replied.

"Okay," Johnson said, "Cuban Embassy, London. Antonio Gomez. Consider it done. Now, there's the matter of five thousand dollars."

The Fat Man choked on a blintz. He waved his arms, trying to slap his own back. His eyes bulged. He moaned.

Johnson had seen Teitelbaum choke before. He leaned over and slapped the Fat Man once between his shoulder blades.

"What are you talking about?" the Fat Man wheezed when his breath returned.

"The five you said I'd get for delivering the letter."

"Wait. Are you telling me you think I'm paying you fifty large to sit on a plane for a couple of hours and deliver a letter to a place you're going already?"

"You told me you'd split the ten long *Señor* Mondongo's agreed to pay for this service."

"I didn't say split it in half."

"Yes you did. You said, one half. I heard you. *Señor* Mondongo heard you." Johnson turned to Mondongo.

"Yes, *Señor* Teitelbaum. You said one half."

"I did?" he said. "I forgot. Well, if that's what I said."

"Yeah, that's it."

"I'll hold it until your return."

Johnson slid the envelope across the table to Mondongo. "Sir, I'm sorry, but I can't do business this way." He stood up to leave.

"Where's he going?" Mondongo cried.

"Nowhere," Teitelbaum said. "Right, Johnson?"

"How do you know, sir?"

"Johnson, you couldn't walk away from this table any easier than I could leave that last blintz." The Fat Man lifted the last blintz between two fingers, held it over his mouth and dropped it into the maw.

Johnson sat down.

"Okay, Johnson, you win. Mr. Mondongo has agreed to one

half up front. One half when the project's completed. I'll pay you through the usual sources."

The Fat Man converted Johnson's pay to legitimate income through Dinesh Ramgoolam and charged Johnson five percent for the service. It was an arrangement Johnson had gotten used to. His paychecks, always for courier services, came from companies he'd never heard of. Johnson deposited the checks in his bank account and Dinesh Ramgoolam did his taxes. Johnson looked clean on paper, but if you asked him where the offices of the South Florida Land Title Company were, he would not have known. The same could be said for the BD&T Recording Studios, Echeverria Entertainment, or Doc Thomas's Equestrian Center.

"Not this time," Johnson said. "I want to feel the cash."

The Fat Man eyes narrowed as he looked at Johnson. "You want what?"

"I want the cash. What's wrong with that?" He turned to Mondongo. "Do you think there's anything wrong with me asking for cash?"

"*Señor* Johnson, don't put me in the middle between you and *el gordo*."

"What did you call me?" Teitelbaum bellowed.

Mondongo leaned back in his chair and held in hands up in surrender. "It was a mistake, *Señor*. I meant nothing by it."

"*El gordo*? Johnson, you speak their language. Tell me what that means."

"I think it means 'fat one,' sir." Johnson swallowed back a smirk. "If I'm not mistaken, I think he just called you the fat one."

Teitelbaum swept the empty blitz plate from the table with the back of his hand and leaned toward the table, his stomach pushing it into Mondongo. "I admit that I haven't taken care of my body. But I have been dieting lately. I've lost weight, haven't I, Johnson?"

"Yes, sir," Johnson said.

"Now, we have a good business relationship, Mondongo, but I will not stand for personal attacks. Do you understand that?"

"Yes, of course, *Señor*. Who in their right mind could not see that you have been losing weight? I mentioned it just the other day to my wife, Conchy, that I was speaking with *Señor* Teitelbaum and how it looked as if he had been dieting and perhaps working out because of the fine tone I noticed in his skin color."

"You said that to Conchy?"

Mondongo nodded. "I did."

"How is she, Mondongo? I haven't seen her since *Noche Buena*, what is it ten? No, twenty years now?"

"Has it been so long?" Mondongo asked. "In exile time runs quickly. But your people, *Señor* Teitelbaum, understand exile. Your people, too, have wandered for many years."

Teitelbaum glanced at Johnson. He leaned back and nodded. "When I was a kid, my folks took a vacation and drove all the way from the Bronx to Miami Beach. So I do know what you mean about exile and wandering, my friend. Believe me I do. Did you ever have one of those Stuckey's Nut Logs you could get along the highways back then? When I think of our wanderings to Miami Beach, I am reminded of those Nut Logs. I must have eaten a crate of them on the trip." The Fat Man turned to Johnson. "Are you familiar with the Stuckey Nut Log, Johnson?"

"I've seen the signs, sir, but I've never actually eaten one."

The Fat Man sighed. "You'll never understand life until you can comprehend exile and nut logs."

"No, no." Mondongo said. "He can understand it, but he'll never appreciate it."

"That's it. You're exactly right."

"You should talk with Mr. Mondongo more, Johnson. You could come to understand a lot about this wretched planet."

"I suppose you're both right, gentlemen. But there's the matter of $2,500 that I'd like to settle before I leave here today."

"It'll be done the usual way, Johnson. No cash. Consider the matter settled," the Fat Man said.

And Johnson did.

CHAPTER 9

Johnson dressed to travel the way he dressed to drive. The evening he and Al left for London, Johnson wore a gray sport jacket over a green pocketed t-shirt, black jeans and black half-boots. In the cab on the way to Miami International Airport, he reached into the jacket's inner breast pocket and ran his fingers over Mondongo's letter. His mind drifted back to Katz's Deli. Mondongo. The Fat Man. Antonio Gomez? He tapped the letter.

"You got a rash?" Al asked.

"No. Why?"

"You keep reaching inside your jacket."

"It's nothing," he said, running his thumb down the envelope's edge. "Nothing."

"Good," Al said.

They checked their luggage curbside and left behind the humid exhaust-blown air as they passed into the airport's cool interior. Johnson carried the blue gabardine trench coat Al had bought him at a secondhand store over his right shoulder. Al wore her coat cape-like across her shoulders. She toted a small leather backpack in her right hand. In it she carried the tickets, passports, and magazines.

The airport's lines, crowds, and hustle caused Johnson to think, this must be what it's like in an airport after a revolution. Everybody wants to take as much of their shit as they can and get the fuck out. People wore fear and desperation on their faces.

"Al," he said as they swung around two guys carrying a GE refrigerator box on their shoulders. "Do you think there's anything strange about the Miami airport?"

"It's an airport, Johnson. They're all strange."

"I used to spend a lot of time in Atlanta's. It was nothing like this."

"Atlanta is nothing like Miami," Al said. "What do you expect?"

"I don't know. Don't things seem a little desperate here?"

"More desperate than Atlanta? I don't know. I'd say Atlanta is the United States and Miami is America. I guess things are more desperate in America."

"Huh?" Johnson said.

Al said, "It's like my friend Brian says, 'Miami is beautiful... and so close to the United States.'"

Johnson laughed.

At check-in, the flight's reality settled on Johnson. Eight hours in those damn seats. Jesus. He followed Al onto the plane like a prisoner being led to solitary. Eight hours. Goddamn, eight hours.

As they passed through first class, Johnson envied the passengers with seats as big as couches. Stewardesses poured champagne into fluted glasses and offered tidbits from the galley that had never seen the inside of a freezer, much less a microwave oven. Music played softly. The passengers spoke quietly. A man sipping champagne looked up at Johnson over the top of his glass. He seemed about Johnson's age. Johnson rolled his eyes at the man, to say 'this is all so stupid, don't you think?' The man ignored him. Johnson moved on.

In coach, row upon row of tiny seats stretched away into the distance. The hold looked as long as a football field and half as wide. It was hot. Johnson smelled baby vomit, cheap perfume, and unwashed bodies. The passengers wore Mickey Mouse ears, Goofy hats and Disney t-shirts. Their faces, all scorched by the Florida sun, were red, freckled and peeling. They could have been cancer patients, or Chernobyl survivors, but Johnson knew them for what they were -- British tourists on their way home after visiting Disney.

"I know," Al said. "You hate Disney."

"How do you know what I'm thinking?"

"Because I know."

"Right," he said.

Al and Johnson disagreed about Disney. Al marveled at the marketing. She said Disney could run the world. They were too damn good. She challenged Johnson to find somebody who did better marketing than Disney.

"I don't care about marketing," he said.

"Marketing is everything, Johnson. And everything is marketing."

"Fine," Johnson said. "Go visit the rat, and get back to me on the fun you had."

"I don't want to go to Disney -- I've already been. I admire their marketing ability. That's all. You ought to admire that, too," she said.

"I don't have to admire shit," Johnson said. "Pretend this. Pretend that. That little fucking rat? Fuck me."

Johnson followed Al past sunburnt children, crying babies, and tired adults. She pointed to their seats and climbed in next to the window. Johnson dropped into the aisle seat, balled his trench coat up and slid it under the seat in front of him. Sunburned Brits scrambled through the cabin stuffing and cramming every available nook with coats, bags, hats, suitcases, coolers and cardboard boxes.

A young blond man wearing a navy-blue jacket and tie stood at the front of the cabin waving to the crowd. He held a microphone up and said, "Folks, my name is Marcus, and I'm the steward on this flight. As we prepare for take-off today, I'd like to remind you that all your belongings must fit beneath the seat in front of you or in the overhead compartments. If you have anything that doesn't fit, we must stow it in the luggage compartment, underneath the plane."

"There you go," Johnson hissed to Al. "I like that guy. He'll bring some order to this fucking chaos."

"This is not chaos," Al said.

"I don't care. I like that guy."

"Now," the steward continued, "I'd like to take this opportunity to welcome you aboard English Airways, and as a final memory of your visit to America, I'd like to lead you in a song that I am sure you're all very familiar with." Music played over the public address system. The steward sang into the microphone, "It's a world of laughter, a world of tears. It's a world of hope and a world of fears. There's so much that we share, that it's time we're aware, it's a small world after all. Come on," he cried. "You know the words. It's a small world after all...."

Al laughed.

"What the fuck is this?" Johnson demanded.

"Bringing order to chaos," she replied. "Or, the best damn marketing."

Adults stopped packing, children stopped whining, infants grew quiet and together they sang, laughing and smiling at one another.

Johnson had plans for just such a contingency. During his forty-one years on the planet, he had developed six rules of personal behavior. The third rule: never take valium while drinking vodka. The double v combination knocked him unconscious. As the flight attendants and passengers sang the Disney theme song, he reached into his suit coat pocket for the Tylenol bottle with one valium in it and a single serve bottle of Smirnoff vodka. He turned to Al and said, "Wake me when we get to London."

"What?"

"I'll be going to sleep now." He popped the valium into his mouth, twisted the cap off the vodka and swallowed the contents of the bottle. Johnson recapped the bottle and stuffed it in the seat pocket in front of him. He thought to ask Al if she wanted to change seats so she'd have an easier time getting in and out during the flight, but passed out instead.

Johnson's issue with valium had more than one side to it. Sure, there was the passing out, but there was also the waking up. The next thing he knew, Al and the steward, Marcus, were splashing water in his face.

"Hey, what the fuck?" Johnson said.

"Good, you're alive," Al said. "We've been trying to wake you for ten minutes."

Johnson breathed; pain, like lightning, flashed through his head. He groaned and blinked to stop from seeing double.

"Will he be okay?" Marcus asked.

"He'll be fine," Johnson said. His teeth hurt. "Jesus, Al, what'd you do, beat me up while I slept?'

"Yeah. I told everyone on the plane that you hated Disney and each of them came by and punched you. They wanted to drop you into the ocean, but I thought that was a little much."

"You hate Disney?" Marcus asked. "How can you hate Disney? Disney is happiness. Disney is love."

"How can you be so stupid?" Johnson asked.

"Sir," the steward said, "I just asked a question. There's no need to get hostile."

"Well, I hate fucking Disney. I'd like to build a big rat trap, catch that little fucker Mickey and cut his fucking ears off with a dull goddamn knife. What do you think of that?"

The steward backed down the aisle.

"Don't pay any attention to him," Al said. "He always gets this way when he's hung-over."

"So, I'm hung-over, goddamn it. But even when I'm not, I hate Disney."

"Johnson, shut up. You slept the whole damn flight. Just get your ass off the plane before they send security to take us off."

Johnson stood up. Hot liquid in his brain rolled from side to side. "Jesus," he said.

Al handed him his trench coat and pushed him down the aisle. The flight crew stood at the cockpit door. The steward cupped his hand over his mouth and spoke to the other flight attendants. They looked at Johnson as if he were a leper. If he felt better, he might have flipped them off. But he didn't feel better.

He and Al walked up the jet-way, down a long blue-carpeted corridor, through double glass doors and into a holding room where hundreds of people waited in line. As they inched toward an immigration check point, something bothered Johnson.

Something more than the hangover. He stared at Al.

She caught him looking, and said, "Yes?"

"Nothing," he said, because he couldn't put it into words. It had to do with being a foreigner. They were someplace other than home and things would be different -- colors, people, what they thought good or bad. He nearly said, "Things are different here. Right?" But he saw something familiar in the distance. The security guards at the immigration desk wore the same uniforms as the guys who guarded the Fat Man's island. Jesus. He might have laughed if he wasn't hung-over. Johnson thought of saying to the guard, "I'm a friend of Steve Teitelbaum," to see if it whisked him through the gates.

Johnson approached the desk and nodded to the guard. "You know," he said, "Your company is headquartered where I live."

"What of it?" the guard said. He looked past Johnson into the crowd.

"Guards I know say the work's okay until a real job comes along."

The guard nodded and smiled. "That's the way of it, eh mate?"

Johnson grinned. The guy spoke English like an English guy. "Right, mate," Johnson said. He winked at Al. She shook her head.

"Station number four," the guard said, and pointed to an open reception desk.

"Thanks, mate," Johnson said.

At the desk, an immigration officer examined his passport, asked him where he was born, if he was in Great Britain on business or pleasure and how long he intended to stay. Johnson said he was from the states, in Great Britain on vacation and intended to stay ten days.

Johnson's and Al's suitcases lazed around the luggage carousel -- the last two on the belt. He grabbed a small metal cart, dropped their bags into it and followed Al to the customs counter. She pushed two pieces of paper across to a spectacled kid in a dark blue sweater with epaulets and a badge. A cowlick swirled over his head. He scanned the papers and glanced up at Al, then past her to Johnson. Johnson braced to be searched. They wouldn't just let him into a whole other country, without a good grilling.

"Anything to declare?" the kid asked smiling, teeth scattered around his mouth like a handful of Chiclets.

"No," Al said.

"You, sir?

"Nope," Johnson said. "Nothing to declare."

"Enjoy your stay in the UK, then."

Johnson wondered for a moment if maybe he should have done a little extra business, then dismissed the idea immediately. Al would have killed him.

"Wait," she'd said to him the day before they left. "The Fat Man is giving you five thousand dollars to take something to London."

Johnson had just opened a beer. He sucked foam from the bottle's top, nodding his head. "Yeah, five long, less the five p conversion to legit." He didn't tell her he'd wanted cash but couldn't get it.

"So, what is that to those of us in the real world?"

"Five thousand dollars. Less the five percent he charges for conversion to legitimate money that I can report to the IRS."

"Five percent to your accountant, Dinesh whatever?"

"Ramgoolam. Dinesh Ramgoolam. And no, the five percent goes to the Fat Man as his percentage. Dinesh gets his taste in accounting fees." Johnson swallowed a guzzle of beer.

"So what exactly are you delivering?"

"I can't say," he said. "But as far as I can tell it's not illegal."

"What do you mean, as far as you can tell? They're paying you five thousand dollars to deliver something and you don't think it's illegal?"

Johnson walked out to the back porch and dropped into a red plastic Adirondack chair. "Listen, some people buy their suits at JC Penney. They cost what, a buck?"

"A buck being one hundred in this case."

"Right, and some people buy their suits from Armani or a private tailor and spend who knows what? Right?"

"Right."

"Think of me as the Armani of delivery men."

Al laughed. "And I am?"

"Whatever you want to be? My lovely assistant. My trusty side-kick."

"Wily adviser."

"Main squeeze."

"Trusted counselor."

"Babe."

"Not a chance," Al said. "Wily adviser or nothing."

"Wily adviser," he agreed. "Wily adviser to the Armani of delivery men."

Johnson surveyed the people in Gatwick International Airport's lobby. So this is London, he thought. The people crowding the airport looked as if they hadn't seen the sun in years. The Africans seemed paler than Anglos in Miami. Even their clothes were dark and brooding, as if the weather had sucked all the color from them.

Al changed money into pound notes and handed it to Johnson. "See," she said, "English money."

He looked at the different sized and colored bills, surprised to see how many new things he'd have to learn. "Shit," he said, "it's really different."

Al laughed. "Of course it is. What did you expect?"

"Well, I guessed it would be different, but not this different. It's like red and yellow. What's that all about?"

"It's so you can tell the bills apart."

"Apart from what?" Johnson complained. "I don't know what they are."

"You'll learn. Don't worry. Oh, yeah," she said, "remember one pound is not one dollar. One pound is a dollar and a half."

"Aw man, what a rip," Johnson said.

"What do you mean?"

Johnson wasn't sure. "Aw, you know," he said.

"No," Al said. "I don't."

"Well, I mean. One of their pounds cost me a dollar fifty."

"Yeah?"

"Well, shit. What's that all about?"

"Local currency and exchange rate," Al said. "But you know Johnson, this is not the time to discuss relative currency value. I'm tired. I want to shower."

"Yeah, yeah," Johnson said. "Go. Go."

Johnson followed Al down an escalator to a train platform. She purchased two tickets from a vending machine and they boarded. Al fell asleep against his shoulder as soon as she sat down. The train was really no different than any he'd ridden in the states. A conductor came through the cars and punched their tickets. The tracks were lined with weeds, stained by oil and fuel, burnt back by fire and frost.

Slowly, Johnson began to notice things that told him he was in England. A Vauxhall car depot. Houses joined at the hips, side by side along the track, with small gardens snaking out behind them. Old brick houses with new dormers and additions. The gray sky, the lack of sun, the greenways and large parks alongside the tracks.

They whisked by a station platform. It was morning, and Johnson recognized rush hour when he saw it. People stood dressed for business. They wore long coats, to their knees and below. Some of the men wore caps, some hats, but their heads and ears looked cold. Johnson had intended to bring just the gray sport jacket for warmth, but Al said he'd need more than that in London. By the look of the people lining the platform he knew Al was right about the weather and the coat.

Seeing all the English people made Johnson feel funny in the bottom of his stomach. He knew tourists in Miami were real greenhorns, easy to take for money, fun, or sex. There must be people in London who took tourists for money or fun or sex. Johnson wondered what he would do if he met up with a guy like himself. Would he get taken? Would he do the taking? He decided the best thing to do would be nothing. Try not to get taken and not take anybody that required a lot of work. He was in a foreign place. They could throw him out. He turned and looked at Al sleeping, mouth open; a little snoring sound crept from her mouth. Jesus, if he got kicked out of the country, Al would be pretty pissed at him. He imagined her shouting, "Goddamn it, I can't take you anywhere. How were you raised for Christ's sake? Don't you know anything?"

He'd try and tell her it wasn't his fault -- that the rules were different in England. Johnson knew there was nothing he would purposely do to get kicked out. He would deliver the letter to the Cuban Embassy. When that was out of the way, he'd settle into the tourist thing. Check out the bars, see what really went on in London.

The train jogged sideways, changing tracks, and pulled under a long low glass-roofed building.

"Victoria Station, London. Last stop," a man's voice said over the loud speaker.

He nudged Al. "I think we're here," he said.

She coughed back a snore, sat up and looked out the window. "Looks like it," she said.

Johnson grabbed his bags and followed Al. They walked alongside the train into the diffused light that brightened Victoria Station. Johnson believed it a light soft enough to be used in heaven. He'd never seen anything like it. Red brick buildings, older than any in Miami, crowded up around him. Pigeons cooed and flew overhead. Mechanical train schedules flipped and clicked with the fluttering sound of shuffling cards. The concourse smelled of electric trains, coffee, and cheese warmed in dough.

"Jesus, Al," he said, "will you look at it."

"Look at what?"

"The station. It's," Johnson stopped and tried to figure out what exactly it looked like. "I'm not sure," he said after a pause, "but there's nothing like this in Miami."

"Johnson, close your mouth," Al said. "You look like some kind of rube."

"Al," he said, "I am some kind of rube."

She rolled her eyes. "Right, and I'm a nun."

Johnson wanted to drop his bags and sit for hours, just watching. "You know," he said, "I've never seen anything like this place before. It's like something out of a kid's train set." He looked up, squinting at the roof, trying to make sure he hadn't stumbled into some giant kid's playroom. Johnson had done enough drugs in his life that the possibility could not be completely ruled out.

"Johnson," Al said, "after we check into the hotel and I get a shower, we can come back here and you can stare open-mouthed at the ceiling all you want, but right now..."

"Yeah, yeah," he said. "I need a shower, too."

He followed Al through the station and out into London's early morning rush hour. Cabs, cars and people swarmed by him. Something was wrong. Definitely out of whack. Maybe he'd developed some inner ear problem on the flight. He tilted his head to the side and hopped on one foot, then the other.

"Johnson, what the hell are you doing?"

"Something's wrong here, Al. I think something screwed up in my head during the flight. Maybe it was the valium." Something similar had happened before. Once, after a bout with a bottle of Jack Daniels and a gram of cocaine, he'd had the distinct feeling of falling up.

"Like what?" Al asked.

"Traffic. There's something wrong with the traffic."

"What do you mean?" she asked. "Didn't you know it went the other way?"

Johnson looked at her to see if she was messing with him. "What do you mean, the other way?"

"The driver's on the right here and they drive on the left."

"What?" he asked. That couldn't be right.

"They drive completely opposite of us. You didn't know that?"

He thought for a second. Yeah, he had heard something about that. "Yeah, I guess I did. It just looks so funny."

Al strode over to the cab stand, opened a taxi door and threw in her luggage. "Come on," she said.

Johnson followed her into the cab.

She told the driver an address. "Near Notting Hill Gate," she said.

"Right, then," he said, and they were off.

"On holiday?" the driver asked.

"Working holiday," Al said.

Johnson said, "Yeah, working holiday."

"Yanks?" the driver said.

"Yeah," Johnson said, "Yanks."

"Where in the states do you live?"

"Miami," Johnson said.

"Oh, Miami," the driver replied. "That's down in Florida? Near Disney, right?"

"No," Johnson spat out. "You're thinking Orlando. We're nowhere near Disney."

"Shame," the driver said. "I understand it's a wonderful place."

Al squeezed Johnson's knee. "What's the weather been like?" she asked.

"Unseasonably warm and sunny. Haven't had a drop of rain in two weeks."

Johnson looked out the windshield and saw the driver turning into the wrong lane. "Watch out!" he cried.

The driver laughed. "I love you Yanks."

"Right," Johnson said. "Right." Johnson leaned back and watched people out the window. He tried to spot landmarks, things that would let him know where he'd been, but buildings cramped his vision and it seemed every other one was covered by scaffolds. He noticed people crossed with the lights and walked stiffly. They passed a Kentucky Fried Chicken and a McDonalds side by side. He'd liked to eat in those places in Miami, back before Al moved in.

"Do you know how many chemicals they pump into those animals?" she'd asked.

"More than I pump into me?" he replied.

She smiled, and said, "No, really."

He said, "Yeah, really."

"Forget it, Johnson. There's no talking to you."

He could have taken it farther, but there was no point. People just believed some things. It didn't matter how stupid some ideas were. People stuck to them. Sometimes Johnson admired that. Sometimes he didn't. Sometimes he wanted a double cheeseburger with fries.

They stopped at a traffic light. Johnson looked out his window at a man sitting in the gutter, drinking a can of Fosters beer. He wore a cardboard sign around his neck: **Irish Gypsy**, written in black magic marker. The guy's eyes were clear but his cheeks and nose were mottled red and blue. He stared at Johnson. Jesus, Johnson thought, I'm really glad I'm not you. The man nodded. The cab lurched forward. Johnson turned his head, to see if the man looked after him, but he couldn't tell. A chill ran up Johnson's spine. He'd been spooked like that before.

The other time was at the Betsy Ross. A Marielito living in the next room told Johnson he had invited a Santeria priest in to exorcise the bad spirits. Johnson, hung over, lay across his bed, tangled in sweaty sheets, listening to chanting in the hall. Beautiful rhythmic chants that reminded him of the Latin Mass. Beneath the chants he heard a goat bleating and smelled cigar smoke. As the chanting came closer he heard hoofs tapping the linoleum in the hallway. They wouldn't, he thought, knowing they would.

The procession passed his door and through the crack at the bottom he saw shadows, heard the tapping of the goat's hooves. He rolled from the bed. The smell of the cigar raised a gorge in his throat. He stumbled into the bathroom and vomited into the toilet. As he rested his cheek against the bowl, the chanting grew louder, drums beat a steady rhythm and behind the drumming he heard the calm bleating of the goat. The chants grew louder and Johnson heard a new voice, shouting in a language he'd never heard before. The rhythms grew faster.

Johnson heard a shout and the sound of a body falling to the floor. He vomited again. Footsteps sounded outside his doorway. Not the tap-tap of the goat's hooves. He rushed to the door and pulled it open and stepped naked into the hall. A dark-skinned woman dressed in white, a white cloth wrapping her head, turned back to Johnson. She moved a cigar from her lips and blew a plume of smoke at him.

"We cleaned you, too, *niño.* We clean everything here."

Johnson looked down at his nakedness. When he looked up the woman had gone on.

CHAPTER 10

Johnson and Al climbed out of the cab in front of a four-story white building. Thin columns supported a tiny balcony on the second floor, which served as cover for the front steps. A knee high, white brick wall enclosed the property. The building's embellishments, ornamented corners and scalloped railings appeared old and tired to Johnson. The place looked exactly like all the others up and down both sides of the block, except for the brass sign on the gate post: *Pembroke House*. Past the gate, poured concrete steps rose from street to double glass doors. Plants cluttered the stairway. Johnson reached for his wallet to pay the driver.

Al touched his arm. "I'll get it," she said. She handed the driver one of the funny colored bills. He handed her back some coins.

"So this is it?" Johnson asked.

"The guidebook claims it's the best place in London."

Johnson could tell by Al's tone that she was disappointed.

"If we don't like it," she said, "we can go somewhere else."

"I didn't say I didn't like it. I was just asking."

"I know you didn't say that. We could have stayed at the Sheraton. It would be just like staying in Cleveland. But this is London. I wanted something different."

"Okay," Johnson said.

"Okay," Al said.

Johnson dropped his bag at the top of the steps and held the door open for Al. An orange cat raced past his foot. A woman inside the hotel shrieked, "Victoria!!!" Johnson turned and watched as the cat raced beneath the cab's tire as it pulled from the curb. He closed his eyes. When he opened them, the orange cat raced in a circle in the middle of the street. Blood leaked from what remained of its tail. The woman vaulted past Johnson, over Al and into the street. A low wail, as cold and chilling as the cat's howls, escaped from her throat as she and the cat began chasing each other around an invisible tree. After ten revolutions, the cat raced off under a hedge. The woman fell to her knees. "Victoria," she wailed. "Victoria."

The woman was the first English woman Johnson had an opportunity to observe in any detail. She had dark hair, dyed. Her breasts looked small, but firm. He figured her to be his age or older. Mascara ran with the tears on her face, and she looked frightening in her grief. She wore a black dress, dark black stockings, and low black shoes. Johnson thought she'd be sort of attractive if she could get over the damn cat.

Johnson knew about cats and people. Regarding cats, there were basically three types of people in the world -- those who worshipped them, those who loathed them and those who didn't care. Johnson didn't care. A cat? A dog? Sure -- one barked, one meowed, but when you got right down to it, both cat and dog ate, slept, and shat on their owner's dime. Some might imagine that a cat would chase mice for you, or a dog would bark at robbers, but it was Johnson's experience that they did neither.

The woman pointed a finger at Johnson. "You let her out! You know that's not allowed."

"What are you talking about?" Johnson said.

"You did. You let her out on purpose."

Johnson laughed. "I didn't know anything about her," he said. "How could I? I've never been here before."

"In the pre-visit packet," the woman said. "Page four, paragraph three -- it reads, 'The true owners of the Pembroke House Hotel are the beloved Victoria and Albert. All guests are asked to do everything in their power to ensure the comfort of the House royalty.' And below that paragraph are the rules," she hissed. "Number one, 'Like true royalty, Victoria and Albert have not experienced the common world of rough and tumble London. They ask your indulgence; please do not allow them out of the hotel.'" The woman pushed to her feet.

"They are royalty," she said. "They will not know how to mix with the commoners."

"Well, I'm sorry," Johnson said. "But I didn't see any pre-visit packet."

"I saw it," Al said, "But I thought it was a joke."

"Hardly," the woman said. Her eyes widened, and she brought the back of her hand up to her mouth.

Johnson followed her stare. A piece of orange tail lay in the gutter. She screamed and collapsed in the street.

A tall man dressed in a blue waistcoat rushed past Johnson. He bent down to the woman, cradled her in his arms and carried her up the steps. "Welcome to Pembroke House," he said, in an accent Johnson didn't think was English. "Please don't mind Sheila, she's very attached to the cats. Follow me. We'll have you checked in shortly." Johnson figured the man to be in his early sixties. He was clean shaven with short cropped gray hair and a strong jutting chin. The few wrinkles that crossed his cheeks looked pressed in with an iron.

Johnson picked up the bags and followed the man through the door into a narrow hallway. The check-in counter protruded from the wall on his right; a stairway rose on the left. The hallway continued past both, running the length of the building. At the hall's far end Johnson spied another door, similar to the one in front. As he looked closer, he discovered his own reflection and realized it was a mirror.

The man in the blue waist coat appeared behind the counter. "First stay in London?" he asked.

Al said, "No, but my first time in this hotel."

"And you, sir?"

"First time," Johnson said.

"Well," the man said. "London is a city with something for everyone. If you ever have a problem or want information, just ask for Spiro. No one knows London like I do."

"Spiro?" Johnson said. "We had Vice President named Spiro."

"Agnew," the man said. "He stayed here after resigning."

"Is that so?" Johnson asked.

The man nodded. "Your name, sir?

"Johnson."

"Mr. Johnson..."

Johnson cut him off. "Just Johnson. No mister."

"Fine, sir," the man smiled. "This is the finest small hotel in all of London. If you're a statesman, diplomat or corporate head looking for quiet London hideaway, more often than not, you'll stay with us."

Al grinned at Johnson. "Told ya," she said.

"You have a reservation?"

"Alexandra Cohen," Al said.

The man flipped through a stack of papers. "Ah, very good, Ms. Cohen," he said. "You'll be in the Armada Room. Just sign these papers, and we'll need an imprint of your credit card."

Spiro pushed some papers across the counter. Al signed them and slid her credit card to the man. "Here are your keys," he said. "Please leave them at the desk whenever you're out. Now, may I take your luggage?"

Johnson watched the man closely. This guy, Spiro, did not need to carry bags, and he knew Spiro knew it too. He had smarts, weight and dignity. CON MAN. CON MAN. The words flashed in Johnson's head like neon on Ocean Drive. He wasn't that good a con man, Johnson thought. Good con men played stupid. This guy played it too smart, too smooth. But it was London. Maybe the cons played a different game here.

Johnson followed Al and Spiro down the hall toward the room. A mirror appeared in every direction he looked. Sometimes he saw himself, or the reflection of Al or Spiro or furniture.

Spiro stopped in front of a doorway. Dropped the bags to the ground. A skeleton key emerged from his pocket. "Madame, sir, your room." He pushed the door open and stepped to the side. The room was slightly smaller than their bedroom at home. The closets and dressers were built directly into the walls. Johnson noticed mirrors of different sizes and shapes on each wall.

"Welcome to the Armada Room," Spiro said. "Make yourselves comfortable. If you require anything, just call the front desk."

"Boy," Johnson said. "You guys sure like mirrors."

"Sir?" Spiro asked.

"Mirrors, they're everywhere."

"The hotel's owner collects them," Spiro said. "I believe the one on that wall," he pointed across the room, "hung in Peter the Great's bath at the Hermitage, in Leningrad. Excuse me, St. Petersburg."

"Interesting," Al said.

"Quite," Spiro said. "The owner believes there is a reflected greatness captured in all mirrors."

"Huh?" Johnson said. "What?"

"I'm afraid you'd have to ask him, sir," Spiro said. "And at the moment, he's traveling."

"That's okay," Johnson said. "I'm not that interested, really."

"If there's nothing else, then?

"Right," Johnson said, as he fumbled for his wallet and handed Spiro the first bill he found.

"A twenty-pound tip is extremely generous, sir," he said.

"What's twenty pounds worth?"

"Thirty dollars and change," Al said. "Give or take."

Johnson snatched the bill back. "What's a good tip?" he asked.

"Two pounds," Al suggested.

Spiro nodded. "Two pounds would be about right, sir."

"Jesus," Johnson said, peering into his wallet. "Do I have any of those?"

"They're generally coins, sir."

"Oh," Johnson said.

"Johnson," Al said, holding two coins in the palm of her hand. "Give him this."

He held the coins for a moment. They had some weight and a woman's profile. Probably some old dead queen, he thought. "Here you go," he said.

"You're very generous, sir."

Johnson saw Spiro smirk and liked him.

Al dropped onto the bed when Spiro left. "What do you think?" she asked.

"I think he's a con man."

"No, about the room."

"It's nice," he said, "but I expected a little more from the finest fucking small hotel in all of fucking London."

"A little more what? Look at the mirrors. Isn't that cool?"

"Okay, so the mirrors are cool. What's all the stuff with the cats about?"

Al giggled.

"I mean, the damn cat ran out the door. How am I supposed to know about that cat shit?"

"Don't worry about it. I'm sure once the cat is back everything will be forgotten."

"Well, you see, that's the problem. Something needs to be forgotten. Something needs to happen for this place to be all right with me. I don't like that."

"They have guests staying here all the time, Johnson. Others must have let the cat out. You're acting like one of those people who believe others are watching them all the time."

"You mean they're not?"

"Fuck you and just so you know, service makes this the finest small hotel in London. Okay? S-E-R-V-I-C-E. We could have stayed at some big chain hotel, but the staff would never know us and service would be second rate."

"I think I like it better when they don't know me."

"We're not in Miami now. None of your friends or business acquaintances are around. Lighten up."

"I'm light," he said. "I was just answering your question, damn it."

"Yeah, yeah," she said. "I need a shower."

Johnson watched Al strip out of her clothes, then rummage through her suitcase for her bath kit. Her thighs and hips were creased with lines from her clothes. He smiled at the thought of her clean.

Johnson picked up the remote control and turned on the television set. He ran through five channels and the screen turned to snow. "Hey, Al, the TV's broken," he said.

She stuck her head out of the bathroom. "I thought you didn't watch TV."

"I don't," he said, "except when I'm on vacation. You should use everything they put in the room. It's the only way to get your money's worth."

"You're a strange man, Johnson."

"Thank you," he said.

Johnson stopped on a talk show where men and women were debating their diets. One man claimed to be more like a racehorse because he ate only grains. Some of the audience applauded, some laughed. The moderator, a blonde woman in a business suit, ran up a row and stuck her microphone beneath a woman's chin. "How do you mean racehorse?" the woman asked.

The man winked at her, "Oh, you know, love."

Laughter racked the audience.

"Goddamn it," Al shouted from the bathroom.

Johnson leapt off the bed and ran to the door. Al stood naked in front of the tub, with her arms folded under her breasts. "This is supposed to be a room with a shower. I told them specifically when I booked this room that I wanted a goddamn shower. Fucking incompetents."

Johnson thought about spelling out the word service, but knew better.

Al stormed from the bathroom to the phone. "This is Alexandra Cohen. I just checked in and there's no shower in the bathroom." Her eyes focused on the ceiling. "I don't give a shit about the damn cat. I want a room with a shower, and I want it now. I am not paying these prices to sit in a bathtub of dirty water. Send someone over to take us to a new room." She slammed the phone down and began pulling on the clothes she had just taken off.

Johnson tried to stay out of her line of sight, just in case there was anything he might have done to precipitate the lack of shower.

"Johnson," she said.

"Yeah?"

"Maybe you're right."

"About what?" he asked. Trying to make sure of things before he leapt into them.

"Everything," she said.

That seemed like an awful big responsibility. "No," he said. "I don't think so. You know what? I was just thinking that I'm never right. Sometimes it appears that I am, but on the whole I think I'm wrong."

"That's not true."

He might have said that it was. He had concluded years back that he had probably always been wrong, but someone knocked at the door. "I'll get it," he said.

He opened the door just as Spiro had raised his hand to knock again.

"There's a problem?"

"Yeah," Johnson said. "My girlfriend ordered a room with a shower. This one doesn't have one."

"A shower? The only room we have available with a shower is the Dunkirk."

"Okay," Johnson said. "We'll take it."

"Well, this is highly unusual," he said. "Moving bags around after you've been placed in your room."

"No," Al said to the man, quietly. "Unusual to me is ordering and confirming a room with a shower and not getting one when we arrive. That's what I call unusual."

Johnson nodded his head. "Back in the states we call that a bait and switch. Are you familiar with the term? Bait and switch?" Johnson watched Spiro closely to see if his eyes betrayed some recognition of the con.

"I can assure you, sir and madam that we at the Pembroke House would not engage in any behavior of the, what did you call it, bait and hook variety."

"Bait and switch," Johnson said. "Bait and switch." The guy

was a con.

"I'll certainly move you immediately. If that's what you desire."

"That would be our desire," Johnson said.

"Follow me," Spiro said.

Spiro led them back to through the hotel to a flight of stairs. A yellow cat lay sleeping in a cubby hole alongside the stairway. Its tail looked fine.

"The cat's back," Johnson said. "And it looks great."

"That's Albert," Spiro said. "The cat you let out was Victoria."

"Listen, don't put that cat on me. I opened the door. It ran out. I didn't chase it out. I didn't even know it lived here."

A small door at the top of the stairs had a sign over it, 'Mind Your Head.' Johnson nodded when he passed it. Just across the landing stood a door marked 'Dunkirk.'

Spiro stuck his key in the door and pushed it open. "The Dunkirk," he said.

The room was bigger than the Armada. It had a sofa, a desk and a television suspended from the upper corner of the wall. Mirrors of differing shapes and sizes covered the walls.

"Does it have a shower?" Al asked

"Yes, ma'am," Spiro said. "The Dunkirk is the best room in the hotel. I'm sure it has everything you could want. If there's anything else you desire, please call the desk."

"I want my bags brought here immediately. I want a shower, and I want the name of the best restaurant within walking distance. Thank you," Al said.

Spiro pulled the door closed after him. Al laughed. "I'm paying for service and we damn well better get it. One way or another."

Johnson looked from the door to Al. "I'm not so sure you should mess with that guy. He looks funny to me."

"Don't be ridiculous, Johnson. This is London, not Miami."

"Okay," he said. "But the guy is more than you think."

"If he brings the bags and finds me a restaurant, then."

"Then what?"

"Then, I don't care if he's one of your funny guys."

Johnson nodded, thinking, yeah, but he's not one of my funny guys. He's one of someone else's funny guys. Al referred to Johnson's business associates as funny guys. The Drool, a professional panhandler, was a funny guy. Teitelbaum was a funny guy. Dinesh Ramgoolam was a funny guy. Anyone who hung out at the Wreck, even a woman, was a funny guy by Al's lights. Al claimed she didn't know any funny guys. Johnson assured her she did, but just didn't know it. "You know," he said. "By your standards I'm a funny guy."

"I know," she said. The conversation ended.

Johnson lay across the bed and listened to Al shower. He'd flipped around the television dial, concluded the TV wasn't broken, but there were only five channels. He settled on a show about a farm family. The weather was cold. Sky overcast. Some of the characters spent their time in the barn worrying about people and some spent their time in the house worrying about animals. Just as he got interested in the show, someone knocked at the door.

"Yes?"

"Your bags, sir."

"Just a second." Johnson snapped off the television, rolled out of bed, and opened the door. Spiro waited, bags in both hands.

"We apologize for any inconvenience, sir," he said as he dropped the bags in the room. "This is, of course, the most elegant of our rooms. Each mirror has its own story. That one for instance," he pointed to a tiny gold frame with streaked, silvered glass, "hung in Versailles. History has it that Marie Antoinette gazed upon that glass."

"Listen, I'm not tipping you again just for bringing our bags to this room."

"That's quite all right, sir. The Madame asked for a restaurant recommendation."

"Yes."

"The best place within walking distance is the Yard House. The food is quite good, and I believe they serve a full lunch. Stop at the desk on your way out, and I'll give you directions."

"Thank you," Johnson said, as Spiro closed the door behind him.

The sight of the luggage on the floor reminded Johnson of Mondongo's letter. He lifted the letter from his jacket pocket and slid it beneath the extra blankets stacked on a high shelf in the closet. He stepped back and surveyed the hiding place. It was good enough as long as no one searched the room, and he couldn't imagine why anyone would. Satisfied that the letter was safe for the moment, he sat back on the bed and tried to remember everything he'd learned since arriving in London. They had great train stations. They drove on the wrong side. They didn't have many television stations. They didn't know the value of a shower. They built a lot of scaffolds. They placed too much importance on cats. Al thought it was a good place to visit. He would net out after the trip. He wondered if they would get out to a real pub soon. Maybe he would just close his eyes for a little bit. It had been a long flight. He was tired.

CHAPTER 11

On his first morning in London, Johnson lay in bed naked while Al dressed for her meetings. "What'll you do today?" she asked from the bathroom. He could tell by the elongation of her words that she was applying her lipstick. He imagined her pursing her lips, then blotting them on a folded piece of tissue. Johnson considered those lip prints pressed so delicately into toilet paper some of the most beautiful things he'd ever seen.

Johnson arched his back, stretching across the mattress. "Not a clue," he said. "I guess I'll just check out the town. See what's happening."

Al emerged from the bathroom wearing a gray jacket and skirt. She had her hair pulled back off her face. Her lips were a dusty red, outlined in a slightly darker shade. She approached the bed and leaned over Johnson. He caught her perfume's scent, a thin high-noted aroma called *L'image*. She kissed him on the forehead. "I'll be back around five," she said. "Have some fun."

"Don't work too hard," he said.

Al turned to him from the door. "Don't you play too hard," she said.

"I'll try not to," he said, smiling.

Johnson lay in bed for a few moments after she left, then got up, went to the closet, and checked on Mondongo's letter. He lifted it from beneath the extra blankets and turned it over in his hands. Mondongo had told him to deliver it as soon as possible. He could deliver it that morning. Shower, dress, take a cab to the Cuban Embassy, tell the cab to wait, walk through the door, say, "Delivery for Antonio Gomez" and be done with it.

There seemed something amateurishly easy and unprofessional about that. If that's all Mondongo wanted, he could have mailed it or used Federal Express. Instead he had gone to the Fat Man and gotten Johnson. Johnson would not only deliver the letter, but see Mondongo got his money's worth. He would not walk into the Cuban Embassy in London until he felt the time was right, and it wasn't that morning. Johnson slid the letter back under the blankets, showered, dressed, and went down to the hotel lounge to check out the free coffee and continental breakfast promised by the note card on his bedside table.

In Johnson's experience a hotel lounge was a dark room with a bar against one wall, textured, Formica topped tables with Naugahyde captain's chairs surrounding a tiny linoleum dance floor with a small riser for the Saturday night band, and a juke box glowing in the corner. Those places smelled of spilled drinks, last night's cigarettes, and any number of regrets. In the Pembroke House, he found a small brass plaque "LOUNGE" hanging on French doors that opened into a bright airy room. Floor-to-ceiling bookcases covered two walls; a large fireplace filled another. Five different sized and shaped mirrors shared the wall with the fireplace. A sunburst-shaped gold mirror hung above the mantel. It reminded Johnson of a tattoo that Al's friend, Judith DelGato, had on her right ass cheek.

In the room's center, two black leather couches sat across a dark wood coffee table from each other. A coffee table book with a floral print book jacket occupied the middle of the table. "The Beauty of English Gardens" was splashed across the book jacket in bold, yellow expressionistic strokes. Three over-stuffed easy chairs were organized into a small conversation clutch around the fireplace. The lounge smelled of coffee and fresh baked goods. A linen covered table, just inside the French doors, held coffee, tea, orange juice and a selection of rolls, muffins and Danishes. Johnson lifted a clean coffee cup from the stack and was about to pour when a voice behind him said, "Sir, I'm sure you'll much prefer the freshly brewed."

Johnson turned. Spiro stood behind him, coffee pot in his

hand, dish towel draping his arm.

"Yeah," Johnson said, "fresh coffee would be better." He held out his cup and Spiro filled it. "Thank you," he said.

"My pleasure, sir. I trust you slept well last night."

Johnson nodded, sipped his coffee and felt it warm his throat. "Spiro, you're a nice guy, right?"

"Sir?"

"You're a nice guy? You wouldn't want to anger a guest, right?"

"Sir, there is no finer room in the hotel. You have a shower."

"That's not it," Johnson said. "The room is great. It's just...Look, here's the deal. My girlfriend and I are here for eight more days. I hate when people call me, 'sir.' Know what I mean? My name is Johnson. Just Johnson. Think you could call me that?"

"Of course, sir...Ahh, Johnson. Of course."

"Thank you, Spiro."

"Of course, sir."

Johnson let that go. The guy was trying. "Spiro, what's the deal with that mirror?" He pointed to the sunburst above the mantel.

"Incan, if I'm not mistaken, sir...Excuse me, Johnson. Looted from the Sun King's palace in the 14th Century by one of Pizarro's men."

"Really?"

Spiro nodded gravely. "A rare and exquisite piece."

Johnson thought of Judith DelGato's ass. "I agree," he said. Then, "You know, Spiro, I've never been in London before."

Spiro nodded gravely.

"I want to see the town. Any ideas?"

"London is a true city of the world," Spiro said. "Museums, galleries, stately homes..."

"No," Johnson said, "that stuff's not really my thing."

"Shopping? Clothiers and tailors with generations of experience. The finest of cloth. The best of leathers." Johnson watched Spiro look him up and down. "I guess those wouldn't be your things, either."

"No, Spiro. They wouldn't."

"They're racing at Kenmore Park, today," he said.

"Really?" Johnson replied.

"Horse racing, sir. I mean, Johnson."

"Horse racing. That's one of my things."

"It's simple enough, sir. Excuse me, Johnson. Take the Underground to Paddington Station. Catch the special to Kenmore Park. If you left right now, I suspect you'd miss the 10:40. There's another train at 11:40 and 12:40. The return trains run at 2:20, 3:20, 4:20 and the last one is at 5:20. Round trip to the track is five pounds."

"What's an underground?" Johnson asked.

"I see," Spiro said. "Have something to eat. I'll be right back."

Johnson placed a plain roll and two pats of butter on a small plate and sat down on the couch facing the door. He broke the roll between his hands, feeling the warmth of something freshly baked.

Spiro returned and handed him small white brochure. On its cover was printed a red circle, bisected by a blue bar. The brochure opened into a map marked by crisscrossing lines of various colors (red, yellow, blue, green, orange, purple and brown) that might have been drawn with an etch-a-sketch.

"That," Spiro said, standing beside the couch and pointing over Johnson's shoulder, "is the most useful document you'll have during your stay in London. The Underground is our subway system. It's the most safe and efficient way to travel around the city. Learn it well and there is no place you can't go. Assuming," he said, "that you are neither color blind or illiterate."

"I'm not any of those things," Johnson said.

"Good," Spiro said. "Now, getting to Kenmore Park." He pointed out the District Line and assured Johnson that he could catch it at the Notting Hill Gate Station, three blocks from the hotel. He told Johnson to ride the District Line to Paddington Station, get off, follow signs to the RailTrack and search out the Kenmore Park Special.

After following Spiro's directions, Johnson found himself in the company of pensioners, hipsters, housewives, businessmen, and touts crunching across a gravel parking lot toward a low-slung wood and cement building. Painted across the top of the building and desperately trying to fade into memory were the words: Kenmore Park Racecourse. A gray sky hung overhead. A cold breeze messed Johnson's hair and flapped the bottom of his trench coat. Behind him stretched the narrow platform that served as the Kenmore Park train station.

Johnson spotted the track's white rail and posts, brilliant against the dark green grass. A line of horses stretched out around the curve. The mounts, all browns and blacks, carried their jockeys like flags flapping on their backs. Johnson heard hooves beating turf; cheers rose from the clubhouse. The horses disappeared behind the building. The cries grew louder, louder, then stopped.

Johnson approached the small battered two-window ticket trailer and passed a five pound note through the window to a young Black woman. She smiled at him, then said something over her shoulder to a redhead beside her. She slid coins and a tiny red cardboard placard back to Johnson. The placard was shaped like a shield and had a loop of red string attached. 'Kenmore Park' was written in bold silver letters on the shield. The crowd around him hung the small shields on their coats. Johnson did the same.

He followed the crowd through a crooked wooden turnstile manned by an old geezer in a green army hat and coat. "G'day, gov," the man said to Johnson as he passed through the gate.

Johnson walked with the crowd through a tunnel beneath the clubhouse that delivered him trackside. Between him and the rail, men stood on chairs and small stepladders holding black slates aloft. The slates were covered with numbers written in chalk. Two other men sat or stood beside each of the guys holding the slates. Before each group, chipped and battered sandwich signs read: *Isaac Hooper, Best Odds/Highest Payouts; Morris Fox, 30 years of service; Thomas Breen, south London's oldest and most trusted name.* Bookies! Johnson thought, as he strolled among the crews spread out like vendors at a flea market. He nodded and smiled to those who made eye contact, though most didn't. He decided bookmaking must be legal in England. A pretty interesting proposition to consider. Johnson knew a few guys who'd be out of work if that happened in Miami Beach. Not the bookies. They'd be fine. But the guys who collected, protected, and smoothed the way with the local coppers, they might have a few problems. Even the Fat Man would lose his little taste of the action.

Johnson stationed himself against the clubhouse wall and watched the bookies work. The numbers on the chalkboards were the odds. A different group of men, huddled 50 yards up the rail, seemed to be the odds-makers. The guys with the slates communicated with the odds-makers through hand signals.

Just before the third race, Johnson approached guys grouped beside the sign *Samuel Halpert, Home of the Big Winners.* Samuel Halpert's crew consisted of three men. One guy stood on small ladder and held the odds board. He had an oversized head and a tearing eye that he wiped repeatedly with a torn yellow rag. On a stool beside the ladder sat a man in a large blue coat that draped to the ground. He wore a black wool watch cap cocked over his eye and sat bent to the small desk on his lap. A jockey-sized bald man stood beside the sandwich sign and spoke quietly to the passing crowd. "Halpert's your man," he'd said to Johnson when he passed the first time.

Johnson wanted to bet the longest long shot. Lacking something from the inside, he figured it was the only way to make money. What could you win on a horse that went off at 5 to 4? Nothing. But a long shot? If it hit? Samuel Halpert's odds board showed the number four horse going off at 34 to 1.

"What'll it be today, gov?" asked the jockey-sized man. He licked his right thumb and pushed his hands out before him, as if prepared to take a big bet. "Halpert's your man. All the winners bet here. At Halpert's it's not really gambling."

"Two dollars to win on the four horse," Johnson said.

"Wrong country, yank. That'd be pounds and three's Halpert's minimum." He said Alpert for Halpert.

"Right," Johnson said. "Pounds. Three pounds on the four horse."

"Three on four," the man shouted. He took a twenty-pound note from Johnson and returned a handful of coins and two bills.

The man on the stool handed the little man a small card. "Three on four," he said.

"Three on four," the guy said to Johnson. He handed Johnson a stiff card with Samuel Halpert written across the middle and the numbers seven zero eight stamped on either end of the card. "Good luck, yank," he said.

"That's it?" Johnson asked, looking at the card. "It doesn't say what I bet."

"Frankie," the little man said, "Seven nought eight. What's the bet?"

The guy on the stool said, "Three on four."

"Okay, yank?"

Johnson nodded. "Sorry, I just..."

"Forget it, yank."

The four horse cantered sideways while parading out to the starting gate. The rider wore a blue checked vest that flapped in the breeze. He rode past Johnson with his crop between his teeth while reaching down and tugging on his boots. Johnson wished the jockey had finished dressing before mounting the horse.

The four horse took to the gate well. When the bell sounded, he broke with the pack. He lost ground before going into the first turn and continued to fall further behind as the race progressed. The crowd had busied itself with other matters when the four horse and rider finally crossed the finish line. Not Johnson. He watched the four horse to the very end. He had to. It carried his money.

Johnson bet five races, all long shots, and lost every one. He was out fifteen pounds or twenty-two dollars and believed it money well spent. Spiro was right to send him to Kenmore Park. He'd had a blast. The horses ran on grass and did more than just run around the track. During the fourth and sixth races, they jumped over hedges, too. There were three different places to buy drinks: the Winner's Circle Bar, the Kenmore Park Pub, and the Turf View Restaurant. A vendor working near the paddock sold him a hot pork sandwich, cut from a whole pig steaming in a large roasting pan. The weather was cold, the air clear. Johnson didn't understand a word the announcer said. And he didn't pick a winner, but he'd had so much fun, he didn't care.

Spiro pushed a tiny carpet sweeper back and forth just inside the Hotel's entrance when Johnson returned from the track.

"Spiro," Johnson said, as he came through the door, "I lost fifteen pounds."

"Sorry, sir. I mean, Johnson."

"Don't be. That was a blast. What should I do tomorrow?"

"Let me think about it."

"You do that," Johnson said. "That was great. Great. So cool. I had no idea that you bet with bookies here. I mean, you can bet with bookies in Miami, but the cops don't like it."

On his second day Spiro gave him directions to Portobello Road. "You can walk there," he said.

"What's there?" Johnson asked.

"Portobello Road," Spiro replied.

Johnson spent the early morning wandering through antique and junk shops. The merchandise had the feel of stolen property. The salespeople seemed like fences. He bought a black cap from a street vendor for three pounds. He put it on. It warmed his head. He thought of it as his Irish Jockey's cap. At 11 a.m., Johnson strolled into the Sun & Moon Pub to celebrate his purchase.

"Half pint of New Castle," he said to a young woman behind the bar. She wore her hair twisted into a knot on top of her head. A safety pin pierced her eyebrow. A brass stud poked from her right nostril. When she turned her back to Johnson, he saw a black snake's head tattooed on the nape of her neck. He knew the snake's body coiled down her back and its tail reached all the way to her ass.

Johnson turned to his left and nodded to the only other customer at the bar. Gray stubble covered the guy's cheeks and head. He rested his chin on his right hand and stared straight ahead at the bar. A cigarette smoldered between his fingers.

The barmaid placed Johnson's beer on the bar. Johnson lifted the drink. "Cheers," he said to the guy.

The guy's eyes shifted to Johnson. "Arrghhh," he replied.

"No talking at the bar before noon," the girl said.

Johnson laughed. "No talking? You're kidding, right?"

"Shhh," the girl said. "Some people like their quiet."

The next day, Spiro sent him to the Brixton Underground station. Johnson walked the Electric Avenue market taking in the aromas of West African spices and PanAfrican incense. He was comforted to see vibrant West Indian colors struggling mightily against London's soiled browns and grays. The Rastafari men, women, and children he passed on the street were no different than those in Miami and he felt oddly comforted discovering a bit of home so far away. Across the avenue down a dingy side-street from the market, Johnson spotted a pub whose name, it appeared, was originally The John Barley. A few slashes of red, black, and green paint transformed the pub's sign to The Bob Marley. Johnson wandered down the alley, stepped into the pub, and pulled the door shut behind him. He squinted into the bar's darkness and reached up to take off his sunglasses, only to discover he already had. The skunky aroma of a powerful reefer hung in the air. A Jamaican dance hall beat played on the sound system, the music circling back on itself in a repetitive riff of guitars and drums. The glowing red tips of fat Rasta spliffs burned brightly at the bar.

"Who be this white bumba clot coming through that door?" a voice sang out of the darkness.

Johnson knew enough Jamaican slang to know that he'd just been called a white mother fucker, and knew he'd just stumbled into a place where white mother fuckers were probably not welcome. "Sorry, gentlemen," Johnson said, holding up his hands. "I can see I've chosen the wrong pub." He backed toward the door. "No blood, no foul."

"You're a yank, then?" someone else asked.

"From Miami," Johnson replied.

"Me cousin in Miami," the first voice said.

"Probably don't know him."

"Be called Eddie, a merciful big clot."

"I know a guy named Eddie," Johnson said. "Rastafari, big time. Part Chinese. Seven feet tall. Dreads thick as rope."

"Be him," the voice said.

Johnson put his fists together in front of his chest and bowed toward the darkness. "Respect," he said.

Eddie's cousin and others at the bar called back, "Respect."

"Come sit side by me, White Clot," Eddie's cousin said. "Drink a Guinness with I and I."

Johnson didn't want to stay, but he saw no way to leave without offending the man at the bar. "Maybe just half a pint," he said and walked slowly toward the bar. A single lightbulb hung down over the cash register. He could see silhouettes of six men and their faces when lit in the spliff's red glow. The men all wore dreadlocks.

"My name's Johnson," Johnson said.

"You White Clot to me, boy," Eddie's cousin said, laughing. "I and I be Pony Boy."

The bartender placed a glass of Guinness on the bar. Johnson put a five-pound note beside it.

"We don't take no money, White Clot," Pony Boy said. "Put it away."

"Thank you," Johnson said. "To your health, then." He toasted them and took a pull from the Guinness. "That's very nice," he said.

"Try this, Clot," Pony Boy said. He offered a smoldering joint the size of a child's forearm.

Johnson piped his hand together and took a slow, deep hit. He nodded to the man as he handed him back the joint. "It's the Emperor's herb," he said.

"Too true, Clot," Pony Boy said, smiling. He nodded slowly. "Tell I and I about me cousin."

The high settled Johnson against the bar. The Emperor's high. There would be time enough for Pony Boy's question. He sipped his Guinness and let the somber facts of his life wash over him. He was in London, stoned in a bar with Rastafari. He had a half pint of Guinness. Stoned in a bar in London with Rastafari. Eddie's cousin, Pony Boy. A Guinness. Johnson nodded. He could now make out the details of the men around him. Pony Boy's dreads crept from beneath a black beret cocked atop his head. He wore round sunglasses, low on his nose. Over their tops, Johnson could see Pony Boy's eyes closed. A pistol hung out of the pocket of his leather jacket. The man beside Pony Boy cradled a sawed-off double barrel shot gun in his lap. Okay, Johnson thought, be cool.

Johnson sipped the Guinness. The music played. The men around him nodded their heads. "Eddie's full high Rastafari," Johnson said. "Got a woman and two kids. Girls, I think. He looks healthy and prosperous. Eddie works as the powerful big bouncer at a strip club in Miami. Heaven's Gate. He keeps me in the Emperor's herb. A fine, righteous smoke."

Pony Boy's eyes opened to little red slits. He smiled at Johnson. "You tell him that I and I send greetings from Brixton. Tell him that we and we meet again."

"If not here, then in the next," Johnson said. Allowing the Emperor's herb to guide his thoughts.

"Be righteous true, White Clot. Be here or in the next."

Johnson settled back into his seat. The dance hall music pulled through his brain like a continuous rope. His mind crawled alongside the rope. Followed its twists and curves. Driven on by beats and calls. One tune broke into another, then another. After how many, he could not count, he allowed the rope to drop away. He smiled to himself and the Emperor, Haile Selassie. He blinked open his eyes. Turned to the bar and drained the Guinness. "Thank you very much, gentlemen. I'll be on my way, now."

"Clot, you come back to see I and I."

"I'll do that," Johnson said. He joined his fists in front of his chest and bowed toward the man. "Respect," he said.

"Respect, Clot," Pony Boy said. "Respect."

On his fourth day, Spiro sent him to the East End. "Get off at Whitechapel, Johnson. Look for the Blind Beggar Pub."

The bartender in the Blind Beggar had asked Johnson if he was there to see where George Cornell was standing when he called Ronnie Kray a fat poof, and took a bullet between the eyes for it.

"No," Johnson said. "I'm here to get a beer."

"Wouldn't you like to see?" the bartender asked. He was a man about Johnson's age with curly red hair, a sweat-stained white shirt, and a hint of brogue in his speech.

"How about a New Castle Brown Ale?" Johnson said.

"It's not like Mr. George Cornell told Ronnie something he didn't already know." The bartender looked up and down the bar, leaned closer to Johnson, and whispered, "Ronnie was a poofter. And a little on the heavy side. So, it appears that Mr. George Cornell took a bullet between the eyes for telling someone the truth. What do you think of that?"

"I think I'd like a New Castle Brown Ale," Johnson said.

"Right, mate. Right. Coming right up."

Johnson turned around to survey the Blind Beggar. The place was bigger than most of the other pubs he'd visited. It was dimly lit and filled with the low murmur of afternoon conversations -- a place you could call home.

"Here you go, mate," the bartender said.

Johnson turned back to the bar, lifted the pint to his mouth and took a pull.

"So, now," the bartender said. "Don't you want to know where Mr. George Cornell was when he took that bullet between the eyes?"

Johnson savored the beer for a moment. Then looked to the

bartender. "Okay, where was Mr. George Cornell when he took that bullet between the eyes?"

"Right where you're standing, mate. That very spot."

After four days in London, Johnson decided it wouldn't take much to make him happy. If he hit a big score, a million or two, he knew just how to live -- one half the year in London and one half in Miami. He loved the whole deal with London.

The Brits knew their driving was fucked up. Every street corner had an arrow and a big sign, LOOK RIGHT, to show you which way the traffic flowed. You could actually pay for things with coins. Money jingling in his pocket had real value, not like the coins back home that collected in the jars in his bedroom. He discovered the phone booths and light poles in the neighborhood around the Pembroke House were covered by multicolored index cards that advertised sex. He'd grabbed some to show the guys back at the Wreck. His collection included a pink card with a line drawing of a buxom woman holding a crop, who offered: "Public School Discipline: Beautiful Strict Governess providing Equestrian, Schoolroom and Corrective Fantasies"; a stiff white card with an "actual photograph" of a "GENUINE 18 YR OLD BUSTY 36-22-34 ALL SERVICES INCLUDING GREEK CITY BASED SEXY & DISCREET"; and a sky blue card with a picture of long boot-clad legs promising, "Beautiful Black Mistress gives a spanking good time NAUGHTY BOYS REPORT NOW!" Johnson smiled every time he remembered the phrase, "Naughty boys report now!"

Johnson liked the fact that the Brits called sausage bangers. He liked the fact that he could probably score some dope from Pony Boy and his posse. He liked the Page Three Girl's tits, and he liked talking with the bartenders. He'd tell them he was from Miami, and learned not to mind that most had never heard of the city. Instead of getting mad at people who talked lovingly about Disney he'd say, no one tells the real story behind Disney. Sure, he'd say, there's the land grabs and the mysterious deaths of the people who opposed the corporation, but nobody talks about the number of children who disappear each day at Disney World.

Thousands since the place opened. People's mouths would hang open in disbelief. Johnson would sum it all up by saying, "Well, things are a bit different in the states."

His listeners would nod, sip their drinks, and say, "The things you don't know. Blimey, mate. Disney?"

Johnson would nod. "Disney is not what it's cracked up to be."

Johnson loved the fact that everyone smoked, that some rolled their own cigarettes. He loved that the pubs filled at lunch time and people tossed back a couple ales, as if it were no big deal.

After a morning and early afternoon of wandering, Johnson would return to the hotel and nap, shower, and dress for Al's return. She would take him to dinner and the theater.

CHAPTER 12

On his fifth morning in London, Johnson showered and dressed. He slid Mondongo's letter from its hiding place, stuck it in his trench coat's inner pocket and carried it with him to the hotel lounge for coffee. Al had left for her meeting an hour before. He wondered how her work was going and decided to ask her when she got home. Boy, she did some funny shit for a living, he thought. Spiro stood on a step ladder at the room's far end, running a feather duster over the sunburst mirror.

"Morning, Spiro," Johnson said.

"Good morning, Johnson," he replied. "Did you sleep well?"

"Fine, Spiro," he said as he poured a cup of coffee, grabbed a roll and some butter and dropped down onto the couch. "Like a baby."

"We're pleased to know that, Johnson."

"Hey, Spiro, how do I get to the Cuban Embassy?" Johnson asked.

Spiro nearly spun off the ladder turning toward Johnson. "Excuse me?"

"Jesus, be careful," Johnson said. "You don't want to hurt yourself. I'm looking for the Cuban Embassy. You know, their embassy here?"

Spiro stepped carefully down off the ladder. "I'm afraid I wouldn't know."

"Any idea how I might find it?"

"I'm sure I wouldn't know that either, Johnson."

Spiro's answer bugged Johnson. The guy prided himself on knowing everything about London. "What about the phone book?" Johnson asked. "They're probably listed, right."

"Maybe," he said. "Excuse me, sir." Spiro folded up the ladder and carried it toward the door.

Maybe? Jesus, that's strange, Johnson thought. The ladder scraped the wall and Spiro cursed in some language other than English. Maybe Spiro had a hard-on for Cubans? Johnson knew plenty of people in Miami who did.

The woman behind the front desk was bent over with her back to Johnson, speaking to the tail-less cat in the soft cooing voice some people reserved for children. The woman's ass, pressing against the fabric of a burgundy skirt, was something Johnson could admire: slim, well rounded, cheeks like cantaloupes. He cleared his throat.

The woman straightened up. She looked about Al's age, had red hair to her shoulders and green eyes. Her lips were pale and her cheeks and nose freckled. She blushed a bright pink. "Pardon me, sir," she said. "But Victoria's had quite a difficult time of it these last five days."

"I know," Johnson said. "I'm the thoughtless monster who let her out."

She smiled at him. "Oh, I'm sure you didn't do it on purpose."

"You're right," Johnson said. "If I did it on purpose, she'd be dead." He smiled. She didn't.

"It's a joke," he said.

"I don't see it as funny."

"No, I guess you don't. Listen, I'm sorry about the cat. If I'd known..." he shrugged. "But look here. I've got some things to take care of. Do you know where the Cuban Embassy is?"

"No, of course not. Perhaps they're in the book."

"The embassy book?"

"The phonebook."

"Good idea," Johnson said.

The woman bent over again. Johnson leaned over to see her ass. The yellow cat leapt up onto the countertop. She looked fine except for the white bandage wrapping the stub of her tail. Johnson swept the cat off the counter with a brush of his arm.

He was always amazed at a cat's ability to land on its feet -- a skill he admired.

The woman stood back up with a phone book and began leafing through the pages. "Cuba. Cuban," she said, running her finger down the page. "There it is. Cuban High Commission. 67 Holborn Street."

"Holborn Street? Any idea how to get there?"

"There's an underground stop at Holborn. I'm sure that it's somewhere near there."

Johnson loved that about London, no one knew where anything was. It was one of the few things about London that seemed like Miami.

Johnson thanked the woman, gave her his room key, and started down the steps. He held the door open for a moment longer than necessary on the off chance that Victoria would try another escape. Nothing happened.

It was an unseasonably warm and dry time in London. At least that's what all the locals told him. The sun shone, but the temperature never climbed higher than forty degrees. He'd come to appreciate his Irish Jockey's cap. In London it had become as indispensable as his sunglasses. It kept his head warm, and he liked the way it looked. He could pull it down over his eyes, or wear it back on the top of his head. Outside the Pembroke House, at the bottom of the stairs, he reached into the coat pocket where he kept the cap. It wasn't there. He checked the other pocket. "Fuck," he said.

He turned and jogged up the steps through the door. The woman behind the desk shrieked when she saw him.

"Jesus," Johnson said.

"I'm sorry, sir," she said. "You startled me."

"I forgot something in my room." He put his hand on the counter for his key.

"You did," she said. "Nothing important, I hope."

"Well, I came back for it, didn't I?"

"Yes, you did."

"Well, it has some importance."

"Yes, it must."

"My key?"

"Your key? Right." She bent behind the desk and fumbled through papers. "Now where did that key get off too? I just had it a second ago."

Johnson had seen it before. At the Betsy Ross. Hide the key, toss a room. A guy could lose everything he owned in five minutes. He didn't wait for the woman to stand up. He ran up the stairs, three steps at a time. The woman shouted after him. Yeah, finest fucking small hotel in all of fucking London. They were a bunch of rip-offs just like any assholes in any other god-damn hotel.

The door to the Dunkirk room was closed. He turned the knob. It was locked. He rapped at the door.

It opened. Spiro said, "Did you bring the..." He looked into Johnson's eyes and tried to force the door closed. Johnson leaned against it, pushing his foot into the opening. Spiro slammed the door, pinching Johnson's foot.

"Ow. Shit," Johnson shouted.

"You shouldn't have come back," Spiro cried.

"You shouldn't be in my room trying to rip me off. Fucking thief."

"So that's what you think? Thief? I am no thief."

The door swung open. Johnson hobbled into the room. Everything appeared in its place, except the mirror from Versailles was gone. A camera lens poked through a small rectangular hole in the wall. Johnson looked from Spiro to the camera.

"What the fuck is that?" he said. "You fucking pervert!"

"And you, Mr. Johnson? Just what are you?"

"Hey, I'm not the one caught in another man's hotel room rigging a camera up behind some phony fucking two-way mirror. Ow, you really fucked up my foot, you know that."

"Right," Spiro laughed. "Play the fool. The ignorant man. You're obviously very good at it. You had us completely fooled, but you took it one step too far."

"The fuck are you talking about? Jesus, maybe my foot's

broken. Why the fuck did you have to slam the door on my foot?"

"Since the Wall fell the rules are different, aren't they Mr. Johnson?"

"Johnson, goddamn it. Just Johnson."

"Have it your way."

"Call me Johnson, goddamn it," Johnson said, "And tell me what the fuck you're doing."

"Doing? Doing? Johnson, what's the one thing we've been trained to do? Never admit anything. You're not armed. I could snap your neck, strip you naked and leave you in a running shower. I could make you disappear. I could walk out that door and deny everything you say." Spiro dropped into a chair beneath the camera. "But honestly, Johnson. Don't you miss it?"

"Miss what?"

"The war."

"What war?"

"Oh, you play the fool well, Johnson. The Cold War. Honestly, don't you miss it?"

Johnson knew he had to think about the answer. If he told the guy he missed it, he might have to say what about it exactly he missed. If he said no, well, who the fuck knew where the guy would go? "Well," Johnson began.

"What am I talking about? What a fool. The Cold War isn't over for you. Is it, Johnson? You still have Cuba and Cuba still has you. How I admire that."

"It's nothing," Johnson said.

"Nothing. Nothing. What do the people at Langley, I mean the old timers, do these days but worry about Cuba and Fidel? Everything else? Gone. Gone. A brief shining moment in the world's history. We knew the score then." Spiro pointed at Johnson. "You and I could not have gone to war. We knew that. But our proxies. We make the snowballs and have some lackey throw them. God, how I loved that."

Spiro's conversation started to make some sense to Johnson. Cold War. Cuba. Proxies. "You're a communist," Johnson said.

"I'm a communist like you're a Republican. We're professionals. The passion of politics is best left to the politicians. They gave the best of the world to us. Absolutely the best." Spiro looked off longingly at the camera. "Where's your posting?"

"I live in Miami."

"Ho, wonderful. On the front line against Fidel. Oh, those mad Cubans." Spiro straightened up. "Of course, I've never had direct contact with any of their operatives, but I understand the women are absolute wild cats."

Johnson thought of Judith DelGato. "Yes, Spiro," he said, "the women are quite nice."

"And what is your cover in the posting?"

"I've got a small delivery company."

"With exactly one employee, right?"

Johnson nodded. "And a bookkeeper."

Spiro clapped his hands. "Of course. Of course. The bookkeeper. Where would we be without our bookkeepers?"

"Doing seven to ten in a federal prison for tax evasion?" Johnson suggested.

"Ha ha ha," Spiro laughed shaking his head. "Americans."

Johnson laughed too. Spiro seemed like a man who knew things. Things that could be extremely funny or extremely not funny. Best, he thought, to laugh along with him.

"So, Spiro, who do you work for?"

Spiro wiped a tear from his eye. "The hotel."

Johnson nodded. "Nice place. They say it's the finest small hotel in all of London."

"It was. Back when a guest's bill didn't matter. When all costs were subsidized by my employers. Oh, back then. Amazing. But now? It's run by impotent bureaucrats with some starry-eyed view of capitalism. It makes me sick." Spiro shook his head. "No one at the top -- not in the Kremlin, not at Langley or the Pentagon -- understood what we in the field knew." He cocked his left eye at Johnson.

Johnson nodded, but he didn't know why.

"The Cold War guaranteed peace. Not peace for everyone. Not a good life for everyone. But no major wars. No wars between superpowers. We had the bomb. You had the bomb. We weren't going to use it. You weren't going to use it. But now, even I, Spiro Dimitry, from a Greek island so covered with goats I slipped on goat shit every day for the first fourteen years of my life, even I could have a bomb." He shook his head. "The world has gone mad." He covered his face with his hands and sobbed.

"Well, you know," Johnson said. "This still looks like a pretty good gig for you. I mean the place is nice enough. And you know, like Mick Jagger says, you can't always get what you want."

Spiro looked up from between his hands and laughed. "And to think we conceded victory to you Americans." He laughed again. "A people whose entire sense of history is based on what they're told by their television, who believe that there is some sense of fairness to be found in the world, who in moments of great crisis quote rock-and-roll drivel. The world is mad," Spiro shouted at the ceiling. "Mad."

"Hey," Johnson said. "I'm just trying to help you out here. You're just pissed 'cause you think they've taken something from you."

"I'm not, what did you say? Pissed..."

"Bullshit," Johnson said. "Sure -- before you didn't mind being a porter, because in your mind you weren't a porter. You believed you were a spy. But to the bosses you were a porter. The same way I'm just a delivery man."

"You don't know. You have no idea. I did important work. I have awards. Medals." He pointed at the camera. "I have movies of your J. Edgar Hoover wearing a dress and being spanked by a young man."

"Spiro, we've all got those. You're a porter. Be a porter."

Spiro shook his head. "If only they'd met you. They'd have realized that our society wasn't bankrupt. They would have seen for themselves what you Americans really are. We would have won. You people would have lost."

"Yeah," Johnson said, "and where would you be right now? Here, that's where. You'd be the porter."

"I am so much more," he said. "So much. A hero of the revolution." Spiro looked from side to side, then stood up. "Come with me," he said.

"Listen," Johnson said, "It's not that I don't want to, but I don't have time right now. I planned to do something else today."

"Follow me," he said.

Johnson grabbed his cap from the bedside table and followed Spiro out of the room, down the hall to a small door over which hung the sign, 'Mind your Head.'

Spiro unlocked the door with a key hanging from his belt and turned back to Johnson, "A porter, eh? I'll show you porter." He ducked through the door.

Johnson followed him into a narrow passage, just wide enough for one person, though tall enough for Johnson to stand. The walls were unfinished plaster and lath. Electrical conduit and pipe snaked and twisted over the plaster. Tiny lightbulbs hung from wires tacked to the ceiling. A thick carpet padded the floor and muffled Johnson's footsteps. He followed Spiro straight down the hall to another door.

"There," he said, "look there."

Johnson pushed the door open and found himself looking through a large window into the hotel's interior hallway. He could see the woman behind the desk, and the cat, Victoria, with its bandaged tail.

"The camera works on a drop mount designed by the East Germans," Spiro whispered as he reached up and pulled down a contraption holding a small camera. "In the days before video we had the quietest most spectacular cameras. We had contests. Best camera work in a hotel room. Finest surveillance pictures from a parked vehicle. Now," he gestured to the camera, "Japanese video. Japanese!" Spiro's shoulders sagged. "There," he said, pointing, "The umbrella stand. I used that to hold my microphones. I could hear the cats purr, a woman sigh, a man fart. I picked up everything anyone said. My tapes showed you more than a man's conversation, my tapes showed his soul. I was a genius."

"I can see that," Johnson said.

"You impudent... You think you know things."

"Hold on right there," Johnson said. "I don't know shit. Okay? I don't know shit about you. I don't know shit about me. I don't know shit about shit. So quit saying that shit."

"I'm sorry," Spiro said. "I just envy you so."

Johnson smirked. "Why? You got this great gig. Seem to have the run of the place. What else could you be? Rich?"

Spiro sighed. "I could be respected."

"Shit, I respect you, Spiro. You were a spy. A damn good spy, I bet. They write books about you guys, make movies. You guys changed the world."

"My side lost."

"Not because of you, Spiro. You were doing a great job. You got my respect."

Spiro lurched toward him and wrapped Johnson in a hug. His breath smelled of coffee and was damp against Johnson's neck. "Thank you so much. Thank you."

Johnson patted Spiro's back and said, "You're welcome."

Spiro wiped his eyes, repeated his thanks.

"It's okay," Johnson said. "But I need to get going."

"The Cuban Embassy?"

Johnson nodded. "But don't tell anyone. My girlfriend Al doesn't know."

"Wonderful," Spiro said. "Don't even tell your lovers your business. Oh, Johnson, you are to be admired."

"Yeah, right," Johnson said.

"If you have any problems at the Embassy, I know a man there. His name is," Spiro leaned close to Johnson and whispered, "Antonio Gomez."

"Antonio Gomez?" Johnson said. "You know him?"

Spiro held a finger to his lips and nodded. "Very capable," Spiro said. "Everything at the embassy passes through him. Some family issue has held him back. Others half as good are running directorates in Havana. A very capable man."

"I have a letter for him."

"You can't get to him," Spiro said.

"Why not?"

"Did your people give you a code? A time to meet?"

Johnson shook his head.

"There's not an office in the embassy with a little sign on the door," Spiro made a small rectangle of his hands, "Antonio Gomez. You can try to hand it to him, Johnson. But he'd be slipping if he let you get that close."

Johnson nodded. "Thanks for telling me," he said. "But do me a favor."

"Anything."

"Do something to the mirrors in my room so I know you're not watching me and Al."

"Of course," Spiro said. "Of course."

"And I'll want to see that it's done, too."

"Of course," Spiro said. "I would expect nothing less."

As soon Spiro said, 'of course,' Johnson knew he was fucked. "I'm not kidding," Johnson said. "No pictures, no sound recordings. Nothing."

"Absolutely, Johnson," Spiro said. "Absolutely. A professional courtesy."

Johnson nodded, turned from Spiro, and started down the small hallway. He looked left and right into the rooms and hallways, through the window-like glass, ladders shooting up to catwalks above his head, where he knew there were other mirrors, other cameras and one at that moment looking into the Dunkirk room. Al had told him once that he was paranoid. This space, these mirrors, the ladders and, of course, Spiro, confirmed in his own mind that sometimes paranoia was an appropriate response. He ducked his head under the low door frame and continued down the hall, past the front desk and the damaged cat out onto the street before Pembroke House.

CHAPTER 13

Al had told him not to expect the sun in London. "It probably wasn't even worth carrying sunglasses," she said. Johnson couldn't help himself and brought them along anyway. After a lifetime in Miami, he considered sunglasses a little more important than trousers. He didn't mind being outside without his pants, but to be without sunglasses was completely unacceptable. And he was glad he'd brought them. In his first five days in London he didn't see a drop of rain, or even a cloud. Jesus, he would have been blinded without his specs. He set them on the bridge of his nose and looked left and right. His only perspective in London had been up or down streets. Unless he was in a park the horizons were blocked by buildings.

It pleased him to know for sure about Spiro. The city seemed more sinister, and Johnson took comfort in the knowledge. He believed you didn't know a town until you knew some of its secrets.

Johnson strolled down Pembroke to the Notting Hill Gate underground station. The homeless crowding the station entrance seemed more pitiful in London than in Miami. Cold and damp, it was no place he'd care to sleep outside. The homeless he knew in Miami seemed wealthy compared to those in London. If you could keep off the crack, they had told him, life was actually good. Very good.

Johnson took the Central line east under the city and got out at Holborn Street. He had become a pro at the underground. He had learned its etiquette by watching the way other people rode. Don't speak to your neighbor. Don't make eye contact. Unlike

New York, he had not seen any rough stuff. He was amused when a street musician entered the train and played for a few stops, even during rush hour. Johnson knew at which end of the station to wait for the least crowded car, knew where to change for special lines and knew which stations served fresh coffee.

At the Holborn stop, Johnson bought a copy of *The Sun* and admired the Page Three Girl on his way up out of the station. He folded the newspaper under his arm and patted his breast pocket for Mondongo's letter. Holborn was a business street and was crowded with traffic and late morning pedestrians.

In London, he discovered, addresses don't run straight from one end of the block to another, but curve back on themselves for no apparent reason. On one side of some streets the addresses get higher while on the other they go lower. He knew it was just another one of those things, like the wrong-headed driving, that you could get used to.

The numbers on the buildings indicated he was nearing the embassy. He decided to take a quick walk past the building, then cross the street and double back. The embassy was housed in a brown building, the walls made of a shiny marble-like stone. It rose four stories. The ground floor had wide windows like a department store, but they had a dark tint and Johnson couldn't see through them. A shiny brass plate on the wall next to the door read *Republica de Cuba*. A security camera pointed down at the front door; another scanned the entire front of the building. A man sat in a small blue car parked in the alley alongside the building. He smoked a cigarette and seemed to be carelessly watching the street. Johnson knew the watch. Let the world pass and only the odd things leap out at you. Only the un-ordinary becomes clear. It was like driving. Everything done on a second level, done back behind thought. You didn't need to remind yourself to stop at a red light, to press the accelerator through a curve. But when tail lights went red, or when a cop ended up on your tail then, like sliding on wet pavement, you noticed all that was around you. You paid attention.

Johnson walked a block down from the building, stepped to

the curb, waited for a break in traffic. He tracked across the street, doubled back, then stopped across the street from the embassy and looked around as if lost.

The guy in the car beside the embassy leaned forward and tossed his cigarette through the window. It lay smoldering on the ground.

Johnson muttered, "shit." The man had noticed him. "Shit." Do something out of the ordinary and they're going to notice. "Shit." Johnson couldn't re-cross the street. That would make the guy real nervous. He might freak. Who knew what he might do?

Delivery was not easy. When the delivery could be worth hundreds of thousands of dollars or fifteen to twenty years in jail a good delivery man developed methods. Johnson's professional instinct told him to linger across the street from the embassy. Told him to watch the doorway and the crowds. And told him to try and think of a way in and a way out. Now, he had fucked up. You never want to deliver to a person who is nervous or angry. You never want to be more than just the guy with the package.

"Fuck." Johnson looked left then right, trying to appear confused. He lifted the London transport map from his pocket and acted lost. He stamped his foot. "Fuck." Why didn't he just walk through the door and deliver the letter? "Fuck." He had to make some fucking production out of it. "Fuck." He should have just walked in, said, 'Hi, delivery for Antonio Gomez.' But no. Fuck!

If he walked off now, he knew that when he returned, this guy or some other guy in the car would be on him like...

A car door slammed across the street. Johnson didn't look up. He studied the map, hoping his intensity would be read as sincerity. He looked at the Central's red line cutting across London, the squiggly blue route of the Victoria line terminating at Brixton. He wondered what went on at Elephant & Castle station.

"May I help you, sir?" asked a man standing beside him.

The voice came to Johnson as if in a dream, carrying a familiar resonance, a tincture of something -- salsa, rum, cigars? A taste familiar in his ears. Miami speaking to him. Cuba speaking to Miami. In London's cold sunshine in September, Johnson heard the sound of the tropics. Eyes focused on the London transport map, Johnson responded in kind, "*No gracias, Señor,*" he said.

"*Habla espanol, Señor?*" the man responded, false surprise in his voice.

Johnson turned his head. The man from the car stood next to him, closer than one would in normal conversation. He had a thick rubbery face; black hair sprouted from his nose and ears. Gray roots belied his jet-black hair. He wore a short gray trench coat over a gray jacket and black tie. Johnson shifted his feet, moving away from the man.

The man inched closer, grinning. "If you intend to cause problems, my friend, I can assure you it will be much worse for you." The man held his right hand in his jacket pocket. His breath smelled of burnt cigarettes and Cuban coffee. Johnson found the aroma comforting.

"Now what problems could I cause you?" Johnson asked, his mouth dry.

"You're from Miami?"

"What?"

"You're from Miami. Miami, Florida. USA. Coconut Grove. Dadeland Mall. You know, Miami?"

"Yeah. So?"

"Friend, why don't we cross the street where we can speak more privately."

"Well, I don't know," Johnson said. "I'm supposed to meet my girlfriend and if I'm late..."

The man poked him in the ribs with the concealed hand. "Don't worry," the man said. "This won't take any time at all."

"As long as it won't take too much time," Johnson said.

"Nothing. A moment. I'll give you a cup of coffee."

Johnson said, "Okay," and imagined himself wielding a machete in Cuba during the next winter's sugar harvest.

The man grasped Johnson's arm as they crossed the street. He squeezed it hard enough to let Johnson know he was there.

The guy was good, Johnson had to give him that. At the embassy, he opened the door and said, "After you."

The room's walls were covered with travel posters -- Havana Harbor, dancers in a tropical night club, the beach at Varadero. A gray metal counter cut the room in half. Four pretty, dark-eyed women in red and blue blazers stood behind the counter and opened tourist brochures to the Brits waiting for information.

"This way," the man said.

He guided Johnson through a doorway and down a hall to a closed door. The man rapped once on the door, then pushed it open. He nudged Johnson into the room. A large man rose behind a desk. He had light chocolate skin and tightly curled hair. "Yes, Javier," he said.

"A friend from Miami."

"Another from Miami?" the man said, grinning.

Johnson nodded. "Well, Dade County actually."

"Still," the man said. "It's nice to have a neighbor visit us when in London." He reached his hand out to shake, "Luis Baste."

"Johnson," Johnson said, taking the man's hand. A picture of Fidel and Che Guevara and a map of Cuba hung on the wall. A picture of Luis Baste beside a woman and two children stood on the desk.

"And what do you think of London?" the man asked, gesturing to a seat.

"It's cold."

"Tell me about it. It's cold. It's wet. I'm afraid I was not really cut out for the climate."

"I was just thinking that myself," Johnson said.

"Have you been in London long?"

Johnson shook his head. "No, couple, three days. I'm still trying to get used to everything here."

The man nodded. "Yes, it's very different from Miami."

"Yeah, like what's this driving thing? And the food's funny and the pubs close so early you can't even get going. What's that all about?"

"One doesn't come to London for its food," the man said. "And somebody told me once why the English insist on driving on the wrong side of the road, but I can't remember now. I suspect the pubs close early so the workers can get up the next day and slave for their capitalist masters." The man laughed.

"That's very funny, sir," Javier said.

"Thank you."

"Still," Johnson said. "I've done my job plenty of times hung over."

"I imagine you have," Baste said.

Johnson watched the man for a moment. He was one of those guys that made you feel comfortable. He was, Johnson searched for the word, disarming.

"So are you the head man here?" Johnson asked.

"No," he smiled broadly. "I'm, oh I don't know..."

"In charge of security?" Johnson suggested.

The man grimaced and said, "Yes, I suppose you could say that. What do you think, Javier?"

Javier held up his hands as if to surrender. "Whatever you say, sir."

"So, Johnson. What were you doing that Javier found so interesting? You're not involved with any of those crazy Miami Cubans, are you?"

Johnson wasn't sure how to answer the question. Involved? No not quite involved. He was just doing his job. "Well, Luis. Um, I'm not really involved. I'm just delivering something to you guys. Something from a guy in Miami."

"And what is it you're supposed to deliver?"

"A letter from a guy named Mondongo. Ever heard of him?"

Javier and Baste began laughing. "You're delivering for Mondongo," Baste said through shrieks of laughter. He wiped a tear from his eye. "Oh, this is too much. Wait, wait." He nudged Javier. "Did somebody from the embassy send you over?"

"What embassy?"

"The American, of course."

"No," Johnson said.

The men laughed again. "Okay. Okay. You're not from the

139

embassy. Let's see Mondongo's letter."

"I can't give it to you," Johnson said.

Baste laughed, "You can't give it to me. Ha ha...let me guess. Hold on." He held his right hand up, while he wiped his eyes with his left. "You can only give it to...to...Antonio Gomez, right?"

"Right," Johnson said, recalling Mondongo's directions.

Javier and Luis Baste hooted with laughter.

Johnson hadn't exactly guarded the letter with his life, and he had delivered hundreds, maybe thousands, of packages. Nobody had ever laughed at him before.

Luis wiped his eyes with a handkerchief. "It's all too funny," he said.

"I'm glad you find this funny," Johnson said. "But no one gets the package but Antonio Gomez."

"Do you know Antonio Gomez?" Luis Baste asked. "Maybe I'm Antonio Gomez. Maybe he is," he said, gesturing toward Javier. Javier bent over with laughter. Tears flowed down Luis Baste's face.

The door at Johnson's back opened. Luis Baste and Javier stopped laughing. Luis sat up straight in his chair. Javier snapped to attention. Johnson turned and found himself looking up into the eyes of a man with the chiseled looks of a Cuban don. Johnson's head reached to the middle of the man's chest. The guy had the features of an actor and the broad chest of a laborer. "Antonio Gomez?" he asked.

"Luis, who is this man?"

"I think it's Carson over at the American Embassy playing with us, again," Luis Baste said.

"Excuse me," Johnson said. "I have a letter for you."

"You do? And just who do you think I am?"

"If you're not Antonio Gomez, you sure ought to be."

The man nodded. "Okay, my friend. Let's see it." He held out his hand.

Johnson handed him the envelope.

He tore it open, snapped out the letter and scanned it. He

breathed deeply, then smirked. "This is too perfect. Just too perfect." Antonio Gomez looked into Johnson's eyes while speaking to Luis Baste. "I think you're right, Luis. Carson's had a hand in this." He then spoke to Johnson. "It was Carson, wasn't it?"

"Who's Carson?" Johnson asked.

"It's all very funny." He tossed the letter onto Luis Baste's desk. "Call Carson. Tell him we weren't fooled, and keep my name out of it." Antonio Gomez turned and left the room.

Luis Baste picked up the phone and dialed a number. He read some of the letter, closed his eyes and smiled. His eyes opened. "Carson. Luis. Listen, don't think we've bought this Mondongo letter for one moment. I'm sure you guys over there thought it was funny. But you didn't get me, or Javier." Javier stood with his arms folded across his chest. He nodded once. "And this courier, Jesus, he's brilliant. The idiot perfected. He acts as if he knows nothing. The name Johnson, an allusion to the president responsible for your greatest foreign policy debacle of the 20th century. Oh, Carson, you Americans are too much. What would we do without you?"

Baste sat quietly for a moment, looking up at the ceiling. His eyes drifted down toward Johnson and his smile began to fade. "Is that so? Really? I don't know, Javier brought him in, I thought...it seemed... Yeah, just a second." Baste leaned across his desk, holding the receiver out. "He wants to talk to you."

"Shit," Johnson said. Who is it?"

"Carson Lea, Cultural Attaché, American Embassy."

Johnson took the phone. He held the receiver to his ear. He heard a man breathing on the other end. He listened for a moment. "Yeah," he said.

"Who the fuck do you think you are?" The man's voice raged on the other end of the line.

"What?" Johnson asked.

"Who the fuck do you think you are?"

"Yeah, I'm okay. No. No," Johnson said. "They're still laughing."

"What the fuck are you talking about?"

Johnson laughed. "No, they're not buying it. Yeah, they get the joke. No, I don't need a car. I think I need to walk a little, but thanks anyway."

The guy was screaming now.

"No, no, that's okay. Do you need to talk to Luis?" Johnson looked at Baste and shook his head. "Right. Right. Useless meetings. I understand. We'll talk later." Johnson reached across the desk and dropped the phone onto the receiver. "Well, fellows you caught us. We thought we had you."

Javier and Baste began laughing. "You Americans."

"Got to go," Johnson said.

"Of course," Baste said. "Javier will see you out."

Johnson shook Javier's hand at the door and began walking slowly away from the embassy. He'd delivered the letter. Handed it directly to Antonio Gomez. It wasn't Johnson's problem that the guy laughed at it, thought it was a joke. Fuck, that didn't matter. He'd done his job. Delivering it was easy. He'd tell Spiro how easy it had been. Nothing.

That guy at the American Embassy bugged him. What the hell was he so pissed about? Not that it mattered. He went through everything he'd done since arriving in London and, except for the herb with Pony Boy, none of it struck him as illegal. The guys at the Cuban or the American Embassy shouldn't be pissed at him. He was just delivering something for a crazy guy from Miami. What the fuck. But he was in a foreign country. He glanced at the traffic and realized that things could all be different. Maybe there were some things that were legal in the states that he didn't even know were illegal here. Jesus. Maybe he'd done something they could get him for. But he couldn't imagine what.

Three blocks from the embassy, Johnson looked back over his shoulder. He turned back just as a black Mercedes limousine pulled around the corner and stopped in front of him. The door opened. Javier leapt out of the car, stuck a gun in Johnson's face, pushed him into the back seat and climbed in after him.

Luis Baste sat beside him, his hands folded in his lap. "That little show back there was very funny, Mr. Johnson."

"Just Johnson," Johnson said.

"But we are no longer amused. Do you understand? We aren't amused."

Johnson nodded and his head was thrust back against the seat by the forward motion of the car. Like all his trips through London, he had no idea where he was going.

"Luis, can I shoot him?" Javier asked, holding the gun against Johnson's temple.

Johnson had a gun pointed at him once before. It was back on South Beach. He was on his way home from the Wreck, after one or two beers more than necessary. He staggered into the bushes to pee and tripped on some homeless guy's bed roll. "Jesus, shit," Johnson said. A mosquito buzzed his ear, a branch swatted his face. He unzipped and pulled his dick out.

A man rose up out of the shadows, shouldering a small rifle. "Hold it right there, fucker,"

"You hold it. I got to piss," Johnson said. He loosed a stream.

"I got a gun," the guy shouted.

Johnson's eyes teared. His bladder emptied. He nodded.

"You're drunk," the man said.

"You're right," Johnson said. He shook his dick and pushed it back into his trousers. "You've been right about everything. You've got a gun. And I'm drunk. Goodnight," he said.

Johnson turned his head slowly, looked up the barrel of Javier's gun and wished he was drunk.

Javier repeated his question. "Can I shoot him?"

"No," Luis said. He patted Johnson's leg. "I thought I liked you."

"I liked you," Johnson said, trying to ease his forehead away from Javier's gun. "I still do. You, Javier, Antonio Gomez -- I think you're all great guys."

Baste held up his hand, signaling Johnson for quiet. "You played us for fools. Fools."

"No I didn't."

"Please, Luis," Javier pleaded. "Just one shot. I'll clean up the mess."

"Mr. Johnson," Baste sighed, "You're in no position to argue."

"You're right," Johnson said.

"Fine," Luis Baste said. "Now that we have an understanding, let me tell you something. Something none of you gringos will ever understand -- and I don't care if you're a Yankee gringo or a Soviet gringo. What's going on between Cubans is not about communism and capitalism. It's a fight between brothers. It's about who is going to inherit the family's wealth. As soon as one of the brothers wins, everybody is going to get together like one big happy family. But do you know who we're going to remember as evil?"

Johnson shook his head.

"Whoever got between us. Whoever took a side. Because whoever took a side was fighting a member of our family. Remember that. We can fight to the death amongst ourselves. But don't ever think you can step between us or pick a side. Because eventually...Eventually..." The man shook with anger. "Do you understand?"

"I think so," Johnson said.

"Good," Luis Baste said.

The car turned left and right, swung wide, sped up a narrow street and pulled up before wrought iron gates. A man in uniform leaned into the driver's side of the car. Then waved it through the gates.

The car stopped abruptly under a portico. Javier pushed his pistol into a shoulder holster, opened the car door, stepped out and pulled Johnson out onto the driveway. Javier stepped over him and back into the car. The door slammed shut. The car sped down the circular driveway and out the gate. Johnson sat up. A blond man in a business suit stood over him with arms folded. Two Marines in dress blues stood on either side of the man, their hands resting on holstered .45's.

"Well, if it isn't our man in Havana," the guy said. "My name is Lea. Carson Lea." The guy wasn't smiling, but he didn't seem pissed off. He also didn't reach a hand down to help Johnson up.

"I've never been to Havana," Johnson said.

"Well, according to the letter you delivered to the Cubans, you know Havana well. You know the routes the Maximum Leader takes from the presidential residence to his mistresses. You know when he swims, where he dines, when he goes bowling."

"I don't know shit," Johnson said.

The guy looked side to side at the guards. "Shoot him," he said. "Throw his body in the Thames."

"Jesus," Johnson said. "You can't do that."

"I can't do that. I can't do that. You," the guy went at Johnson like he was going to kick him.

"Fuck fuck fuck," he said, stamping his feet. "You pieces of shit in Miami. Is it the sun? Does it fry your brains? We work hard to get a deal with the Cubans. No more Mariels. No more rafters. We'll control the maniacs in Miami. We get a deal. Not a great deal. Nothing for us, but for you guys. You know what happens to tourism in Miami every time the Maximum Leader decides to send another 100,000 of his poor huddled masses yearning to breathe free to your city? In the fucking toilet. The fucking toilet. So what do you do in return? Deliver a letter to the Cuban Embassy, telling the Cubans you intend to hit Fidel using old KGB operatives. What is this *step down or die* bullshit? Why the fuck would you tell these guys you're going to kill Fidel? I don't get you people."

"Is that what that letter said?"

"You didn't know what you were delivering?"

"No," Johnson said. "It was just a letter given to me by an old guy in a bar on South Beach when I told him my girlfriend and me were going to London. He said his wife and son had stayed on the island, that the kid had grown up to be a big man. Had a job at the Cuban Embassy in London."

"Goddamn it," the man shouted, kicking Johnson in the ribs. "And what name did he tell you?"

"Jesus Christ," Johnson cried, rolling into a ball to protect himself. Lea wore fine leather shoes. Johnson felt as if he'd been kicked by a slippered foot.

"What name?" the man repeated.

"Antonio Gomez," Johnson shouted.

Lea stomped his feet and jumped up and down. "Goddamn, goddamn. Fuck. Fuck. Fuck. Fuck. Fuck. Fuck."

Johnson peeked out from under the cover of his arms.

The guards at the gates had turned and were staring into the compound. Lea shouted, "What the fuck are you looking at?" He gestured to the Marines. "Bring him inside."

The Marines grabbed Johnson roughly by either arm and dragged him up a walk to the embassy's side door. One of the Marines wore too much cologne. The smell reminded Johnson of South Beach. He turned and looked at the guy, just a kid. Like all of them down on South Beach. Out to get laid or killed. Here this poor fucker was stuck working with this tight ass, Lea. Jesus, there was no justice.

Johnson had seen Leas before. Driven them all over hell and gone. The cut of the suit, the style of shoes. The guys were politicals. Fly into town, get met at the airport, out to the Fat Man's house for two hours of talks. Back to the airport and on the next flight out. How many had Johnson driven in secret, only to see their faces behind candidates on election day, or in cabinet positions? They all wanted what the Fat Man had. Money. Other people's money. "I can turn it on," the Fat Man told him. "I can turn it on like a faucet. It could run forever. These guys are nothing without me."

Johnson shrugged his shoulders. "Fellas," he said. "I can walk on my own."

Lea looked back at them over his shoulder. He nodded and the Marines released Johnson's arms. Johnson followed Lea down a corridor into a small elevator. He pushed a button marked six, the doors closed, and the car began to rise.

Johnson wasn't sure what to do. The Marines stood on either side. Lea stood at his back. He wasn't sure why he was getting this kind of treatment all of a sudden. Gomez must have been a pretty important guy. He wished Spiro had given him more information on the guy. Now he was going in blind. Who knew what these guys were up to? Who knew what Antonio Gomez had done?

The elevator stopped and the doors slid open. The Marines stepped out, let Lea pass and they followed him down to a heavy wooden door. Lea unlocked the door with a key attached to his belt. "After you," he said to Johnson.

Johnson stepped into room that looked like something out of a movie. White sheer curtains hung on three windows. The room held a couch, a desk, two chairs and a gleaming decanter full of a brown liquid. A blackened fireplace was built into one wall. A picture of former President Reagan hung behind the desk.

"Would you like a drink?" Lea asked, closing the door and walking across the room to the decanter.

Johnson didn't answer. He looked from side to side, trying to figure out what the guy was up to.

"Oh, don't worry," Lea said. "The room's secure. We de-bug it every week and nobody but our friends really care what we're doing any more." He held the bottle up to the light. "This a fine bonded bourbon from a small distillery whose original owner fired Jack Daniels for making poor product."

"Okay," Johnson said. "I'll try one."

Lea nodded. "That's a boy. Did you, by any chance, mention Antonio Gomez to Luis back there?"

"I met him," Johnson replied.

"Who?"

"Antonio Gomez."

"When?"

"At the Cuban Embassy. Just now. He came into the room while I was there."

"How do you know?"

"Six feet tall. Black hair, lots of it slicked back, graying side-burns. Chiseled looks like Cesar Romero, or somebody. That him?"

"That's classified," Lea said. "I can't tell you." He poured the whiskey into two cut glass tumblers. He motioned Johnson to the couch and sat in the armchair directly across from him. Lea crossed his legs, straightened the crease on his trousers and touched his tie. "Antonio Gomez? Hmmm." Lea took a sip of whiskey.

Johnson tasted his. A fine bourbon. Smooth, sweet, hot. "That's a good bourbon."

"Just another reason why the good old US of A is number one in the world."

"Yes, sir," Johnson said.

"And do you know how we've stayed number one?"

"A good draft and a great farm system?"

"What?" Lea asked.

"It was a joke. You know sports, number one, draft, farm system."

"Oh, a joke," Lea said. "A joke. That's very funny. You telling me a joke." Lea said "hahaha" when he laughed.

Johnson promised himself never to tell the man a joke again.

"But jokes aside, we've stayed number one by staying on top of the other guy's business, by knowing every move he makes." The man looked left and right and Johnson sensed Lea was about to tell him something he thought important. "It's the IKPA rule."

Johnson nodded his head. "The IKPA rule?"

Lea grinned at him. "It's an acronym. For Information -- Knowledge -- Power." His grin widened. "I made that up myself. IKPA." He winked at Johnson.

Johnson didn't know whether to laugh or cry. He took a gulp of whiskey. He closed his eyes for a moment, letting the whiskey run down to his stomach before speaking. "That's beautiful," he said.

"Thank you," Lea said. "Thank you. I'd write a book about the IKPA rule, but the agency's non-disclosure rules." Lea waved a hand. "It's not possible. I can't even let myself think about it."

"Well, that's a shame," Johnson said. "An idea like that would probably change the world."

"That's what I think," Lea said. "Absolutely." He sighed. "But so few will ever know of IKPA. It disappoints, but I know my sacrifice is in the service of a greater goal."

Johnson nodded his head. "What's that?"

"The security of the United States of America."

"Oh right," Johnson said. "Right."

Lea shifted in the chair, leaning closer to Johnson. "Tell me everything you know about Antonio Gomez."

"There's not much to tell, really. Say," Johnson said. "Do you suppose I could have another drink?"

"Yes, of course." Lea fetched the decanter and poured Johnson's glass full.

"Thank you. As I said, there's not much to tell, really. This guy, this old Cuban was next to me in a bar on South Beach. That's in Miami, you know."

Lea nodded.

"And I'm telling the bartender that my girlfriend, Al, and I are going to London."

"Your girlfriend's name is Al?"

"Her name is Alexandra. I call her Al."

A smile rose and fell on Lea's lips.

"Well, I'm telling this guy and he's joking about me seeing the queen and some other bullshit, when this old guy from down the bar says, excuse me, *Señor*, but are you truly going to London? I tell him that I am and he tells me the story of his family. It's Miami, there's a million of those stories. The revolution. Fidel is a commie. People leave. Their family stays behind. They expect to go back. They don't. Shit, if I've heard one of those stories I've heard a million of them. Well, the guy says his kid works for the embassy and could I drop off a letter while I'm there. Something from his father. What could I do? Say no? Two days later I picked up the letter from the bartender and tried to deliver it. The rest you pretty much know."

Lea said, "That's very interesting. You have just given me the I in the IKPA equation."

"It's nothing," Johnson said. "Anything I can do to help."

"Do you think the old man was really Antonio Gomez's father?"

"Well I did, until I met you. Now, I'm not sure."

Carson Lea nodded. "There are some things men like me will always understand that men like you could never fathom."

"That's why you get to drink this fine bourbon and have such a nice office, huh?"

Carson Lea nodded.

"Well, good for you and good for me," Johnson said. "I appreciate you looking out for me." Johnson drained his glass and stood up. "Can I go now?"

Carson Lea sighed and nodded. "I guess so. Though, Johnson, I must tell you that the I you've given me has not been very helpful."

Johnson nodded his head. "That's been the story of my life, sir."

"I can see that." Carson Lea stood up. "What's the name of your hotel? I'll have the driver take back."

"I don't remember. It's some little hole in the wall. You know, it doesn't even have a shower."

"Welcome to London, Johnson. It probably makes you even prouder to be from the good old USA."

"That it does, sir. The place is near the Notting Hill Gate underground station. Could I get a ride there?"

"Of course. You've done a great service for your country today. I'll see that it's not forgotten."

"Thank you, sir." Johnson brought his hand up and saluted Carson Lea.

"Johnson, no saluting."

"Oh, I'm sorry, sir."

Carson walked him out of the side door of the Embassy. A dark blue 1992 Ford Crown Victoria stopped in the driveway. Seeing that car made Johnson proud to be an American. "That's a great car," he said to Carson Lea.

Carson looked at it, then back to Johnson. "It's okay. I prefer a Mercedes."

Johnson knew Carson Lea to be a complete and total asshole then; he'd only thought it before. Johnson almost gave him his, 'give me a Crown Vic over any other car' speech. He'd given it naked and clothed, drunk, sober and high; it rolled off his tongue like a prayer.

America's a big country, he'd say. You need a big car in a big country. Then he'd go after which ever car had been praised. Ah, he'd say, the Mercedes is an over-rated piece of German engineering. A truly good car should have a number of things the Mercedes would never think to have. First and foremost the most important thing about a car is its ability to stop. The Crown Vic has a beautifully smooth braking system. Then, it has style, pick-up and class. The trunk is are roomy, the rear seats are broad. You can drive all day and be as comfortable as sitting in an easy chair. Cops assume you're some old duffer who can't afford a Caddy. You get one with cruise control, set it at sixty-five miles an hour and three days after leaving New York you'll find yourself at the Pacific.

Carson Lea opened the rear door for him. "Thank you for all your help, Johnson. If there's anything you need from the embassy while you're here, remember, we never met." He stuck his hand out for a shake.

Johnson took it and winked at him. "Met who?" he asked.

"Exactly," Lea said.

Johnson slid into the back seat. It was like being back in the states. The driver was even on the left side.

Johnson told the driver to take him to Notting Hill Gate. The conversation with Lea and the bourbon combined to tire him out. It didn't matter. He'd done his job, delivering the letter. What could he do about the shit that followed? He glanced up at the rear-view mirror and noticed the driver watching him. "Yeah?" he said.

"So, you're a yank?" the man asked. He had a small head, patchy hair.

Johnson nodded.

"Where are you from?"

"Florida," Johnson said. "Miami."

"Oh, near Disney World," the man said. "Me and the missus

have been saving for a holiday to Disney. They tell me it's heaven on earth."

Johnson nodded. He said, "Yeah, that's right," and spent the rest of the ride looking out the window.

At Notting Hill Gate station, he thanked the driver and slammed the door. Johnson felt a cold or some other bug coming on. He was tired. Needed to sleep. The weather was colder than he thought. He knew what he needed -- a hot shower, a nap. Rest. He admitted to himself it was a hard day's work delivering the letter. He'd tell the Fat Man the entire story. He'd understand. And if he didn't, well? Maybe Johnson shouldn't have told them that the letter came from a maniac named Mondongo. Maybe they wouldn't have laughed at him. Sure, Havana had Fidel, but Miami had Mondongo. If Antonio Gomez, Luis Baste and Javier were sensible men they could laugh at the mirror images. Fidel existed only because of Mondongo. But there was no way of knowing if they were sensible men. They may have been Cuban versions of Carson Lea, and he was an absolute asshole. Johnson was done with the whole mess, and damn happy about it, too.

He walked slowly up the steps to the hotel door and pulled it open. A yellow streak shot past his foot. He turned as a cat darted across the street and under a parked car. Sheila bowled Johnson over as she sprinted by. She dove onto her knees and pleaded with the cat to come out from under the car.

Johnson stood up and brushed himself off. He could see that Sheila wanted no help from him. He stepped into the hallway and saw himself full figured in the mirror. He flipped the bird at his reflection. Spiro was behind the mirror laughing at him, Johnson knew it. Well, fuck that, he thought. He stuck out his tongue, then put his thumb on his nose and wiggled his fingers. He made a fist with his left hand and grabbed his bicep with his right, pumping it up and down. Finally, he grabbed his crotch and mouthed, 'eat this' at his reflection.

Spiro came up behind him and said, "How did it go with the Cubans? I've always found them to be a very volatile people."

Johnson spun around, still holding his crotch. "Damn, I hate that," he said.

"Hate what?" Spiro asked, staring at Johnson's crotch.

"Nothing," Johnson said.

"I see," he said, looking up into Johnson's eyes. "But how did it go? Did you threaten them? Expose some secrets? Were they shaking?"

"No," Johnson said. "I wasn't there for that. I just delivered a letter."

"What did it say? Don't tell me," Spiro cried. "Rapprochement? Detente? You don't know...you'll be losing your way of life! How I miss the Cold War." A tear ran down his cheek and he brushed it away. "Now I'm crying like an old woman."

"Spiro, come on, in America they think men need to cry more."

Spiro eyes grew larger. He punched his right hand into his left. "We could have won. You're over there crying. Capitalism -- a morally bankrupt concept that tells men they need to cry more. Hah! We could have won. We would have won."

Johnson patted Spiro on the shoulder. "Come on, Spiro," he said. "You know it's not over. It'll never be over. They say it's over. But we know it ain't over."

"What do you mean?"

"Listen, if it ain't the US and Russia..."

"Soviet Union," Spiro said.

"What?"

"Not Russia," he said "Soviet Union."

"Okay," Johnson said. "If it's not the US and the Soviet Union it'll be somebody else. You just need to make yourself available. That's what I did. Started in one line of business. Did that for a while. Opportunities started to dry up; I hooked into something else. Just make yourself available. Business will come your way."

"That's the difference," Spiro said. "You people have always looked for business. I'm looking for a cause."

"There's always the United Way," Johnson said.

"The what?"

"It's a joke."

Spiro nodded. "I'm glad you find this funny."

"Jesus, lighten up, Spiro."

The door opened and Sheila whisked past them with the yellow cat cradled in her arms. "Is he okay?" Johnson asked.

"No thanks to you," she snapped.

"Well." Johnson didn't know what else to say. He turned back to Spiro. "Tell me about your friend Antonio Gomez."

Spiro shrugged his shoulders. "He's very professional."

"Is he dangerous?"

"All men are dangerous," Spiro said.

"What the fuck is that supposed to mean?"

Spiro looked right and left. "Do you always play the fool this well, Johnson?"

"What the fuck is that all about?"

"Johnson," Spiro said. "All men are dangerous." He spoke slowly, emphasizing each syllable. "Do you understand? It's a simple idea."

"Oh, okay," Johnson said. "I get it. All men are dangerous."

"Good job," Spiro said. "Now, if you'll excuse me, I have to go unplug a toilet." He grinned at Johnson. "You lose Cuba, you'll be unplugging toilets, too."

CHAPTER 14

Music played in the Dunkirk room as Johnson stuck his key into the lock. Spiro probably left the radio on. He turned the key and pushed against the door. It didn't budge. He tried it again, turning the key in the opposite direction.

"Who's there?" Al shouted.

"Me," he said.

"Just a second," she said.

A bolt clicked and slid. The door opened.

"Oh, Johnson," she said, "Hi... Today's meeting broke down into some brainstorming bullshit about branding. I couldn't take it anymore, so I came home early." Al wore a man's white dress shirt, unbuttoned, and a pair of black bikini underwear. She had a bottle of red wine, half empty, in one hand and a glass full of wine in the other. French-sounding accordion music played from the clock radio. "We've been trying to wait for you. Really, we have."

Johnson stepped into the room and pushed the door shut behind him. A naked, dark skinned woman lay on her stomach across the bed. She had thick, shoulder-length black hair, small-ish breasts, and a towel across her ass. She grinned at Johnson. *"Hola, amigo,"* she said.

"Como esta, Señora," Johnson said, and wondered why he spoke so much Spanish in London. He understood it at the Cuban embassy. That made sense. But everywhere else? Some of the English he'd heard didn't seem right either. Pony Boy and his guys spoke hard core Jamaican English. The guy next to him in the Sun & Moon Pub, whose entire vocabulary seemed to be

"arghh." The woman in The Guardsman Pub near Buckingham Palace he thought was speaking French, but discovered she was from Scotland.

He turned to Al. "She's lovely. Where did you find her?"

"She was lying across the bed when I came in. I thought you found her."

"Como se llama?" Johnson asked.

"I speak English," she laughed. "What do you think, Johnson, you are in Miami?"

"How did she get here?"

Al narrowed her eyes. "You didn't let her in?"

Johnson shook his head.

"She was here when I got here," Al said.

Johnson turned to the woman. *"Señora..."*

"Helena Sanchez," she corrected him. "Helena Sanchez-Brito, but Helena will do. Don't you remember?"

"Helena, what are you doing here?"

"You invited me, remember? I work with Antonio Gomez. He wants you to deliver a message to his father. Tell the old man the revolution was beautiful, and he should not have fled Cuba. Tell him his wife died four years ago cursing his name. Tell him things have been better without him."

Johnson laughed. "You took off your clothes to tell me that."

"No, Johnson," Al said, waving her hand. "I took off her clothes."

Helena moved her head in a circle, stretching her neck. "Eyiieee," she cried. "You most certainly did."

Johnson thought of asking Al if she took the clothes off every interesting woman she met. He decided he'd wait till they were alone.

"Here, Johnson," Al said. "Come sit down over here." She gestured at the overstuffed chair. "Have a glass of wine." She poured another glass. "It looks like you've had a hard day."

Johnson waved his hand. "A normal one. So normal, it doesn't feel like I'm on vacation."

"You're on vacation, Johnson. Sit."

Johnson heard sex in Al's voice. He knew that if he ran his fingers between her labia she would moan and they'd come out wet.

Al handed him a glass of wine and brushed her lips against his. "Sit," she repeated, "you're on vacation."

Johnson took the glass of wine. "Sure," he said. "But let me lose some of my clothing." He stripped naked, then pulled a denim shirt over his shoulders.

Helena Sanchez laughed. "You two must do this all the time."

"Whenever we can," Al said. She sat down on Johnson's lap and stuck her tongue in his mouth.

Johnson closed his eyes. It had begun again. He reached out to Al's nipples and rolled one between his fingers. He felt a hand brush his chest and opened his eyes to see Helena Sanchez standing over Al. Al stroked Helena's pubic hair with one hand and probed her mouth with the other. He reached out to Helena's tits and closed his eyes. Hands roamed over his body. Nipples firmed and tightened between his fingers. Bodies firm and soft. Skin -- delicate and warm.

Al had brought it to him again. He was never sure how it worked between Al and women. He'd seen her do it -- start talking to a woman, then wink and laugh. A private laugh, telling them if you think you like men, think again. She didn't brag as Johnson had heard men do. She just told them, I am a woman who knows how to please women. A woman who pleases herself through other women. If they got that far, other matters arose. Johnson, for instance. He knew his presence complicated things. In a bar, on a train, in a restaurant, Al and the woman would be past the look. They would be negotiating. The woman deciding if it was worth it. Al letting her know that it was worth it for all the world. The woman would look past Al, gesturing to Johnson. So who's he? Do you know him? Is he something to you? Is he part of the deal?

Johnson watched Al's answer. He waited for hesitation. He waited to see if they had met a woman Al desired so greatly that she'd leave him behind. He watched her eyes. Her lips. Her hands. "He is the deal," she would say. "He makes it better. He makes it real. He is a witness. You need a witness for the kind of sex we will have. No one would believe it otherwise. We might not believe it ourselves. He will see it. He will remember it. Him being there. You knowing he's watching. You knowing there's a cock made hard by this sex." Al would run a finger under the woman's chin or over her thigh, then stand up. "Johnson," she'd say, "we're going now."

Al and Johnson would stand, and nine times out of ten, ninety-nine times out of one hundred, nine hundred and ninety-nine times out of a thousand the woman would stand up as well.

Sometimes Al worked too well. The woman, made weak in the knees, would stumble. Others quaked and moaned through orgasms on the spot. Al touched their hands. "If you think that's nice," she'd say, "that's nothing. Come on. Come on."

Sometimes they would start messing around in the car as Johnson drove home. They'd touch each other and giggle. The women wouldn't know what Al thought was okay. They'd be hesitant. Nervous. She would touch them everywhere. Kiss their necks. They'd moan. Al would find out their secrets. She probed and plunged. By the time Johnson parked the car she knew spots that made them weep.

Johnson wasn't sure of his role in all of that. What was he doing there? What did this woman want? When he asked her the first time she said, "I want you and every woman I meet." Then she laughed.

"No," he said. "Really?"

"Johnson," she said. "Do you like apples?"

"Yeah, I like apples. Macintosh."

"Okay. You like Macintosh apples. Why?"

"They taste good. I like them. I've always liked them."

"Johnson," she said. "You taste good. I like you. I've always liked you."

Johnson lay on his back on the floor of the Dunkirk room. Al straddled his cock and rode up and down as if on a horse. Helena Sanchez stood over Johnson's face. Al spread Helena's pussy wide and licked and sucked the woman's clitoris. Al pushed her fingers into Helena's vagina, then fell face forward on to Johnson. Her lips and cheeks were covered with juice and saliva. She rubbed her face against Johnson's. "Does her pussy look good?" she asked.

"Yes," Johnson replied.

"Do you want to fuck it?"

"Yes," Johnson sighed.

"Do it through me," she said. "Fuck me so hard. Fuck me. Fuck her," she cried. She sat up and pushed her face into Helena's crotch. "Do you feel how good he's fucking me?"

"Yes," Helena moaned. "Fuck her so good," she said.

Johnson thrust his hips off the floor. Pushing into Al's pussy. Feeling each and every part of himself collapse into the head of his dick. Johnson never knew whether he was going to be alive at the end of such bouts. He never knew if he was alive during such bouts. He thrust his cock harder. Al moaned louder. Helena Sanchez chanted, "fuck her, fuck her, fuck her."

"I'm going to cum," Johnson said.

"Not yet," Al pleaded. "Not yet."

"Not yet," Helena cried. "Make her hot."

Johnson cried out when he came. He yipped like a dog and writhed beneath Al. She rode him, up and down. He jerked and squirmed. His cock softened and fell out. A glob of sperm slid down his leg. It cooled. Johnson shivered.

Al continued to wriggle on top of him. She pulled Helena to the floor. The two women rolled together. They moaned and made sucking sounds. Al giggled. Helena hissed, "So you like that?" Al moaned as if something touched her very deep. She breathed faster and harder. Her body began shaking. Helena repeated, "Yes yes yes yes." Their cries built to a frenzy. Johnson wondered how long they could sustain it. When it broke. They both cried out, sharp and loud. They laughed -- rolled apart, then together and were quiet.

Johnson sat up and looked at the woman. Helena rested her head on Al's stomach. She moved her fingers in small circles through Al's pubic hair. Al had her left arm draped across her eyes. Her lips were swollen. She could have been sleeping.

Johnson's knee popped as he stood up. He saw his reflection in the mirror. His face red and blotchy. It was then he remembered Spiro's camera. "Fuck," he said.

"Did you say something?" Al asked.

"No," Johnson said. He leaned closer to the mirror, trying to see through to the other side. He couldn't. He mouthed the words, "Fuck you, asshole."

"Johnson, what are you doing?"

"Nothing," he said. "It's just..."

"Don't worry about Spiro," Helena Sanchez sighed.

Johnson turned to Helena. She sat up beside Al, grinning.

"Who's Spiro?" Al asked.

"The porter here," Helena Sanchez said. "I sense Johnson has some concerns about the noise. Isn't that right, Johnson? The noise?"

Johnson looked from Helena to the mirror. He saw his face, the face of a doomed man, staring back at him. "Yeah, the noise," he said, watching his reflection speak for him.

"We didn't make that much noise," Al said. She brushed her hand against one of Helena's nipples. "At least I didn't hear too much noise."

"Yes," Helena said. "Who hears or speaks well during sex? I know I don't."

Johnson watched his face and let his imagination run off and play with itself. Helena knew Spiro. Spiro probably let her in. They were working together. There were probably men on the other side of the glass right now waiting for the opportunity to...the opportunity to? Johnson couldn't figure out what they wanted from him. He replayed his visit to the Cuban Embassy. What was really there? Antonio Gomez? Helena had given him a message for Antonio Gomez's father. They must know the father did not exist. Was it a message for Mondongo? Did the twerp from the American embassy know what was going on? Johnson didn't believe so.

Al stood up and shook the tangles out of her hair. "I don't know about you guys, but I think it's a little chilly here."

"When I first got here I was cold all the time," Helena Sanchez said.

Al pulled on the white shirt and grabbed her glass of wine. "To warmer weather," she proposed.

Helena Sanchez picked up her glass and stood beside her. "To warmer weather and the revolution." They knocked their glasses together and drank.

Johnson watched their reflections in the mirror. How many times had he seen Al's luminous white skin beside a darker Latin woman? How many times? Eight? Maybe ten. Ten? Jesus. Ten Latin women. But how many women total? How many times had this happened? Al and Helena talked quietly behind him. They touched each other and laughed. Johnson tried to count how many times he and Al shared each other with a woman, shared a woman between themselves. The count, he figured was near thirty. Thirty different women in two years. Jesus. Thirty. Each one was different. Some even dangerous. A blonde named Heather thought Al should run away with her. Every day for two weeks at 6 p.m., she showed up in front of Johnson's house howling that Al and she were meant for each other. One day she wasn't there. Johnson didn't miss her exactly, but something seemed lacking from the day. Later, someone told him Heather had died in a car crash. Johnson wondered if she died on the way to his house. He didn't ask.

When he turned around Al and Helena were dipping their fingers in their wine glasses, painting each other's nipples, then sucking them clean. Johnson knew Al loved that. He watched Helena Sanchez and tried to decide if she was any more of a threat than the other women Al brought home. She'd delivered a message from Antonio Gomez. Was she any different from the UPS delivery woman that Al invited in for a glass of water and two hours in bed? Probably. But there was nothing he could do about it. He reached for his wine and sat down on the bed.

Helena Sanchez turned to him. "Do you just sit there and

watch?"

"Sometimes," he said. He placed the wine on the table next to the bed, plumped the pillows and lay back. Johnson believed sex with two women was like a fine meal. Watching two women please each other was a sweet and filling dessert. During sex it's all close work; through watching you get perspective. You come to know perfection and flaw. You see beauty and horrors and absolute proof of what Johnson had known for years. Sex is better for women. Sex is deeper for women. The storm that builds while two women make love is longer and more intense than anything a man can bring. Johnson sat back on the bed and watched the storm build between Helena Sanchez and Al.

Al had pushed her fingers into Helena, leaned back and watched the woman, eyes closed, writhing on her hand. "Your pussy's so hot," Al said. "Do you like your pussy so hot?"

"*Si*," Helena Sanchez sighed. *"Si, es spectacular."* Helena began a rhythmic dance.

Al sipped her wine, then crouched down to the floor. She spread Helena with both hands, and placed her face up in Helena's crotch. She moaned, then hummed on Helena's clit.

Helena snapped her teeth and growled. She held Al's head against her with a hand and ground her pelvis into Al's face. Helena lifted her glass of wine, threw her head back and poured the wine into her open mouth. She closed it to swallow -- a trickle ran down her cheek. She opened her eyes and scowled at Johnson.

Helena tossed the glass toward him. It arced high above the bed and landed between Johnson's legs. A drop of red wine stained the sheets. Johnson smiled at the moment's beauty. His cock grew hard. Helena Sanchez crumpled to the floor. She and Al entwined their bodies. Johnson spat in his hand and began stroking his cock as he watched the women on the floor. Al's fingers pushed deeper into Helena. Helena pushed Al's legs apart and dove face first into her crotch. Helena hummed and moaned on Al's clit. Al stuck her head up and flexed her neck, stretched her neck, moaning at the ceiling. The head of Johnson's cock flared; he stroked slower, feeling the moment seconds away. He reached for Helena's empty wine glass. His sperm shot into the glass and mixed with the remnants of wine. Johnson said, "Fuck me," when he came. He milked his cock dry and lay back on the bed. He closed his eyes and listened to the women please each other. He listened to the sucking, licking and moans. The short cries, the whispered pleas. He listened to the shift of bodies and the verbal emotions -- fast, faster, faster, until the quaking, moaning and shifting combined to a quivering moment where cries of pleasure filled the room. The cries built to shrieks and then died in long slow moans.

Helena giggled.

Al said, "Thank you."

Johnson sat up on the bed. Al and Helena lay across the floor. Al on the bottom, Helena's head resting on her stomach. Their faces were red and slick with saliva and juice. Eyes closed, they both smirked at something.

Johnson had seen that smirk before. It said, "We know good and better. This is better." Johnson knew it was something he was not supposed to see. He was let into a private circle, a secret club. Women had let him see something -- know something -- he wasn't supposed to. It was a beautifully dangerous position. It allowed him to believe that he knew things. Things so basic and elemental that all other things to be known sprang from this knowledge. People created gods, fought wars, invented capitalism, so they could deny and defeat what Johnson had learned over and over again when he was in a room with Al and another woman. Women do not need men. In fact, Johnson believed, they were better off without them. But it was not an idea he ever mentioned to Al. Instead, he thanked the women in the only way he knew how.

Johnson sat up on the edge of the bed and cleared his throat. "You guys need anything? More wine? Cold water?"

Johnson saw Al's stomach rise and fall as she chuckled. "Johnson," she said. "You're wonderful." She smiled. "I need some wine."

"Me too," Helena Sanchez said, without opening her eyes.

Johnson looked around for the bottle. They had drained it. "The bottle's empty. I'll get some more," he said.

"Just call for it," Al said. "I'm sure they'd bring it."

"No, no," Johnson said. "I'll go get it." He had a pressing desire to get out of the room. Back home everything he could have offered would have been out of the room. It was his method, to leave the room and allow the Al and the woman to talk. To settle any matters that hung in the air. Johnson had learned that there could certainly be many. After sex of the kind that Al and Johnson generally had with a woman, all the barriers would come down. Social, political, hygienic. It didn't matter how many times had Johnson heard women discuss him like he was nothing more than a talking dildo. Al always defended him, but he preferred not to have to deal with it. Instead, he made his offer. Would they like anything? Was there something that would make them more comfortable? And if all that failed, he'd just say, 'I'll be back.'

He pulled on his jeans, buttoned up his shirt and pushed his feet into his boots before turning back to Al and Helena. They lay together on the floor, Helena head resting against Al's stomach. The blinds were drawn in the room and London's gloomy sunlight cast a gray tint through the drawn slats. The light from the bathroom fell in a square across the women's bodies. Al's head and torso and Helena's face and neck were framed in the light. They smiled, lips together, eyes closed. Johnson wondered what they were thinking about. Or were they still in that place where there were no thoughts?

"I'll be back," he said, and pulled the door closed. He stopped in the hall to make sure he was completely together. He planned to go to the front desk, ask for a bottle of wine, have them open it and return to the room. He started down the hall, watching his reflection in the mirror at the far end. Spiro materialized behind him. Johnson turned. At the same moment he felt a hand on his shoulder.

Spiro nodded, then gestured, "I believe you two already know each other."

"We meet again, Johnson," the man said.

Johnson turned to face Antonio Gomez.

"I would like you to take a ride with me," the man said.

Johnson looked back over his shoulder. Spiro had disappeared. "You know I'd really like to, but I've got company in the room and my girlfriend's expecting me back in a few minutes."

"Don't worry about your girlfriend, *Señor*. Helena Sanchez will more than keep her occupied. As I am sure you have already seen."

Son of a bitch, Johnson thought. "Well, you know, I didn't bring a jacket and..."

Antonio Gomez held a finger to his lips and shook his head. "The car's warm. It's just outside. I promise, you won't be cold and I'll bring you back. Promise," he said holding his right hand over his heart.

"Okay," Johnson said, "As long as you'll bring me back. You know I'm from Miami and it's not too cold there."

"Believe me, *Señor*. I know where you're from."

"Let's go then," Johnson said, turning toward Gomez.

"Not this way." Gomez pointed. "We'll be going that way." He put both hands on Johnson shoulders and turned him around. "That way."

Johnson shrugged. He didn't know there was a back way, but he didn't feel as if he were in any position to disagree. He started down the hall and saw an open door with a stairwell for the first time. He pointed through the door. "There?"

"Si, Señor," Antonio Gomez said.

Johnson turned into the hallway and through the glass he saw Al and Helena Sanchez sitting naked on the floor talking. He turned back to Antonio Gomez. The man shook his head and held a finger to his lips. "Don't," he whispered, with such menace that Johnson knew he wouldn't speak.

Johnson walked down the stairs feeling like a beaten man. They had watched him and Al and Helena and something about it seemed wrong. Helena must have known all along that they were being watched. Helena must have been laughing the whole time. Goddamn, he thought. Goddamn. The steps were wooden and firm under Johnson's feet. They passed room after room, and through each mirror they saw what took place on the other side. It gave Johnson a moment of panic to think that every mirror he'd ever seen was two way. Johnson saw no sign of Spiro. He expected him to be there running cameras, but Johnson and Antonio Gomez were alone. They reached the bottom of the steps and Johnson pushed open a door to the outside. He squinted against the light.

CHAPTER 15

A Mercedes limousine sat idling in the parking lot. White puffs chugged from the exhaust pipe, traffic rumbled beyond the garden wall and two small birds, Johnson guessed them to be sparrows, flitted around the gritty pavement. It struck him that Antonio Gomez was taking him out to die. There could be no other reason for it. He was having a clairvoyant experience. When your life becomes clearer than it's ever been before -- there can be no other reason. You're going to die. I am going to die, he told himself. He focused on his situation, thought through it all -- die.

He imagined telling his friends back home how funny it seemed. "Yeah, I was killed by a Cuban. In London, for Christ's sakes. Jesus, you could understand Miami, even Havana. But London?" Johnson smiled when he imagined their laughter. Goddamn it, he thought. I'm just going to die. Even Al's not going to know what happened. Goddamn it. Johnson wasn't ready to die yet. He thought someday he might be, but not today. Goddamn it.

Antonio Gomez gestured toward the car door.

Johnson turned toward the man, put his hands on his hips, and said, "Are you going to kill me, or what?"

Antonio Gomez snorted. "Kill you? Kill you? Is that what you think? Would I kill a dog that shit on my shoes?" He shook his head. "I might rub his nose in it. I might beat him with a newspaper, but I wouldn't kill him."

"You're going to beat me with newspaper?" Johnson had heard of people using bags of oranges and rubber hoses, but never newspaper.

"Oh, Spiro is right," Antonio Gomez said. "You are stupid." He reached down and pulled open the door. "Get in the car."

Johnson slid into the back seat and Antonio Gomez dropped in beside him. Johnson recognized the driver, Javier. Antonio Gomez settled himself in with great rustling and adjustment. He said, "*Vamos*," and the car rolled forward, through a gate and out onto the streets of London.

Antonio Gomez sat back in his seat. "The English and the Cubans have a lot in common," he said to the window.

Johnson knew Gomez was addressing him. He'd seen men who believed they thought great thoughts do that before. Johnson hated when people did that. He also wasn't too happy that Gomez said he was like dog shit. "Yeah, you're right," Johnson said. "There's that language thing you guys got going."

"What?" Antonio Gomez said, looking over his shoulder at Johnson.

"You know, that language thing."

"We speak different languages," Antonio Gomez said.

"I know that," Johnson said. "But you both, Cuban and English alike, speak a language."

Antonio Gomez sighed. "No, my friend, the comparisons go much deeper than that." Gomez chuckled. Johnson knew the man was laughing at him. "England is an island. Cuba is an island. Both are located just off great continents, homes of powerful nations. Both have charted their own ways in the world. Their peoples, through desire and inner strength, have made their nations' roles in the world far grander than anyone would imagine."

"Yeah, you're right about that. Look at how successful the Miami Cubans are. Goddamn. I mean, who would have thought it? Not me."

Antonio Gomez snorted. "The Miami Cubans. Deserters. Worms. American toadies."

"Oh," Johnson said. "Sorry, I forgot."

Antonio Gomez continued to look away from Johnson and

out the window. The man's breathing had become louder. Johnson watched his back rise and fall with each breath. I must have really pissed him off, he thought. Well, fuck him, he pissed me off too. Johnson decided to ask the question. "That Helena Sanchez, you sent her to get me?"

Antonio Gomez looked over his shoulder at Johnson and nodded his head.

"You were watching the whole time?"

Antonio Gomez smirked, an eyebrow went up and he nodded. "I thought that trick with the wine glass was pretty good."

That really pissed Johnson off. Fuck him. "Well, I had fun. You know the talk on the street in Miami is that all the young girls in Cuba are fucking tourists for a little spare change. But I didn't think Fidel would have his women out whoring so old perverts like you could watch."

Antonio Gomez wheeled around and swung an open hand at Johnson.

Johnson ducked and the slap glanced off the top of his head.

The limousine stopped abruptly, throwing Johnson on the car floor, against the front seat. Javier leaned back over the seat, pointing a pistol at Johnson. "Now, can I kill him?" Javier asked.

Johnson looked from the pistol to Antonio Gomez. The man smiled at him. Horns honked behind the car.

Antonio Gomez shook his head. "No, you'll get the car bloody. Just drive."

Javier disappeared over the seat. Johnson felt the car lurch forward.

"So you see what you've fallen into, *Señor* Johnson. I think you're playing way above your head."

Johnson climbed back up onto the seat. He leaned against it and closed his eyes. "Yeah, I think you're probably right. So what's this all about? Why do you even care?"

"Maybe you could tell me what this is about. You come from Miami to London. You stay at the Pembroke House. You go to the Cuban Embassy, then to the American Embassy. Tell me about that."

"There's not much really," he said. "My girlfriend, Al, had to come to London on business. She asked me if I wanted to go along, I said yes. Sometime after that I was in a bar on South Beach telling the bartender, a friend of mine, that I was going to London. This old guy at the bar comes up to me and says..."

Antonio Gomez held a hand up. "Javier," he said. "Fuck the car. Shoot this lying shit eater."

The car swerved to the side of the road and stopped. Javier turned back and placed the gun in Johnson's face.

"Aw fuck," Johnson said. "I'll tell. I'll tell."

Antonio Gomez nodded. The driver sighed and turned back to the wheel. "*Señor* Johnson, if I were you I wouldn't tempt the fates many more times. Our friend Javier is dying to shoot someone. Isn't that right?"

"*Si Señor,*" the driver said.

"The truth, *Señor* Johnson and, how do you Americans say? And nothing but the truth."

So help me God, Johnson thought. Johnson wanted to stall for a moment, but he wasn't sure why. Did he need time to think? He wasn't sure. After all, why not just tell them the truth? Who could it hurt?

"*Señor* Johnson?" Antonio Gomez said. "You make me believe that you have something to hide."

"In Miami," Johnson began, "I have a private delivery business. My main client knew I was going to London and he arranged for me to combine business and pleasure by delivering that letter to the Cuban Embassy. That's it."

"Do you know who the letter was from?"

"Just like I told Luis and Javier. They know. Some crazy old guy named Mondongo."

"Mondongo?" Antonio Gomez said, eyes widening. "My god, not Mondongo. Did you hear that, Javier? The letter's from Mondongo."

The driver nodded. "I heard."

Antonio Gomez turned to Johnson. "My god, a letter from the man whose name is tripe."

"What?" Johnson said. "What did you say?"

"The man's name, Mondongo. In English it would be tripe. Cow guts." Antonio Gomez laughed. "You are a pawn, Johnson, moved as easily by Mr. Tripe in America as you are by me in London." He slapped the back of the seat. "Javier, pull over."

The driver pulled the car to the side of the road. "This is where we part company Johnson. Enjoy your stay in London."

"Hey, wait a second." Johnson pointed at the clothes he had on. "It's cold out there. You said you'd give me a ride back."

Antonio Gomez smiled at him. "I lied."

Javier pushed the gear shift into park, got out of the driver's seat and opened Johnson's door. He reached a hand into the back seat and grabbed Johnson's shoulder. Johnson shook him off. "I'm coming. I'm coming," he said. Johnson turned to Antonio Gomez. "You know, liars really suck."

Antonio Gomez laughed. "Go, Johnson. Go."

Johnson stepped out onto the curb. Javier pushed the car door closed and grinned at Johnson before he dropped back behind the steering wheel. The limousine pulled from the curb and drove slowly down the street.

Johnson rubbed his arms against the cold. Goddamn, he thought. What the fuck am I going to do? He had no identification and no cash. He had intended to grab a bottle of wine from the hotel's lounge, put it on the tab and hurry back to the room. Now he was in a strange city, didn't know his way around. Though they seemed to speak English, it felt like he didn't know the language. It sounded like they were speaking Portuguese to a cat. Johnson imagined himself staggering through the streets of London, wearing plastic garbage bags stuffed with newspapers to keep him warm. Lost. Broke. He'd become a beggar at the entrance to the underground. Al would pass him. He'd reach for her, but in his disheveled and vermin-ridden state she would not recognize him and she'd shrink from his touch. Johnson mouthed the phrase he planned to repeat over and over while he shook the coins in his begging bowl. "Spare change for an American down on his luck. Spare change for an American down on his luck."

He would spend his hard begged money on drink. His skin would darken with grime, shrink against his bones, and he would die. All that would remain of Johnson would be the bundle of rags he'd wrapped about himself and the small stain on the sidewalk where he died. God, he thought, a tear running down his cheek. I could have been something. I could have been something good. He wondered if Al would call his mother to tell her he had disappeared -- that he was gone and not coming back. He wasn't sure if he wanted Al to do that. The news would kill his mother. Oh God, he thought, why have you forsaken me? He hugged himself for warmth, looked at the bleak London sky and closed his eyes against the future.

He stood wondering how long he would last. Six months? A year? It took a long time to die. A long time. He shook his head and opened his eyes. Across the street stood Spiro, on the front porch of the Pembroke House with his arms folded over his chest.

Al was right, he thought, that's the finest fucking small hotel in all of fucking London. Johnson waved at Spiro. Tears of happiness flooded his eyes. He started across the street. A horn honked and a tiny London taxi screeched to a halt, its bumper just nudging Johnson's leg. Johnson didn't care. He waved to the driver and shouted, "Sorry. Sorry."

He crossed the street and scampered up the steps. "Spiro," he said. "I'm so happy I found my way back."

"You told them everything, didn't you?" Spiro said, scowling.

"There was nothing to tell."

"I told them they'd have to kill you to get the information. I told them you were a man. You disappoint me, Johnson."

"They pointed a gun at me," Johnson said.

"Did they chamber a round? Did they pull the trigger? They pointed a gun at me," he simpered. "They pointed a gun at me. American crybaby." Spiro untied the blue waist coat and pulled it open.

Johnson shrank back, putting his arms up in front of his face.

"What are you doing now?"

"I thought you had a gun," Johnson said.

"If I had a gun you should rush me."

"But you'll shoot me," Johnson said.

"Damn Gorbachev! If I could have only introduced you to him. If he saw you, it would be the United States breaking up. It would be the United States suffering through a radical transition to a managed economy."

Johnson didn't know what the fuck Spiro was talking about. He didn't care either. He was cold. He wanted to go in and lie next to Al's naked body.

"This is what I came to show you." Spiro pulled open the waistcoat and his entire shirt underneath was covered with rows of medals. Ribbons, gold and silver coins, crossed leaves, hammers and sickles.

Johnson had never seen so many medals in one place. "Jesus, where'd you get those?"

"In the service of the cause. In the service of the proletariat."

"That's pretty good, Spiro. I've never seen that many medals on a man."

"This isn't all of them. These are just the ones that don't fit on my uniform."

"Wow," Johnson said. "That's really cool."

Spiro's jaw jutted out. "Thank you," he said.

"You're welcome."

Spiro looked down at him. "What did Gomez do when you gave him the information?"

"He laughed at me."

Spiro's eyes widened. "Laughed?"

Johnson nodded.

"Heh," Spiro said. "It's better not to die for information people laugh at."

"That's what I think," Johnson said.

"And?" Spiro said.

"He slapped me once."

"He did?"

"Yeah. I ducked, but he still hit me."

Spiro nodded. "You should not have ducked. That shows weakness. But he slapped you. That's good."

"Yeah, then threw me out of the limousine."

"No he didn't. I saw it. The driver got out, opened the door, then you got out."

"Well, I didn't mean he literally threw me out. I meant he said, 'get out of the car.'"

"After he laughed?

"Yeah, right after he laughed."

Spiro pulled his coat closed. "The girl left right after you did."

"My girl?" Johnson asked, his heart speeding up.

"No. The Cuban."

"Good," Johnson said, then something crept into his mind. "Hey, Spiro, did you let her into my room?"

"Yes," he said. "You appeared to enjoy her company."

Johnson nodded. "You know, I don't like it that you watched Al, Helena and me. I think that kind of sucks."

Spiro shook his head. "It really shouldn't bother you. I'm a professional. No one in that room did anything that, say in the old days, I could have used to blackmail you. There were no animals, everybody seemed about the right age. All in all, Johnson it was pretty tame."

"What do you mean by that?"

"All I'll say is, you lack imagination, Johnson." Spiro waved his hand, then turned and opened the door. "After you, sir." Spiro bent low and swept his hand toward the door. A yellow flash raced by. Spiro snatched the cat by the scruff of its neck and held it in mid-air. He turned and winked at Johnson.

Johnson walked through the door pissed at Spiro. But he had to admit that there wasn't much he could do. They'd never said they were friends, though Johnson liked him. It was like having a bartender you tip well treat you nice. You had to wonder why. Did he really like you or was it the tip? Al told him it was the tip. "Because," she said, "I don't care how good a friend someone is. They are not going to spend eight hours walking back and forth

behind a bar bringing you drinks for nothing. Would you do it?"
    Johnson had to admit that he wouldn't.

CHAPTER 16

The Dunkirk room smelled of Al's shower -- damp, musky and sweet. The scent of her oils and unguents reminded Johnson of his house in Miami. He felt home and relaxed as he closed the door. Little evidence remained of the afternoon they had shared with Helena: the bed covers had been straightened, stray clothes gathered. The mouth of an empty wine bottle poked up out of the waste basket. Three smudged glasses stood on a tray in the corner. Al walked out of the bathroom wearing only a white towel draped over her shoulders. The damp, curling tips of her hair lay dark and wet against it. When she and Johnson first started hanging out together, his friends joked that he was getting young quiff. As he watched her cross the room, he could see that Al left her youth somewhere about a year back. It made Johnson glad. Her body had softened and developed a fleshy roundness that he hoped might cushion his falls.

"You were gone a long time," Al said, rubbing a pinkish cream on her arms. "Helena Sanchez scared you, didn't she?"

In Miami, the frightening women were lesbians who tried to get Al to leave him. He hadn't thought that about Helena. Maybe Al knew more than he thought. "Yeah," he said. "She did."

"Don't worry about her. She had fun, but I don't believe we're her cup of tea, or should I say cafe con leche." Al smiled at the joke. "She probably won't be back. She'll keep this afternoon a secret, and think about it when she wants to think about something really hot."

Johnson nodded. He could imagine thinking about it, too.

She stood in front of one of the mirrors looking at Johnson

through the reflection.

Johnson imagined Spiro on the far side watching.

"I still don't get it," she said. "How did you meet her?"

"She worked at the company where I delivered the Fat Man's package. I invited her by, but I didn't think she'd show up."

"Well, you thought wrong."

"What a surprise," Johnson said.

Al turned from the mirror and put her hands on her hips. "What's wrong?"

"I don't like London."

"What do you mean, you don't like London? What specifically?"

"I don't know."

"Johnson. What don't you like?"

"You're going to think it's stupid."

"No I'm not."

"Promise?"

Al nodded her head and made a cross over her heart.

"I hate that mirror."

Al looked over her shoulder. "That mirror?"

Johnson nodded. "Can we put a towel over it, or something?"

"You hate that mirror, so you don't like London?"

"Well, yeah," Johnson said. "I told you it was stupid."

"No, it's not stupid, just a little strange," she said. "But that's what has always attracted me to you. That little strange thing."

"Good," Johnson said. "I'm just going to hang a towel over the mirror, okay?"

"Johnson, if hanging a towel over the mirror makes you happy, hang the towel."

"Thank you," he said.

Al sang while Johnson showered. He could hear her over the rush of water. She sang show tunes, that's what she told him. Show tunes. He liked that about her. Show tunes. The only show tune he knew was "Somewhere," from West Side Story. Though when he first heard it he thought it was just a song. Marvin, a transvestite at the Betsy Ross, sang the tune whenever he was sad and drunk. Marvin smoked Eve cigarettes and drank gin from a tumbler with one ice cube. His legs looked good in a skirt, but he had a man's face and no amount of makeup or hair was going to change that. He was always sad and often drunk. Johnson had heard him sing 'Somewhere' so often he'd memorized the words.

Al sang began singing it one day, walking from the kitchen to the back porch at Johnson's house.

"Hey, where'd you learn that?" Johnson asked. "I knew a guy on the beach used to sing that all the time."

"It's from West Side Story," she said.

"What's that?" he asked. "Some movie?"

"They made a movie out of it," she said. "But originally it was a Broadway show."

"Huh?" he said.

"You know about Broadway shows, right?"

"Yeah," Johnson said. "Of course." But he really didn't know. He knew there were plays on Broadway. He knew they had musicals. But he'd never seen one.

For the next three days Al set out to teach him about American Musical Theater. Each night she came home from work with the video of a different musical in her briefcase. The first night she brought home *West Side Story,* which Johnson found pretty good. When they sang "Somewhere," Johnson believed he'd learned something about Marvin. The next night Al brought home one called *The Man of La Mancha.* Johnson thought it was okay, but fell asleep halfway through it. He couldn't remember the name of the one she brought home next. Something about a guy and a girl. They sang and danced. Johnson fell asleep. The next day he told Al that American Musical Theater wasn't really his thing.

"I can see that," she said. "I'm sorry."

"What for?" he asked. "You didn't write the things."

"No. I'm sorry you don't enjoy them. I think there's something mindlessly American about them. They're fun, in a kicky sort of way."

In a kicky sort of way. Only Al said shit like that to Johnson. In a kicky sort of way.

Johnson rinsed the soap from his hair and stood under the hot water trying to wash London's cold from his bones. When his toes felt warm, he turned off the shower and stepped out of the tub.

Al sat in the overstuffed chair trimming her pubic hair with a small pair of nail scissors. The towel Johnson had draped over the mirror was beneath her.

Johnson took the towel from his waist and covered the mirror. "Jesus Al, I hate that thing."

Al looked at him from the corner of her eyes. "You're not going round the bend on me, are you?"

Johnson laughed, "Of course not."

"What's the sudden fascination with this mirror?"

"Honestly?" he asked.

Al nodded.

"I don't like the way I look these days. I'm getting older and that mirror reminds me that it's happening."

"Oh," Al said, a deep sympathy in her voice. "You're looking just fine."

"That's what I try and tell myself, but you know me, Al."

She chuckled and busied herself trimming. "Yes I do, Johnson, and I love you anyway."

Al had never told Johnson she loved him. After they'd been together about six months, he'd asked her why she hung out with him. "Why me?" he asked.

"Why you, what?"

"Why do you hang out with me?"

Al looked at him, smiled, then tapped her cheek with the index finger of her right hand. "What did we do last night?" she asked.

"Last night? Last night we went to the fights at Jai Alai."

She nodded. "The night before that?"

"You know."

"Where'd we go?" she repeated.

179

"That dance thing on the beach. The fuck was it called?"

"Alain Morrissey Dance Workshop."

"Right? See? I knew you remembered."

"What did you think?"

"About?"

"Either?" she asked.

"The fighters were all pugs, except for that fly-weight just up from Cuba. The hell was his name? Pedro Perez. He was all over the place. That kid's left hand is like a swarm of bees. Sting. Sting. Sting. Kid's good. He's going somewhere..."

"And the dancers?"

"Not a pug in the group," Johnson said. "That thing with the gold scarves. It was like, I don't know, the sun rising in your rear-view mirror after you've driven all night. When you see it, man. Very cool. It shocked me that they were able to get to that. It was great."

"That's why I hang out with you, Johnson."

Johnson nodded, said, "I see. And why is that?"

"Johnson, are you having fun?"

"Yeah. A blast."

"Is it interesting?"

"Yeah," he smiled. "Sometimes, too interesting."

"Well, I want my life to be fun and interesting. I've known people...people in my family whose lives sucked. And, in the end, Johnson, all we have is our lives. You, Johnson, are fun and interesting to me. You help make my life interesting. My life will not suck. Sure, you can be an asshole, but so can I. Does that answer your question?"

"What do you mean, asshole?"

"Fuck you," she said. "We got a deal."

They had a deal, something it seemed to Johnson they both understood. You gained or lost in a deal. Someone did something, you did something in return. When their conversation drifted to the point where most couples said, "I love you," they'd say, "We got a deal."

Hearing Al say, 'I love you,' stopped Johnson's progress across the room. Naked and chilly, goose bumps raised on his arms, his penis shriveled to the size of a walnut, he was glad the mirror was covered. He and Al shared their most intimate moments with strangers and near strangers. But that moment, while he watched her trim the hair around her pussy, was their own. He thought he might tell her the truth about the mirror. Then, he'd have to tell her about the hotel and Spiro. It would get more complicated. Then there was the truth about the American Embassy. The Cuban Embassy. Antonio Gomez. Helena Sanchez. There was too much. He wasn't sure how she'd react. Fuck it. "I love you too," Johnson said. "I really do."

She looked up at him from the work between her legs. "Yeah," she said, "we got a deal."

That night Al took him to a play called *The Grand Magia.* It was a story about a magician who tricked a man named Arturo into believing time had stopped for twenty years. Near the play's end, the magician clapped his hands and told Arturo the trick had ended. Arturo refused to believe him. But Johnson believed him. Johnson believed the magician, Arturo, the entire play from the rise of the curtain. When Arturo began arguing with the magician, Johnson leapt up and shouted, "Believe him. It's been a trick."

As the shout passed his lips Johnson realized what he had done. He dropped back into his seat. Heads turned. Some people hissed. A few chuckled. The actors ignored him. The guy sitting next to him, who had belched garlic a couple of times during the show, said, "Pretty good, mate. But I don't think he heard you."

Al hissed at him, "Are you fucking crazy?"

Johnson didn't know what to do. His face felt hot. He tried to sit lower in his seat and cover his face with his hands. Jesus, he thought, how the fuck did that happen? How did I let myself do that?

Were the actors were so good, the play so true? Johnson knew you could be tricked. He'd seen people do it. Shit, it had been done to the Miami Cubans for thirty-six years. Time passed. Things changed. But the right magician could convince you otherwise.

Johnson didn't hear the final words of the play. The lights went dark. Applause began. Al and the man beside him were clapping. Johnson began clapping too. He slapped his hands together until his palms stung. He clapped a steady dull beat. The heat from his palms spread out to his fingers. Johnson knew when he stopped, the pain would end, the heat would cool and time would have passed. Time passed. Things change. The next time anyone asked him, 'what do you think?' he would tell them, 'Time passes -- things change. No matter what the magicians tell you -- things change.'

The actors returned to the stage and bowed. They smiled and acknowledged the audience. A curtain dropped. The applause died down. The house lights came up. Johnson sat staring at his hands, the palms red and sweaty. Already he could feel them change and he knew time passed.

Al nudged him. "Are you okay?"

Johnson looked at her, then at all the people filing out of the theater. Some were pointing at him. He nodded and smiled. "I'm fine," he said. "That was one fuck of a play, huh?"

"Are you okay?" she repeated.

"Yeah, I'm fine," he said. Johnson turned to face her. She looked worried. His hands had cooled. His palms still stung. He leaned over and kissed her cheek. "I'm fine, Al," he said, lingering close to enjoy her smell, speaking softly to her ear. "Come on, I'll buy you a drink."

He stood up and turned around. The theater had emptied out. A young guy in a dark suit stood at the back of the house, holding his hands behind his back. Johnson waved. The guy nodded.

Johnson looked down to Al. She sat staring up at him. Her eyes seemed shinier than usual. A tear slid down her cheek.

"Jesus, Al, what's wrong?"

"You've got to promise me that you'll never do that again."

"What? The shouting at the actors? I promise," he said. She was taking it a little too hard. They didn't know any of these people and would probably never see them again.

"You promise," she said.

"Al, I apologize if I embarrassed you."

"It's not that, Johnson. It's not... It's like my mom. Don't go crazy on me, Johnson. Don't..." Al sobbed and tears ran down her face.

Johnson sat down beside her. "Jesus, is that what's bothering you? Al, don't worry, I'm not smart enough to go crazy."

"Don't joke about this, Johnson."

Johnson didn't think it was a joke. He believed it the same way he believed in Santeria and the mysteries of the Catholic Church. He knew you needed to be smarter to go crazy. He wasn't smart. He said, "I'm sorry," put his arm across her shoulders and hugged her.

The guy who had been standing at the back of the auditorium stood in the aisle next to them. He cleared his throat. "Sorry folks, we're closing the theater."

"Yeah," Johnson said. "We're going."

He walked out to the aisle and waited for Al. She looked bewildered. He'd never seen her like that. She'd been pissed at him plenty -- sad once or twice, but this hurt looked deeper. Johnson wanted to make it go away. He had to stop himself from joking. When things really got away from him, the only thing left to do was joke. He didn't say anything; he but took Al's hand and walked her down and out of the theater to Shaftesbury Street.

A group of men beneath a lone streetlamp on the traffic circle laughed, and an empty beer can skittered across the pavement.

"What should we do, Al?" he asked.

"Walk," she said. "I'd like to walk."

They walked slowly along Shaftesbury to the intersection. The cross street was Holborn. Johnson looked twice at the sign. London proved itself huge and tiny all at once. You could, if you wanted, actually walk places. They had gone to the theater district, walked to the Shaftesbury Theatre and now, Johnson found himself on the same street as the Cuban Embassy. He saw the building ahead, lighted by a streetlamp: the video cameras hanging off the front, Javier's car parked in the alley alongside. An ash glowed in the car and Johnson knew that Javier or someone very much like him sat there watching.

"We better go back the other way," he said. "I don't want to get lost."

"Whatever," Al said.

He took her arm and turned her around. "Do you want to talk about this?"

"Johnson, I'm not here to tell you about my past. Are you here to tell me about yours?"

Johnson recollected being drunk and telling her everything that ever happened to him. "No. I guess not."

Al stopped and turned toward a shuttered business beside them. "Do you remember much from when you were eleven?"

"I'm not sure. What grade would you be in?"

"Sixth."

"Sixth grade. Sixth grade." Johnson remembered a crucifix hanging in the classroom. Some classmates' names. He couldn't remember if his teacher was a nun or not. "No, I don't remember much."

"Did you ever do something as a kid that you regretted?" Al asked.

"Sure," Johnson said. "My life has been pretty much a long string of mistakes and regrets."

"I'm serious."

"Oh, and I'm not?"

"I pushed my mother," Al said. "I thought it was funny. I'd say hey, who are you? Do I know you?" Al looked into Johnson's face. "See?"

"See what? You were joking."

Al waved in disgust. "She was going crazy. On her way to full blown paranoid schizophrenia, and I helped. I fucking helped, as sure as I'm standing here, right now. Goddamn it. I made my mother crazy."

"No, you didn't."

Al wiped her nose on the sleeve of her jacket. Johnson fished a handkerchief out of his pocket and handed it to her.

"We went to doctors together -- my mother, father, brothers and me. The doctor told me not to reinforce, that's just the word he used, 'Alexandra, don't reinforce your mother's delusions.' God, delusions. But that's just what I did. I thought it was funny."

Johnson wondered if Al was fucking with him for calling out in the theater. "You were a kid," he said. "You didn't know what you were doing."

"Fuck you, Johnson. Don't you tell me what I knew. I knew just what I was doing. I was fucking with my mother and it worked. You know anybody on Thorazine?" She didn't wait for him to answer. "It fucks people up. Drooling, ticks. They get orange tans. I did that to my mom, and now I don't even know if I'm sorry." Al broke down into sobs.

Johnson pulled her close. He'd never seen Al do this, this woman thing. It embarrassed him. They were in public. Cars whizzed by. Surrounded by traffic and sirens' wails, her sobs shook both their bodies like orgasms of sadness. When she stopped, Johnson stepped back and felt tears in his own eyes. "What can I do?"

"Don't fucking go crazy on me, Johnson. Don't go crazy."

"I'm not smart enough to go crazy." A small truck lumbered by.

"You may be right," Al said.

Johnson heard a joke in her voice.

She smiled at him. "Thank you, Johnson."

"Hey," he said. "We got a deal."

Al nodded. "Yeah, we got a deal."

When they arrived back at the Dunkirk Room, the night maid had removed the towel from the mirror and turned back the bed. Toffees in paper doilies lay on both pillows. Two bedside lamps lit the room with a faint yellow hue. Johnson pulled off his clothes and fell across the bed. He didn't care if Spiro was watching. He wasn't going to put the towel over the mirror anymore. He wasn't going to talk with Spiro anymore. He and Al had three days more in London and he was going to use them right. He would ride trains, walk through neighborhoods, sit in pubs and talk to the locals. The Fat Man couldn't say shit to him. He'd delivered what he was supposed to, even though there was a lot more involved than he'd known. He would just be a tourist. Go back to the Kenmore Park Race or maybe find a place that sold *The Miami Herald.* He could see if anything had happened in Miami since he left.

CHAPTER 17

Al was up and out before Johnson rolled out of bed. She kissed his ear when she left and told him to have a nice day. He drifted back to sleep. When he opened his eyes, the clock next to the bed said 9:30. He sat up and saw his reflection in the mirror on the opposite wall. His hair looked as if he had just crawled from a wind tunnel. A line of drool had dried on his chin and his left cheek was creased from the sheets. He scratched the top of his head then flipped the finger at Spiro. He mouthed, Fuck You, stood up on the bed and shook his dick at the mirror. Johnson didn't care anymore what Spiro saw. There was nothing he could do to protect himself. Nothing. He couldn't call the police. He couldn't go to the embassy. He could tell Al, but why? She already thought he was going crazy. If he told her that there were cameras behind all the mirrors, she would think he was nuts for sure. Loser. No matter which direction he looked, they had him.

Loser.

He stuck his tongue at the mirror, then went to shower.

Johnson dressed in his best Miami outfit: blue Jeans, green t-shirt, cowboy boots and sunglasses. Funny British money in his pocket, trench coat over his arm, cap on his head, he felt prepared to greet the city. His plan: get on the underground. Go to either Shepherds Bush or Charing Cross. Get off and find a pub. The rest would take care of itself.

He stepped out of the Dunkirk room into the hallway. The Pembroke House smelled of coffee and cleaning fluids. A vacuum cleaner groaned in some other part of the hotel. Just another hotel, Johnson thought. Nothing special going on here. He didn't stop at the lounge because he knew Spiro would be there, waiting. Spiro was everywhere Johnson went in that damn hotel. Fuck him.

He slid his key across the front desk to Sheila. She nodded to him, but didn't speak. Johnson stepped over the two cats rolling together in the hall. One still had its tail bandaged. He stepped out into bright sunshine. The weather disappointed him. He had come to see London, all of London, including its lousy weather. The time left in his visit was growing shorter and he hadn't seen any fog or rain yet. How could he talk about London, if he began by saying the weather was great?

Right, people would say. You like rain and fog?

No. No. The weather was beautiful. Not a drop of rain. Bright sunshine. Beautiful. Then you've never seen the real London.

Johnson knew that. He'd not seen the real London.

Ten thirty on a Thursday morning, the street in front of the hotel was quiet. As he stepped through the gate and began down the sidewalk car engines revved behind him. He looked over his shoulder as two black Mercedes pulled from the curb and accelerated up the street. The cars jumped the curb, drove up onto the sidewalk and blocked Johnson's progress forward and back.

"Shit," Johnson said as the car doors opened. He turned right, vaulted a knee-high wrought iron fence and ran up a narrow alley. The alley opened into a yard surrounded by an eight-foot white brick wall. A gun fired behind Johnson. A brick shattered, raining stone chips in the yard.

"Javier, no shooting," a man shouted.

Johnson crossed the yard at a run and jumped up grabbing the top of the wall. His left hand landed on something sharp. "Ow shit," he cried. His grip failed and he slid back down into the yard, staining the white bricks with blood. Shards of broken glass topped the wall. He looked from the glass to his cut hand. "Fuck," he said.

Johnson heard steps behind him. He turned left. A wooden gate stood open near the corner. He called himself an asshole, raced through the gate and found himself in a block long alley. Each end opened to traffic. Volkswagen-sized garbage cans, London's version of dumpsters, stood at irregular intervals up and down the alley.

Whoever was chasing him had two cars and they were probably on their way to block either end of the alley. Goddamn it, Johnson thought. He ran down the alley pushing on locked gates. At any moment he knew cars would round the corner. He scrambled up onto one of the dumpsters and stepped on top of the wall. The wall ran away from him in both directions, shards of broken glass cemented into the top.

Johnson knew he could run all day in London and never get away. These guys knew the town. He didn't know shit. A flat roofed garage backed up to the wall. Johnson tight roped down the top of the wall, glass crunching beneath his feet. He leapt onto the garage as tires squealed around the corner. He fell onto his stomach, flattening against the roof. A car accelerated as it passed. Johnson heard the squeal of brakes and the sound doors opening.

"Did you see him?" a man shouted. Antonio Gomez?

"No," another answered. Carson Lea?

"Well, he's here," Gomez said. "He's probably in one of the dumpsters. We'll find him. *Señor* Johnson," Antonio Gomez sang out, "Ollie Ollie North-en free."

"Very funny, Antonio," Carson Lea said.

"I am student of your culture, Carson."

"We're flattered by your interest."

Fucked, Johnson thought. That pissant Lea. Fucking Gomez. He should have stayed in Miami. Goddamn. Fuck. He crabbed down the roof, hung from a gutter, then dropped into a yard. He heard the lids of the dumpsters crash open and the sound of men rummaging in garbage. Jesus, Johnson thought, I'd rather go with those guys than crawl in a bunch of maggots.

Johnson squeezed his hands together, crept out onto Pembroke Court. He ran down the street and up the steps to the Pembroke House. Spiro stood on a ladder inside the front door dusting a light fixture. Johnson kicked the door three times. Spiro looked down at him and grimaced. Johnson held up his hand; drops of blood fell onto the porch.

Spiro scrambled down the ladder and pushed the front door open. "Did you fall?"

Johnson looked back over his shoulder. "They're after me," he said, ducking past Spiro. "The Cubans and the guy from the embassy are after me."

"Really?" Spiro asked. "For what?"

"How the fuck should I know? I didn't hang around to ask."

"I love this," Spiro cried, "the old days are back!" He looked out into the street, then pulled the door closed. "Come with me." Spiro led Johnson down the hallway into a tiny closet, through its back wall and into a large wood paneled room. He slid closed the door and pushed a bolt into its lock. "You know," Spiro said, rubbing his hands together, "I could beat you to death in this room and no one would hear your cries." He knocked on the wall. "Craftsmanship. You can't buy things like this anymore, not for any price."

"Good to know," Johnson said.

Spiro gestured toward a small porcelain sink. "Wash your hands," he said.

Johnson turned the water on and watched small drops of blood fall into the sink. The idea of his blood spilling in London chilled Johnson. He felt colder than he had in a while. He shivered as the warm water rinsed the blood away. The cut was not as bad as he first thought. The gash ran at an angle from his palm to the base of his little finger. Fuck me, he thought.

"Are they clean?"

"Yeah," Johnson said.

"Did you use soap? Scrub the wound?"

"No, that'd hurt."

"Do you want me to do it?"

"I'll do it. I'll do it." Johnson picked up the bar soap and slowly massaged it in his hands. The soap stung. Tears formed in his eyes. Ah, London. This is one fucked up town.

"Rinse them and come here," Spiro said.

Johnson looked over his shoulder at Spiro. He sat at a table with a white towel spread out in front of him. He wore a doctor's reflector on his head. A tray of silver surgical implements lay beside the towel.

Johnson almost laughed. "What are you going to do with that stuff?"

"Fix your hand."

"Yeah, right. So let me see, here. You're a porter, a cameraman, a spy. What else? Did I leave anything out? Oh, right. You're a doctor. I forgot."

"It's a good thing I like you, Johnson." Spiro grinned at him. "December third nineteen seventy-three. In this very room I removed three bullets from a man's leg. Then I went and killed the man who put them there." Spiro lifted a small silver bowl from the white tray and spilled three nicked pieces of lead onto the towel. Spiro's grin hardened. "Sit down, Johnson."

Johnson believed everything Spiro said. There was no reason not to. He sat on the chair and placed his hand out on the table. Spiro adjusted the reflector and leaned forward to the cuts. "This," he tapped Johnson's left hand, "is nothing. A bandage. Couple weeks you won't even notice."

"Spiro," Johnson said, "Do me a favor?"

"What?"

"Wash your hands."

He stood up quickly, embarrassed. "Yes. Yes of course. Of course."

Johnson looked around the room as Spiro washed his hands. It seemed a funny place but then everywhere he'd been in the back of the Pembroke House seemed funny. This room had been built with some idea in mind. Quiet. Safety. Something. Johnson couldn't quite put his finger on it. "Spiro, what's the deal on this room? What did you use it for?"

"This room served many purposes. If the walls could... Well, that's the beauty of this room. The walls could never talk. The room is bug proof, absolutely. No listening devices. No cameras.

A safe room. A place to put things and people."

Johnson nodded. "Have you used this room often?"

Spiro sighed. "There was a time when I had so many people coming in and out of this room that it looked like a train station. If Scotland Yard knew who'd been through here." Spiro laughed, then shook his head. "Good days gone forever." He shook the water from his hands and dried them on a white towel. He sat back down in his chair and said, "First." He sprinkled a powder on the wound, then pinched the sides of the cut together and held them in place with bandages shaped like butterflies. He pushed a silver tube across the table. "Rub this salve on it about every hour. That'll keep it moist and it shouldn't bleed again. If it does, just hold a piece of gauze on it until it stops."

"Fine," Johnson said, "but what the hell can I tell my girlfriend about this?"

"Tell her the truth."

"The truth?" The thought had never crossed Johnson's mind.

"Not the whole truth. Tell her how you cut your hand, but come up with a different reason for doing it."

Johnson nodded. "Like what?"

"I don't know your friend, Johnson. That's what you have to decide. Remember there are events and history. Events happen; we have history to explain them."

Johnson liked the sound of that. He thought he might use it in a bar some time. Then he thought, no, nobody in the places he went would get it.

His hand wasn't bad. It tingled when he squeezed it into a fist, but it wasn't real pain. He held it in front of Spiro's face. "Thank you."

"It makes me feel alive. It's a shame you weren't shot. Bullet wounds were my specialty."

"They shot at me but missed. Maybe next time you'll get lucky."

Spiro looked thoughtfully toward the ceiling. "Maybe," he sighed. "We can hope."

"Well, for your sake, I hope somebody gets shot soon. But I

hope it's not me."

"Whatever," Spiro said. "Whoever."

Johnson stood up and paced around the room. Spiro had helped him with his immediate problem, but the bigger issues hadn't gone away. The guys from the embassies were still after him. "You know, Spiro, I was chased just now by people from the American and the Cuban Embassy."

Spiro's eyebrows went up. He nodded his head. "Can only mean one thing, Johnson."

"What?"

"They want to talk to you. If they wanted to kill you, you'd be dead. There's no need to move in close for a kill. You can do it with a car or a truck. Drop a load of bricks on your head. No need for conversation. One minute you're Johnson. Next minute you're not."

"You're probably right."

"Probably?" Spiro sneered. "Heroes of the revolution aren't probably right. We are always right."

"Right," Johnson nodded. "You're right. So, what would you do if you were me?"

"I'd talk to them. They are going to talk to you whether you want to or not. So it's better to do it on your terms than theirs."

Johnson nodded, but he wasn't sure what his terms would be. "I don't have any terms," he said.

"I could help you define your terms, Johnson. I am, shall we say, intrigued by the interest both the Cubans and Americans have taken in you. If one or the other was chasing you, I would say, who cares? But both? I've taken an interest. I want to see how this plays. In the old days, we might have just poisoned them all. Good times gone forever. Don't worry, Johnson. I'll help with your terms."

Spiro picked up the tray of instruments and slid it into the cupboard. He gathered bloody gauze and dropped it into a lidded waste basket.

"I don't have anything to really worry about, though. You said they don't want to kill me."

Spiro nodded. "They don't want to kill you now. Maybe they will after they talk to you. Maybe they want to know what you know before you die."

"You didn't say that before."

"I wasn't interested then. I am now."

"Jesus," Johnson said. Goddamn fucking London. Goddamn. Johnson's goal in life was to have it last as long as possible, then to die in his sleep. He knew that living in Miami ran counter to that prospect. He could count nine times that he'd nearly died in Miami, and he was sure that there were another ten or twelve that he hadn't noticed. But he didn't expect this kind of shit in London. London, goddamn it. People told him it was safer. Better. You could relax. Well, fuck them. They had no fucking idea. "I don't want to die here."

Spiro sighed. "I am afraid you don't have much say in the matter. Gomez is very good. And while I have heard that the American is an ass, they have others much better at such things. Just hope they don't want to kill you."

Johnson thought about running. He could get to the airport, try and get an earlier flight out. "I could run away? Get back to Miami. Lay low."

"If you weren't an independent you could run. But alone, without cash and support, they'd have you in two -- three hours."

Johnson closed his eyes and put his head down on the table. "Damn. Damn. Damn."

"Johnson, pull yourself together. Think of the glory. I don't know what you've done..."

"I delivered a fucking letter," he cried.

"Well, you delivered a letter that was so important that both the Americans and the Cubans are after you. You should be proud. You should revel in the moment. You will never be more alive than you are right now."

"And I'll never be more dead than the moment they kill me." He slammed his left hand on the table and cried out in pain. He looked through his tears at Spiro. "I'll tell you everything I know, then you could go and get killed. How's that? You revel in the moment. I'll be a porter in the finest fucking hotel in all of fucking London. I'll be the finest fucking porter in the finest fucking hotel in all of fucking London. Fuck. Fuck. Fuck."

"If only they could see you. Andropov. Gorbachev. They would see what I've known all along. They gave the world away. You are a weak people. We could have beat you. We could beat you still."

"I'm not talking about my people. I'm talking about me, goddamn it. I'm talking about my life."

"Your life. Your life? What is that? What do you think? You'd be the first person to die, ever? Your life. Johnson, shut up, or maybe I'll change my mind and leave you on your own."

"You wouldn't do that?"

"Shut up, Johnson. I am sick of your whimpering." Spiro rinsed his hands at the sink, pulled paper towels out of a dispenser and tossed them in the trash. "First thing, you must arrange to meet Gomez. Tell him you'll be at the Headless Woman Tavern at five today. Tell him you want to talk. If he asks you any questions tell him the truth. You don't know what he's after."

"What if he asks about you?"

"He should have no reason to ask about me, but if he does, tell him I've taken an interest."

Johnson nodded. This fucking Gomez guy wants who knows what from me and the maniac Spiro has taken an interest. Johnson wondered what his role in all of this was. "What do you think is happening here?"

Spiro shrugged. "Who knows? You may have seen something or someone you weren't supposed to. Maybe they think you work for an organization that scares them. Maybe they just don't like you. How should I know? I'm just a porter."

"I was wrong about that, Spiro, you're more than a porter. I can see you are a hero of the revolution."

"Johnson, please. You bore me."

Spiro was right. Johnson no more believed Spiro was a hero of the revolution than that he was a warrior in defense of democracy. You worked for somebody. It helped pay the bills. For the right amount you could hire anyone to do anything. "Well, thanks for your help, anyway. I suppose I should call Gomez."

"Johnson, you can't call the Cuban Embassy, ask for Gomez and think they'll put him on the line."

"Okay, you're the expert. What can I do?"

"Gomez isn't here."

"What?"

Spiro rubbed his hands together. "Gomez isn't here officially. The Brits know he's here, the Americans know he's here. I know he's here. You know he's here. Officially, he isn't here."

"What?"

"If the Brits cracked down and threw all the people in my line of work out of London, or tried to, the people in Havana or Moscow would do the same thing. Then, you'd have no one around making sure nothing of importance was happening. No people watching. No indication of how things are going. No news. No knowledge. Paranoia increases. Soon you have threats, then action, then?" Spiro threw his hands up in the air.

"Then you have war?" Johnson suggested.

"War is possible. But war is not what war used to be. Sure, war is a problem. You get all the dead and wounded. Industrial infrastructure destroyed. Cities, regions bombed back to the stone age. But worse than war is instability. Countries prefer stability. There is nothing left to win. The US doesn't want Cuba or Russia or London. The Russians don't want America. The powerful want to maintain their power. They want the weak to be weak and happy as opposed to weak and angry. They want an agreement. An agreement that nothing happens that they don't know about. What? You think NATO cares about Bosnians? Serbs? They care about stability."

Johnson nodded his head. "The world isn't a stable place, you know."

"I didn't say they were good at what they did. I only described what they're after."

"That doesn't put me any closer to Gomez."

"How did Gomez get to you?" Spiro asked.

Johnson thought for a moment. "Helena Sanchez," he said, imagining Al's tongue licking the woman's clit. "Helena Sanchez."

"Start there," Spiro said.

Johnson saw Spiro grinning at him and remembered that Spiro had probably watched him and Al tumble around with Helena. Johnson blushed. "How do you know I can get in touch with her?" Johnson said.

"She's a woman."

"Yeah?"

"Well, she's a woman. A girl hired to do whatever. She's probably a switchboard operator or something at the Embassy."

Johnson looked to see if Spiro was teasing him. He wasn't. It pleased Johnson that Al wasn't in the room. She'd have gone off on Spiro, explaining to him that a woman can do anything a man can do and probably do it better. She'd have told him that the root of all society, *all* society, she'd say, repeating the phrase for emphasis, was based firmly on the woman's back and in her womb. And any man or woman who was too stupid to see that was probably too stupid to live. Man, he was glad she wasn't there.

"Switchboard operator?" Johnson asked.

"A woman," Spiro said, exasperation making his voice whiny.

"Okay," Johnson said. "A woman."

Spiro pointed at a black phone on the wall. "Make your call, Johnson. Five o'clock, the Headless Woman Tavern."

Johnson picked up the phone. "I don't know the number."

"0171-234-2078" Spiro said.

"What?"

Spiro sighed. "Dial 0 1 7 1 2 3 4 2 0 7 8."

Johnson spun the dial and listened to the phone ring. He was surprised how similar the sound was to the American ring.

"Embassy," a woman said, her voice sounding like Miami. Johnson wondered what was going on in Miami at that moment. Probably nice weather. "Embassy," the woman repeated.

"Helena Sanchez," Johnson said.

"One moment," the woman said. She could have been a doctor's receptionist in Coral Gables, a clerk along Eighth Street.

After a moment of silence, a woman said, "This is Helena Sanchez, how may I help you?"

Johnson heard the voice and recollected the cool smooth feel of the woman's ass. The silky texture of her skin. "It's Johnson," he said. "Tell Antonio Gomez that if he wants to talk, I'll be at the Headless Woman Tavern at five p.m. today."

"Oh, Johnson," she said, "Nice to hear from you. How's Al?"

"Like you give a shit. You set me up, and you used Al to do it."

"Are you trying to tell me you didn't have fun?"

"Are you trying to tell me you did have fun?" Johnson said mocking her.

"I had a, *como se dice,* a blast?"

"*Correcto,*" Johnson said. "*Pero,* you know what you did."

"*Si, y yo prefiero. Lo siento.* I mean, I'd like to do it again."

"Really. Well, you know where we're staying. Call anytime and leave a message at the..."

Spiro hissed at him. "Make sure she tells Gomez."

Johnson nodded, thinking of Helena Sanchez's tits. "Don't forget to tell Antonio Gomez. Five o'clock, Headless Woman Tavern."

"I'll tell him."

"Thanks," Johnson said. "Don't forget to call."

"I won't."

"*Hasta luego,*" Johnson said.

"Bye-bye," Helena Sanchez said

Johnson hung up the phone and thought of waking up some morning between Al and Helena. He grinned at the idea. When he turned around Spiro stood glowering at him across the room.

"Is sex the only thing you ever think about?"

"No," Johnson said. "I like to drink, too."

"You are really a pitiful character."

Johnson grinned. "Yeah, I know. What do I do now?"

"Wait," Spiro said. "Go back to your room. Watch the television. You Americans love TV. Watch it."

"I don't watch television," Johnson said. "I hate television."

Spiro grinned. "An American who doesn't watch television. I don't believe it."

"I don't care."

Spiro nodded. "I've got to finish my dusting."

CHAPTER 18

Back in the Dunkirk room, Johnson stood over the bathroom sink examining his damaged left hand and Spiro's repair work. The guy was good, he had to admit it. The cut, drawn closed by tiny bandages, crossed his palm like a frown. No blood leaked from the wound; the seam appeared flawless.

Johnson looked at his reflection in the mirror and wondered how he would pass the time until Spiro came to get him. Like a mouse bolting a corner, his conversation with Helena Sanchez skittered through his mind. The smooth taut skin on her ass, the fullness of her lips made his cock hard. He smiled, undid his jeans, pushed them to his knees and spat on his hand. He closed his eyes and wrapped his fingers around his cock -- sliding his hand back and forth from head to balls. He imagined Helena and Al before him on the floor -- tongues out, fingers deep in each other's crotches. He imagined moans and sighs, squirming desire, scrambling muscles tight, quaking, someone knocking at the door. No. Wait... Someone rapped again.

"Yes," he said, his voice thick with sex. He coughed to clear it. "Yes?" he repeated, louder, his dick shriveling.

Spiro said, "I brought you a sandwich."

"Just leave it beside the door," he cried.

Johnson tucked in his flaccid self and zipped his fly.

The tray beside the door in the hallway held a sandwich -- a thick piece of meat between brown bread -- a glass, and an over-sized can of Foster's Ale. Johnson opened the beer and poured it into the glass. A rich head crept toward the rim of the glass. He tasted the beer. The sandwich was lamb on buttered wheat bread. A slash of dark yellow mustard crossed the meat. John-son ate the sandwich and drank the ale. The clock read 11:45. He had hours to wait.

He lay across the bed and lifted a book from Al's night table. The *Let's Go Guide To London*. Johnson had never read a guide-book before. He believed there was something weak in them. No one gave you a guidebook to the place you lived. You just lived there and that was it. You discovered on your own the good and bad places, or you didn't. There were plenty of people in Miami who'd never been to the Ocean Wreck, Johnson's favorite place. He wondered if it would be listed in a *Let's Go Guide to Miami*. He thought he might buy one when he got back to the States just to see.

The tidbits of London's history, its places to shop and eat proved no match for Johnson's desire to sleep. The book covered his face like a tent as he dreamed of Helena, Al and him sitting on the back porch of the house in Miami. Johnson was the only one naked. The women talked about men they'd had in the past. They laughed, joked. Johnson's name never came up. He asked them if they wanted to have sex or what? They ignored him. He was about to ask the question again when some sound interrupted. His eyes popped open. He looked at the clock radio beside the bed. 2:47 p.m. "Just a second," he said, rolling out of bed. He stood before the door, rubbing his eyes. "Yes?"

"It's time," Spiro hissed through the door.

Johnson opened the door. Spiro stood before him in a long brown cloth coat with a Greek fisherman's cap. "It's not even three o'clock," Johnson said.

Spiro shook his head and frowned. "It's time," he said. "Get your coat. Come with me."

Johnson grabbed his coat and cap and turned back to Spiro. "I have to pee," he said.

"Make it quick."

Johnson peed and splashed water on his face. He looked into his own eyes and wished he could be stronger. He followed Spiro through the Pembroke House's public rooms back into the working corridors and, finally, to a small loading dock with a garage-style door. Spiro sat down on a small wooden stool beside the door.

Johnson leaned against the wall. "You said it was time. What are we waiting for?"

"Another five minutes at most. They're very punctual. You're not to speak to anyone until I do so. Do you understand?"

Johnson squinted his eyes. "Well, let's see. I'm not supposed to speak to anyone until you do. Okay. Yeah, I think I got that. Anything else?"

"You shouldn't look them in the eyes, either. Don't acknowledge them, just stay out of their way. Do you understand?"

Johnson nodded his head. "Yes, I guess so."

"Good," Spiro said, looking at his watch again.

A horn honked on the other side of the garage door; a motor revved. Brakes squealed, gears ground, then whined as something backed toward the door. A car door opened and slammed shut. Keys jingled in a lock and the garage door shot open, revealing the back of a small panel truck. A round Black guy in a denim coat and a black bowler looked briefly from Spiro to Johnson, then threw three bundles of laundry onto the loading dock.

Spiro hissed at Johnson and gestured with his head toward the truck. As they passed the guy going into the truck, Johnson said, "Nice hat." The guy looked at him, wide-eyed with fear. Spiro punched Johnson's shoulder, knocking him against the side of the truck.

"Jesus," Johnson hissed.

Spiro punched him again and whispered, "No talking," into his ear.

Johnson almost said, Okay, Jesus, lighten up. Instead he nodded.

Spiro and Johnson dropped onto bundles of laundry as the truck's rear door slammed shut, leaving them in total darkness as they rattled through the streets of London. The truck smelled of diesel and clean laundry. It was cold. At first Johnson was thrown all over the truck, but after a while he learned how to balance himself and keep his shoulders and head from being jostled against the door. He felt something move next to him.

"Soon the door will open," Spiro's voice came out of the dark. "Do not. I repeat, do not speak to or acknowledge anyone, unless I do so first. Do you understand?"

"Yes," Johnson said. "I understand."

"You'd better," Spiro said.

The truck turned hard to the left, stopped quickly. The driver ground more gears, backed the truck up and stopped. The door flew open, the light blinding Johnson. Through slitted eyes he saw men, mostly Asian and Black, slinging bags of laundry from the back of trucks onto an overhead conveyor system, where the bags hung like carcasses at a slaughter house.

They were parked at a long loading dock. Truck after truck, back open, mawing to be filled with laundry. The air smelled dry and warm. Machinery rumbled and sighed. Huge washers churned; dryers tumbled. The laundry workers wore white uniforms and hats, the drivers all blue denim. No one spoke. Bundles of laundry drifted overhead. Spiro gestured and Johnson followed him from the truck.

Spiro led him down the loading dock to a truck nearly filled with bundles. Spiro stood off to the side, Johnson behind him, as the driver threw bags into the back of his truck. When he finished, Spiro stepped onto the truck. Johnson followed him. The door rattled closed.

The bundles in the new truck were still warm from the laundry. The air smelled fresher and the driver moved more fluidly. In the dark, Johnson wondered if Spiro was in with Gomez and Lea. He dismissed it immediately. If it was true, there was nothing he could do about it. If it wasn't, there was no need to get all worked up over it. So far, Spiro had been pretty good. He had fixed Johnson's left hand, sent him lunch and was now accompanying him on this trip to who knew where. He would have to thank Spiro when it was all over. Maybe take him out for some drinks and talk about Miami. Johnson wondered whether he could move as smoothly through Miami as they were moving through London. That would be something, he thought. But Miami was Miami and London was London. There were other ways in Miami, though. Other ways to do things.

The driver made three stops, behind two small hotels and one pub. Each time he opened the back of the truck Johnson wanted to speak to him, but didn't. The guy had a dark beard and small knit cap on his head. At each stop, Spiro looked off into the distance. He didn't speak to Johnson or acknowledge his presence. He just stared. Johnson wondered at what. The future? His past? Was he thinking of his goat shit covered island, the defeat of capitalism or the dusty chandeliers at the Pembroke House?

At the fourth stop, Spiro was standing when the door flew open. He glanced at Johnson, then hopped down out of the truck and through a small door in a brick wall.

Johnson followed him down some metal steps into a basement. The room smelled of beer. It was cool. The walls were made of bricks. In the corner of the cellar barrels were stacked on end. Spiro crossed the room and went up another set of stairs through a door and into a pub's tap room. Above the door the bust of a headless woman, with nicely rounded breasts and blood dripping from her neck, hovered over gold letters reading Headless Woman Tavern.

Spiro nodded to the bartender. "I'll have a cider and you?" He turned to Johnson. "Beer," he said.

"Give him a Boddingtons," Spiro said.

The bar man pulled two drinks, set them before Spiro and Johnson. He moved back to the corner of the bar and stared up at the television.

Spiro sipped his cider.

Johnson took a pull from the ale. "You know in the States people say they drink beer warm in London. I don't think this is warm."

Spiro looked at him from the corners of his eyes. He took another sip. "Johnson, in ten minutes, some men are going to arrive here and have a talk with you. Don't you think you should be focusing on what they might have to say?"

"No," he said. "I don't know anything about any of this stuff. I delivered a letter. I didn't come here looking for trouble from Antonio Gomez. I came here to be with my girlfriend, drink a lot and see London. And you know what? I've been here almost seven days now, and I really like just fucking off in pubs. So you focus on what they might say. I'll focus on the beer and the fucking off." Johnson picked up his glass and took three good swallows. He belched, then set the glass on the bar. "Anything else?"

Spiro shook his head. "No," he said.

Johnson turned around and leaned back against the bar, surveying the room. Light came in through leaded windows. Each table had an ashtray. All the tables were empty except for one in the far corner. An old guy in blind man's glasses sat with both hands wrapped around a pint of beer, three quarters full. The room smelled of cigarettes and it made Johnson want one. He imagined that if he lived in England no one would hassle him about smoking and he would still be able to light up. But then he thought no, it was nice to be able to breathe again. He inhaled deeply, feeling the air fill his lungs. There was no longer any snap, pop or whistle in his lungs. They were clear and he liked that.

"Did you ever smoke?" Johnson asked Spiro.

"What?"

"Did you ever smoke? You know, cigarettes, cigars."

"No," Spiro said. "Never."

"Well, I used to smoke. I just quit. I don't know, maybe six months ago. And I still miss it."

Spiro grunted.

"You know, there's a lot of things in life that I do and have done that are not good for me. Drugs, booze," Johnson held up the glass. "Sex. Since the nineteen eighties, sex for sure."

"You come from a bankrupt society, Johnson. Consume, consume, consume. Drugs, drink, sex, new cars. You feel empty and fill that emptiness with these depraved desires. No one like you could have existed in the old Soviet Union. The people, in service to a greater good, did not have these desires, these perversions.

And those who did, those who flew in the face of the greater good, were sent to camps for re-education."

"Sorry I missed that."

"Laugh your little laugh. Re-education would have made you a man."

Johnson snorted. "Yeah, well they have re-education camps in the States, too, Spiro."

Spiro turned and looked at him, wide eyed. "They do?"

"You bet. They've got two major ones. One in California and one in Florida, where I come from. They're called Disney, but they're re-education camps."

Spiro looked at him for a moment, then burst into laughter. "Johnson," he shrieked, "that's a joke, isn't it?" He laughed some more. "Disney, re-education camps in America. Hah, hah, hah."

Johnson drained his beer. "Bartender," he said, "I'll have another." Then looking to Spiro, "Pretty funny, huh."

"Very funny."

"But it's true," Johnson said. "At Disney they..."

A tiny bell jingled.

Johnson looked over his shoulder.

Javier stuck his head into the pub and looked around. His face showed no emotion. He ducked back out. The bell jingled as the door closed.

Johnson turned to Spiro. "I guess they're here."

Spiro nodded. "They're here."

"Good," Johnson said.

"Good," Spiro agreed.

The bell sounded again. Javier came through the door first, followed by a young guy Johnson didn't know. Then came Antonio Gomez and, finally, Carson Lea. Javier and the young guy split up, sitting on opposite sides of the room. Lea and Gomez walked up to the bar.

"Spiro," Gomez said, reaching for Spiro's hand. "I'm surprised to see you here."

"I've taken an interest," Spiro said, shaking hands with Gomez.

Gomez nodded. "Do you know my associate, Carson Lea? He's from the American Embassy."

"I don't believe so," Spiro said, extending his hand. "Spiro Dimitry."

"Nice to meet you, Spiro," Carson Lea said, smiling.

"Carson," Gomez said, "Spiro works at the Pembroke House. You may remember me mentioning that hotel."

"It's one of the finest small hotels in all of London," Spiro said. "Of course, I'm merely the porter there. But you can take my word, it's an excellent hotel."

"So Antonio's told me. I admire your work there, Spiro."

Spiro raised a hand. "Please, you're too kind."

Gomez turned to Johnson. "And *Señor* Johnson. It's so nice to see you again. So nice. You, of course, know Carson Lea, from the embassy."

Johnson nodded. "Yeah. Hi." His palms were sweating. His mouth dry. During the introductions between Spiro and Carson Lea he had drained his second pint and at that moment needed to piss.

"Great," Antonio Gomez said, clapping his hands together. "Let's get down to business, shall we?"

"I have to piss," Johnson said. He turned away, looking for the rest rooms.

"We're busy men," Antonio Gomez snapped. "First we'll talk. Then you'll, you'll..."

"No," Johnson said. "First I piss, then we talk."

"The man's got the weakest bladder in the West. He needs to piss," Spiro said. "Let him piss."

"I'm sorry," Antonio Gomez said, rubbing his temples with both hands. "I'm sorry. Go. Go."

Johnson said, "Bartender, where are the rest rooms?"

The bar man jerked his thumb back over his shoulder, never taking his eyes off the television. "There, mate," he said.

Johnson looked from Lea to Gomez. "Be right back." Jesus, Johnson wondered, what the hell kind of guy has a problem with me pissing? Jesus. He pushed into the rest room and came face to face with Luis Baste, leaning against the wall smoking a cigarette.

He straightened up and snubbed out the smoke when he saw Johnson. He reached into his jacket, came out with a pistol and placed the barrel against Johnson's forehead.

Johnson's eyes crossed on the barrel. He brushed it away from his head. "I really need to piss." He stepped to the urinal, unzipped his fly and loosed a stream of urine. His eyes teared. He felt the gun against the back of his head.

When he finished, he turned around, facing the gun again.

Baste never spoke.

"Are you supposed to shoot me?" Johnson asked.

Baste shrugged.

"Good," Johnson said. He rinsed his hands and dried them. "See you later," he said.

"Hey, Spiro," Johnson said, coming out of the bathroom. "There's a guy from the Cuban Embassy in the bathroom with a gun."

"I know," Spiro said.

Antonio Gomez waved his hands in the air. "And if Mister I Have to Pee-pee didn't have to go in the bathroom, you wouldn't know that right now, would you? But no. You had to pee-pee."

"A man's got to go when a man's got to go," Carson Lea said.

"Spiro, what do you mean, you know?" Johnson asked.

"They knew we were coming here. If it was important enough to meet us, they'd put a man with a gun in the bathroom. Seems logical to me. I'm surprised even you didn't think of that possibility."

Johnson was pissed. "Well, even if I did think of it, which I am completely willing to admit I didn't. Even if I did think of it, what the fuck could I have done?"

"I don't know. You could have asked me to, oh, I don't know -- arm the bartender. Put a sharpshooter in the corner."

The bartender hefted a sawed-off shot gun. The blind old man pointed two pistols across the table.

"Just like the old days," Spiro said, slapping his hands together. "Mutually assured destruction. Now that we're all on the same playing field, let's begin the negotiations, shall we?"

Johnson smiled, he couldn't help himself.

"Spiro," Gomez said, "you completely misunderstand our intentions. We're here to talk with *Señor* Johnson. We wish him no harm."

"And Johnson and I wish you no harm, Antonio. But no harm from an equal is better than no harm from, what should we say? A super-power."

Antonio Gomez smirked at Spiro. "Javier," he said. "Bring me the briefcase."

Javier crossed the room and placed a briefcase on the bar on front of Antonio Gomez. It was a rich black leather with fine gold locks. They snapped like a ticking clock under Antonio Gomez's fingers. He opened the case to reveal a stack of file folders. He lifted out the first one. "*Señor* Johnson," he said, "I'm going to show you some photographs. I want you to identify the people, if you know them."

Johnson looked at Spiro. He nodded. "Sure," Johnson said. "No problem."

Antonio Gomez turned over the first picture. It was a black and white, 8 x 10 photo taken in a jungle somewhere. There were three people in the picture: Fidel, Che Guevara and some other guy. They were real young. They held their pistols pointed skyward. They all grinned at the camera.

"That's Fidel Castro and Che Guevara," Johnson said. "Who's the third guy?"

"You don't know him?" Gomez asked.

"Nope."

The next picture was another black and white 8 x 10. It was of a gathering at the Orange Bowl in Miami. John Kennedy stood on a raised platform, Jackie stood next to him. Kennedy shook some man's hand, grinning for the camera.

"That's President Kennedy and his wife, Jackie, right?" Seemed kind of a silly question.

"Do you recognize anyone else in the picture?" Gomez asked.

"No. Should I?"

"Here, look at this one," Gomez said, flipping over another.

Two men wearing golf clothes stood in front of a beach house. Johnson saw Florida in the picture. They were in Miami. One of the guys was Richard Nixon. The other?

"I know Nixon, for sure, but who's the other guy?"

"You don't recognize him?" Gomez asked.

He placed the picture on the bar. Johnson leaned over his shoulder to look at it.

"That's guy the same guy as in the other pictures."

"You're right," Gomez said. "You don't recognize him?"

"Shit," Johnson said. "That's Mondongo. That's the guy." Johnson flipped back to the first picture. Che, Fidel and Mondongo. Then Kennedys and Mondongo. And Nixon and Mondongo.

Gomez flipped over another picture. Ronald Reagan leaned over, hand cupped before his mouth, speaking into another Mondongo's ear. They both wore tuxedos. Mondongo grinned as Reagan spoke.

"Mondongo," Johnson said. "They're all Mondongo."

"You're sure?" Carson Lea asked. "You're absolutely sure."

"Yeah, I met the guy twice."

"How about this guy?" Gomez asked, flipping over another picture.

Johnson smiled when he saw it. The Fat Man. He looked smaller in pictures, but it was him. He stood out in front of his house gesturing with a donut toward who knew what. Johnson had seen him do that, use a donut as a pointer. He imagined the Fat Man's voice squeaky and out of breath, shouting, "You fucking idiot, what do you think you're doing?" It made Johnson feel good to see something from home. He wondered what the Fat Man was doing right then. He realized he didn't even know what time it was in Miami.

He said, "Yeah, that's a man I do some work for occasionally." Then he asked, "Do you know what time it is in Miami?"

Carson Lea looked at his watch. "It's eleven in New York."

"In Havana, too," Antonio Gomez said.

"Then it must be eleven in Miami," Johnson said. Eleven o'clock in Miami. Johnson smiled at the thought.

Antonio Gomez sighed. "It appears that it is. Can we get back to the business at hand?"

"Sure," Johnson said. "It was just the pictures. You know, pictures of home."

The Cuban nodded. "Tell us how you know these people."

"Teitelbaum, the Fat Man, is a guy I do work for. Mostly I drive him around. Sometimes I do delivery work for him. Take a package here. Pick up a package there. He doesn't go out much. But when he does, I'm his driver. That's what I do in the States. I deliver things. Mondongo? I met him twice. I told the Fat Man that I was going to London with my girlfriend and asked if there was any way I could make it a working vacation. It was the Fat Man that put me together with Mondongo, and he asked me to deliver a letter to you at the Cuban Embassy here. That's pretty much it, except for all the shit that's happened here."

Antonio Gomez nodded. He turned, and said, "Javier, get Luis out of the bathroom. Wait for me in the car."

"Si Señor," he answered.

Luis Baste eyed them all suspiciously as he passed through the bar. "Antonio?" he said.

"The car, Luis. Just wait in the car."

Gomez waited. When the tiny bell above the door jingled, he took a deep breath, nodded, then turned to Lea. "Carson, can we speak alone for a moment?"

Carson Lea nodded.

They walked across the room and stood in the corner talking.

Johnson turned to Spiro and shrugged.

Spiro winked and gave him a thumbs up.

"It's going pretty good, huh?" Johnson whispered.

"It's going as good as expected," Spiro replied.

Gomez and Lea returned to the bar. Gomez cleared his throat, glanced at Lea, then Spiro and finally Johnson. "The world is a strange place," he said. "A strange and very volatile place.

Change defines the events. Inertia and momentum propel us into the future and toward change. Do you understand what I am saying, *Señor* Johnson?"

Johnson shrugged. "Things change. I know that."

"Good, *Señor*." He lifted a sealed envelope from the briefcase. "This document outlines some drastic changes that will be taking place in Cuba in a very short time. I wonder if you would be so kind as to deliver it to your friend, *Señor* Mondongo."

"I suspected as much," Spiro hissed. "Gorbachev, Gorbachev, Gorbachev is always portrayed as the traitor to the revolution, but it was Andropov all along. Don't trust the spies, they always told us. Even those of us who were spies. Don't trust the spies."

Spiro spat on the floor. "I'll have nothing to do with this." He stood up from his stool. "Alex, Patrick, we're done here."

The blind man took off his dark glasses and put his pistols in a shopping bag. The bartender ducked under the bar and all three -- Spiro, the blind man and the bartender -- walked out of the Headless Woman. The bell tinkled angrily as they left.

Gomez and Lea shrugged.

"Will you deliver the letter?" Carson Lea asked.

"Why me?" Johnson said, wondering aloud. "Why don't one of you guys deliver it?"

"People notice our movements. People notice the movements of our people. You're nothing. I mean unknown," Antonio Gomez said.

"Yeah," Johnson said, "I've been working on that. You know, Mondongo paid me seven long to deliver that letter to the embassy."

"Seven long? I'm afraid I don't understand."

"Long?" Carson Lea said.

"As opposed to large. Seven long. You know. Seven thousand dollars."

"You must be joking?" Antonio Gomez gasped. "You can't expect us to..."

"Outrageous," Carson Lea said. "You weasely little prick, you think you can hold up the United States government for... Do you know the shit I can bring down on your head?"

Johnson nodded. "Fellows, I want to help out, but I've got expenses. Do you guys work for free? I didn't think so. If you asked me to -- I don't know, shine shoes for the government, I might do that for free, but you're asking me to do my job. My job is delivery. If I do your stuff for free and word gets out, I'm ruined."

Gomez and Lea sputtered with anger.

"I'm not an unreasonable man," Johnson said. "Make me an offer."

Gomez looked as if he were about to have a heart attack. Lea shook his head. "I knew there were fuckers like you out there, but you're the first one I ever met."

"That's just what I thought about you, Carson. But that's personal. This is business. Make me an offer."

"Three thousand five hundred dollars. One half of Mondongo's payment."

"You're shrewd, Carson, playing on my patriotic sensibilities. Four thousand and you've got a deal."

"We could shoot you," Gomez said.

"Okay, okay. Three thousand five hundred dollars and no shooting." Johnson reached out to shake Carson Lea's hand.

Lea looked from the hand to Johnson's face. He laughed. "Don't be ridiculous." He turned to Gomez. "I'm out of here."

"What about the money?" Johnson said.

"Don't worry about the fucking money. I'll see you get it. Just take the fucking letter." Lea turned and stormed out of the pub. The guy Johnson didn't know, who sat across from Javier, followed him out the door.

"So, *Señor* Johnson, " Gomez said, "you will do this for your price?"

"Yeah, I'll do it. That's what I do. Deliver things." His beer was empty. He wanted another. Johnson decided there was nothing quite so pitiful as an English pub without a bartender. "What do you do, Antonio?"

"Anything my country asks of me."

Johnson nodded. "What's the letter say?"

"I haven't read it, but have been told it speaks of coming changes, and asks the reader to respond not as an exile, but as a Cuban."

"Do you know Mondongo?"

"His name is not Mondongo. And we've never met."

"He may not get the message."

"Change is coming whether *Señor* Mondongo gets it or not."

An idea struck. "Is this letter from Fidel? Is he stepping down?"

Antonio Gomez grinned at Johnson. "I wouldn't know, *Señor*. *Pero,* if anything should happen to that letter between the time that you accept it and the time it is delivered to the right party, I am afraid there is no place on this planet where you could hide."

"I am a professional, Antonio. Delivery is what I do."

The Cuban nodded and slid the letter down the bar to Johnson. "Enjoy the rest of your stay in London, *Señor*."

"Thank you, Antonio."

The bell over the door jingled. Antonio Gomez was gone. Johnson picked up the envelope. It was light, felt like no more than one or two sheets. The paper was a fine grade of linen, closer to cloth than paper. Blue wax sealed it shut. Johnson held it up for a moment, thought of Miami on the day Fidel stepped down. He hoped that's what the letter contained. It would be a hell of a party.

He slid the letter into his pocket and looked at his empty glass. That beer -- what was it called? Boddington's -- tasted great. Johnson ducked under the counter and stuck his glass under the tap. He pulled the lever forward, but unlike American taps the beer didn't flow. He pulled the lever forward like a pump at a well. Beer gurgled from the faucet and filled his glass, overflowing and running onto the floor. Johnson lifted his glass from beneath the tap, the beer flowing still, and shook drips from his hand. He lifted the glass to his mouth and took a sip just as the bell over the door jingled.

Two workmen walked in wearing overalls and caps. They stepped to the bar and said, "Two avers." At least that's what it sounded like to Johnson. He put his glass on the bar, ducked under the counter and walked out onto the street.

The sun setting made the streets seem lonely. It was only then that Johnson realized he didn't have a clue where he was. Well, that's not true, he thought. I'm in London. I've just made another thirty-five hundred dollars. He walked to the corner and flagged the first cab that came by.

"Notting Hill Gate," he said.

"Right, sir," the driver said.

CHAPTER 19

Johnson leaned back and, as he inched through traffic and hurtled down empty streets, watched London pass through the cab's windows. Humans crowded the sidewalks, crowded the town. It was a false front. There was the London you saw on the streets, the London you saw in theater or pubs, on the underground. But there was the other London, the one Johnson had fallen into. Fallen into because of some crazy old Cuban in Miami. Fallen into because of his work with the Fat Man. No, he admitted to himself, he fell into it because of all of those things and because of who he was. Things happened to Johnson because he made them. They were not all good things, or all bad things, but they were things. That's most important, he thought. Have things happen. Imagine how boring it would be if they didn't.

The cab's brakes squeaked as the driver pulled to a stop and pressed a button on the meter. "Five pounds ten, sir."

Johnson fumbled through his wallet. Handed the man a ten-pound note. "Keep the change," he said.

The man turned full face to Johnson. "Thank you very much, sir. That's very generous."

"Yeah, I know," he said.

Sheila refused to look at him as she slid his room key across the desk.

"Good evening, Sheila," he said.

She grunted.

"Was that one of the cats I saw in traffic, just now?"

Sheila's head jerked up, eyes wide.

Johnson winked. "Just kidding," he said.

Johnson entered the Dunkirk and flipped a bird to the mirror. There was nothing he could do to get away from it. He just had to remember that Spiro watched all the time. Or that Spiro could be watching all the time, and there wasn't shit he could do about it.

The room looked exactly as he'd left it, except no lights were on and the tray of food was gone. In two days, when he and Al had left London, the room would look exactly as it had when they arrived. There was nothing they'd done in the room that would indicate they had stayed there. Johnson looked around and thought that was good. This was not a place he wanted to leave a mark. The room was nice enough and it may have been the finest fucking small hotel in all of fucking London, but it was just a room.

He dragged his suitcase out from under the bed, then slid the letter for Mondongo into the inside zippered compartment. He patted the suitcase and said, "thirty-five large." The idea of actually netting on the London trip made him a little giddy. He'd tell Al, but if she found out how he'd been spending his time, she'd probably be pissed. She just didn't get it. It was important to do business. You couldn't turn it down, you couldn't say, not today. Take it every time it's offered that you can legitimately complete the gig. If he had known before leaving for London that he would have fallen in with the people he did, he might not have taken the deal. If he had known that he was going to meet Spiro and piss off two embassies, he might have passed. Jesus, he might have passed. But if he'd passed, he would not have had the money to travel. He would have stayed in Miami, and if his past was any indication, there was plenty of trouble waiting there for him.

He lay back across the bed, pushed his shoes off with his toes and closed his eyes.

Johnson heard movement in the room and opened his eyes. It was dark, and somebody was skulking around his room. Jesus Christ, the letter. He lay still, his eyes open, staring into the dark. He would wait; if all they wanted was the letter, he would let them have it. He didn't want to die in this room, and knew he would give up everything to avoid it. He was ready to grovel, beg and cry. It didn't matter. He didn't want to die, not for Americans or Cubans or the goddamn Chinese. He was not going to die. "Don't kill me," he shrieked. "Please don't kill me."

"Johnson, wake up," Al said. "You're dreaming." A table lamp in the corner clicked on. He saw Al's face.

She grinned at him. "Boy, that English beer knocks the hell out of you."

"What do you mean?"

"I mean, and Johnson don't take this wrong, I know you're probably spending all your days in pubs and then you come home and sleep. You're in London, Johnson, you should take advantage of your chance to see the sights. I know..." her eyes widened. "What happened to your hand?"

"I hurt myself," he said.

Al shook her head and dropped down onto the edge of the bed. "Johnson, it's your vacation, but that's not an excuse to hurt yourself. I'm not saying you should quit drinking, just maybe slow it down a little."

"I wasn't drunk when this happened."

"I know," Al said, patting his head. "I know."

Johnson thought about arguing, but decided it didn't matter. If she wanted to believe he had been drunk, that was better than explaining what had really happened. "Well, I'll try and take it easy next time."

"That's all I ask," she said. Al stood up and began taking off her work clothes. Johnson was always amazed at the transformation from work Al to play Al. Her work clothes were not severe, but conservative, very conservative. The first time Johnson had seen her dressed for work, he hadn't recognized her.

"Jesus, you look so different," he'd said.

"I'm supposed to. I'm going to work. They expect me to look different."

The shower came on in the Dunkirk's bathroom. Johnson sat

up on the bed and tried closing his hand into a fist. It had swollen a little and the skin felt tight. He held the hand up in front of the mirror. His mind felt fogged. The chill was everywhere in the room. He took off his clothes, letting them fall into piles on the floor and stepped into the shower.

Al rested a foot on the tub's edge and leaned pulling a razor up her left leg. "You really should be more careful, Johnson."

"Yeah, I shouldn't get out of bed in the morning," Johnson said, pushing his head under the stream. The water was warm. It drummed against Johnson's skull, erasing all other sounds. He closed his eyes and let the sound push all other thoughts out of his mind. He emptied it for a brief moment and then, as if swimming up from a deep pool, he pulled his head from beneath the stream and opened his eyes. Al had her other leg up on the tub's edge. She put a hand on Johnson's side and reached past him with the razor.

"Careful, Johnson, it's sharp," she said.

Johnson cupped a hand over his balls. "You be careful."

"Don't worry," she said.

Johnson watched Al shake off the razor and turn back to shaving her legs. "Do you do that every day?"

She nodded her head. She looked flushed and wet. "Every day, pretty much. Some days I don't." she shrugged.

"I could never do that," he said.

"Sure you could. You can do anything you want."

"No," Johnson said, laughing. "I don't mean I want to shave my legs. I mean, I couldn't shave like that. Not every day."

"Why not?"

"There's so much to shave for one thing. The other thing is, I already shave my face. That's enough."

"Okay," Al said. "But if you ever want to shave your legs, I'll support you."

"Al, are you telling me that I strike you as the kind of guy who wants to shave his legs? Cause if you are, you got it all wrong."

"No, I am not saying that I think you want to shave your legs, but if you do it's okay with me."

"What else?" Johnson asked.

"What, what else?"

"What else could I do?"

"Anything, Johnson. Dress up like a woman. Pretend you're a king. Shave your head. Grow a beard. Anything."

"Fuck right now?"

"Drop the soap and find out."

Johnson dried his right leg and ruminated on how good sex was in the shower. It wasn't the shower necessarily, but the sensation. The deal with sex was stimulation. The shower just stimulated more parts of the body. He wondered about shower-like places. Bathtubs, pools, oceans, streams, lakes. Where else? A bus on a bumpy road. In a carriage, on a horse. In space. Weightless sex? Goddamn! WEIGHTLESS SEX! An epiphany. He wondered if anyone had done it yet. Was NASA keeping that a secret? Johnson couldn't imagine going into space and not wondering, even if only for a moment, about sex without gravity. Could you get a hard-on in space? He couldn't think of any reason why not, but there was the question. Like so many of the questions Johnson had about the world, nobody had bothered to find the answers to this one, and if they knew -- they'd kept it a secret from him.

"Al," he yelled from the bathroom. "Do you know if anyone's had sex in space yet?"

"What?" she asked.

"Do you know if anyone's fucked in space, like on the shuttle or the moon?"

She stuck her in the door. "You're a funny guy, you know that?"

"Do you know?"

"No," she said. "But I don't think anyone's done it yet."

"Imagine," Johnson said, "Someone, out there right now, is going to be the first person to fuck in weightlessness. Imagine."

"Two people," Al corrected. "Two people."

Johnson nodded. "Right, right, two people," he said, but his thoughts had turned inward. He'd seen video of astronauts tumbling through space ships. He'd never thought much of the space program before, regardless of the civilian benefits. He hated Tang. But weightless sex? "You know, Al, I'd like to go into space."

"I can see you would, Johnson."

"No, really," he said. "I could be the first man to have sex in a weightless environment. You could be the first woman."

"An honor, to be sure, Johnson. But I don't think we fit the space agency's profile of likely candidates."

"You're probably right," he said. "But still..."

"When we get home, we'll drive up to Cape Kennedy. You can ask if anyone's had sex in space yet and if not, volunteer." She took the towel from her head and wrapped it around her waist. "There's no harm in asking."

"Would you go with me?"

"Anywhere, Johnson. Anywhere."

Johnson thought for a moment. "Do you have any idea the number of different positions that we could try? Man oh man. Space sex. I'd love to do it there."

"Shut up, Johnson. You'd love to do it anywhere."

"True," he said. "But everybody's had sex anywhere. I want to be the first to have sex in space."

Al chuckled. "I admire your interest in adding to our knowledge of ourselves -- one small fuck for a man and all that -- but don't get your hopes up. I don't think they serve cocktails on the shuttle, either."

"You mean, I could be the first person to have a cocktail in space, too?"

"No," Al said. "I don't think you could."

Johnson nodded. "But I can dream, can't I?"

"Of course you can, Johnson. Of course."

As Al and he dressed, Johnson wondered about sex and drinks in space. If he buried face in Al's crotch and she did the same to him, could they tumble around? They'd have to be careful not to nudge any of the controls. Maybe NASA could design a special, what did they call them? Module. A special sex and cocktail module, so if things got a little crazy it wouldn't interfere with the normal running of the ship. He thought about their clothes drifting alongside them. Al's lingerie floating about, ready to be grabbed from the air and slipped into and out of. Toys, condoms drifting around. Maybe a little cocaine floating through the air. Johnson could swim over and snort it like smelling a flower. Cocktails in space. Little plastic packets of whiskey and beer. Johnson knew he'd spring for a bottle of Dom. Special occasions deserve special drinks. He imagined Helena Sanchez in the mix. The three of them, Al, Helena and himself, tumbling around.

"You know, Al," he said, pulling on his left shoe, "that space thing could be a lot of fun."

"It will be for someone, Johnson, but I'm afraid it won't be you. And besides, do you think they'd just let you have sex? No way. They'd hook wires up all over your body. Check your heart rate, perspiration, everything." She waved her hand. "Forget it, Johnson. It wouldn't be worth the hassle."

He nodded because he didn't want to think about the down-sides or the impossibility. It was a dream. It'd been a while since he had one. He wasn't letting it go.

"And they'd video everything."

Johnson glanced at the mirror. "Yeah, I suppose they would," he said.

"I hate that video look," Al said. "It's so cheesy. I'd never let myself be videoed. It'd be different if they used film. That's not so garish. But video? Video could make the Palace at Versailles look like a cheap motel on Eighth Street. Not that I have any-thing against the cheap motels on Eighth Street, but that video look."

"I see what you're saying," Johnson said, his dream evaporat-ing. "What are we doing tonight?"

"I thought we'd go over and stumble around the theater dis-trict. Find a place to eat, get a bunch of drinks, maybe come home and fuck."

"What if we got take-out from some place and just stayed in

tonight?" Johnson suggested.

"We're leaving the day after tomorrow. Don't you want to see more of London?"

"I've seen an awful lot of London, Al. And the bartenders can serve beer fine, but they can't make a proper drink. The food sounds good on the menu, but when you go to eat it, something's missing. I don't want to ride the underground. I'm tired, Al. I'm tired."

She put her hand on his forehead. "Are you sick?"

"No," he said. "London's been a lot more work than I thought. I think I'm just a small town guy."

"You lie down on the bed. I'll call the front desk and see if they can recommend a take-out place. Chinese?"

"Fine," Johnson said sprawling across the bed. "Chinese is fine."

Al reached for the phone. It rang before she touched it. She jumped back and laughed. "Jesus," she said. "That's not supposed to happen." It rang again. She looked at Johnson and grinned. Al lifted the receiver from the cradle. "Hello," she said, "yes, of course." Al put her hand over the receiver. "We have a call."

Johnson sat up on the bed. The list of potential callers ran through his mind. His mother died. The Fat Man was looking for him. Mondongo was in town.

"Hello?" Al said. She smiled. "Helena," she said to Johnson as much to the receiver. "Helena, how are you? Really? You want to come over?"

Johnson nodded.

Al winked at him. "No, we were going to stay in. Get some Chinese take-out. You're welcome to come by. No. No, we'll split the cost. Helena. No. I insist. Fine. Okay. We'll see you in forty-five minutes, an hour. Fine. Yes. I look forward to it too." Al hung up the phone. "I see you're not too tired to entertain."

"Who said anything about tired?" Johnson asked.

CHAPTER 20

Johnson sat in the chair across from the bed playing with a tiny silver earring Helena Sanchez had left behind the night before. It had been a grand time. Helena brought salsa tapes and a boom box along with Chinese take-out. The food was passable, the sex memorable. Johnson had stepped on the earring that morning as he emerged from the shower. A tiny silver hoop with stick figures of a man and woman hanging from it -- his London souvenir.

The clock radio said it was eleven-thirty. The free breakfast would be over in the lounge. Johnson dressed, grabbed his cap, coat and sunglasses thought he'd take a walk to a neighborhood pastry shop.

Johnson danced down the Pembroke House's front steps feeling drained and giddily happy. He looked up into the sky and adjusted his sunglasses against a weak, late morning sun. There were no great victories in his life, but any number of successful holding actions against complete disaster. The letter had been delivered. He was picking up some work on the flip side. The night before with Al and Helena made everything about the world so much better. He felt tuned. Ready. Fuck, he felt great.

When Luis Baste and Javier stopped him at the corner of Notting Hill Gate, across from the underground station, he thought they had a message or something from Antonio Gomez.

"Luis, Javier," he said, loud enough to be heard over the traffic. "How are you?"

Luis Baste smiled at Johnson. "We came to let you know that Antonio Gomez is on a flight back to Havana."

"Really," Johnson said. "Good for him. Gone home to see the family?"

"He's gone home to be tried for counter-revolutionary activities."

"I'm sorry to hear that," Johnson said, feeling the nibble of panic in his heart.

"He'll dance before the firing squad by the end of the month."

"Shit," Johnson said. "Is there anything I can do?"

Javier laughed.

"What's so funny?" Johnson asked.

Luis Baste smirked. "Johnson, you'll be dead long before Antonio Gomez."

"What?"

"We're going to kill you."

"They want you to kill me?"

"No. That first time at the embassy, you played Javier and me for fools. We don't like you. So we're going to kill you. This is not about countries or politics. This is purely personal."

Javier nodded, smiling.

"You can't fucking kill me," Johnson's voice rose to a shriek.

"Yes we can," Luis Baste said. "We're professionals."

"I really want to shoot you," Javier said. "I wanted to shoot you in the face that first day, but the shit eater Gomez wouldn't let me."

"We wanted you to know it was us," Luis Baste said. "And now, you do."

"Here?"

"No, of course not. Some place more private."

Johnson turned as if to run, then swung back with his right leg, trying to kick the toe of his cowboy boot through Javier's left shin. He'd seen Jackie Chan do the kick in a movie. Johnson listened for cracking bone. He heard none. Javier cried out and fell into Luis Baste. Johnson turned and ran. He raced across Notting Hill Gate Road, weaving through traffic. He could tell by the honking horns that Javier and Luis were behind him. He ran into the Notting Hill Gate underground station, bolted the turnstile and pushed his way through the crowd on the down escalator toward the District Line. He ran through a crowd of American high school girls, knocking one to the ground. They screamed, "Asshole... You fucking asshole." Johnson looked back. Javier and Luis Baste pushed through the crowd of girls. They were called assholes, too.

Johnson knew they couldn't kill him in the crowd. They'd already told him that much. He could call a cop. But what good did that do? They worked at an embassy. They probably had permits for their guns and some fucking immunity bullshit. Shit, they could just turn and walk the fuck away. Fuck. They didn't even have to kill him now. They could wait. What did Spiro say? Hit you with a truck. Drop a load of bricks on your head.

Johnson stopped at the busiest part of the platform and wriggled his way into the crowd's center. Luis Baste eased up next to him. "Johnson," he said, quietly. "It was going to be quick. Now? Javier is very angry. We're going to kill you very slowly, then we're going after that whore girlfriend of yours."

An approaching train drowned the sound of Johnson's, "Fuck you." He spun at Luis Baste and pushed him hard, hoping to get him out onto the tracks. Luis fell to the ground. He smiled up at Johnson and drew his finger across his neck.

Johnson jostled his way through the crowd into an already full train car. At the next four stations, -- Queensway, Lancaster Gate, Marble Arch and Bond Street -- he stepped out of the car. At each station, he saw Javier to his left and Luis Baste to his right. Luis smiled and waved. Javier patted the pistol beneath his jacket.

Johnson bolted the car at Oxford Circus and wound his way to the Victoria Line. He walked fast but didn't run. Over his shoulder Johnson spied Luis and Javier spread out behind him, ensuring that he couldn't double back.

The Victoria Line. The blue line that zig-zagged across London. Johnson climbed into a car crowded with West Indian people -- Jamaicans, Bahamians and Rastafari. He stepped out at each station to make sure that he hadn't lost them. They were always there. Luis Baste smiling, waving. Javier, patting the pistol. At Victoria Station, Johnson stepped out of the car and recollected how beautiful the place had been on his first day in London. How sweetly diffused the light was. How heavenly. He stepped back into the car.

At the Brixton Station, he ran up the steps toward the Electric Avenue Market. Luis and Javier hung on his tail. Johnson slowed to a walk at the market stalls. He slowed down to take in the aromas of the spices and the incense. To admire the beauty of the colors. Johnson took his time. Making it a point to remember each and everything he saw, each and everything he felt. He looked into the eyes of the vendors. All Africans. Eddie, the doorman at Heaven's Gate, had told him once when they were stoned, "All of us. I and I. We and we. Are all Africans. And we and we all go back someday."

"When?" Johnson asked.

"Not in this world," Eddie replied.

Luis Baste and Javier were fifty yards from Johnson. They walked together, eyes locked on him. They believed they had him and had relaxed. They had him and they knew it.

Johnson stopped at a spice booth, directly across from the dingy alley that hid The Bob Marley. He looked for a moment at a photograph of the *Holy Most High Selassie I, Jah Rastafari*, the Emperor of Ethiopia and Jah's heaven-sent savior. He bore no resemblance to anyone Johnson had ever prayed to. An African man, in a military uniform. His black beard was flecked gray; his eyes cast upward. Johnson closed his own eyes and breathed in the smells and memories of Africa, then bolted across the avenue and down the alley. He heard Luis and Javier's shoes slapping the pavement behind him.

Johnson raced through The Bob Marley's door and into the darkness. Dance hall music played. Reefer smoke filled the air.

"White Clot," Pony Boy called from the bar.

"Respect," Johnson said, saluting him with his fists.

"Respect," Pony Boy called back.

"Two men are about to come through that door. They're

going to kill me," Johnson cried, as he crossed the bar. "Is there another way out?"

"What you think, Clot?" Pony Boy asked.

"Can I use it?"

"Respect, White Clot. What you think?"

"Right now?"

A hand reached out of the darkness, grabbed Johnson by his coat and yanked him around the bar. A rectangle of light fell across the room. The hand pushed him through the door.

Johnson found himself in a rubbled lot, on the backside of the pub. The door closed. Dance hall rhythms carried through the wall. Pony Boy cried out, "What bumba clot come through me door?"

Luis Baste shouted, *"Come mierda, pendejo."* Eat shit, asshole. "Where is he?"

Pony Boy said, "No respect." A volley of gun fire followed.

Johnson waited. The music played on. The door opened. He jumped back.

Pony Boy gestured with is head for Johnson to reenter the bar. "Respect," he said.

"Respect," Johnson said, stepping into the gloom. The burnt Sulphur aroma of gun powder mixed with the musky smell of the Emperor's herb. Dance hall played, its upbeat energy at odds with the room's tableau. Three figures bent over the bodies that were once Javier and Luis. Johnson stepped closer. Blood from both men pooled, oil black on the floor. Half of Javier's face was gone, the remaining teeth crooked into a smile. Luis leaked blood from his neck and chest. One of the figures leaned close to him with a pistol pointed at his head.

"Don't," Pony Boy said. "Let he meet Jah on his time. Dead be quick, soon."

Dead be quick, soon. Tears welled in Johnson's eyes, not over Javier and Luis, but himself and Al and all he loved. Dead be quick, soon.

Pony Boy touched his shoulder. "Best be gone from here White Clot. Tell me Eddie in Miami the Emperor smiles on him and his. And tell none <u>ever</u> what was done once here."

CHAPTER 21

On the morning of Johnson's last full day in London, Al sat in a chair across the room, reading to him from her guidebook. "...the lowest gate of the tower fronts onto the Thames..." She'd finished her work and was looking forward to a whole day off in London. She'd dressed in jeans, hiking boots and a Brown University sweatshirt.

Johnson lay naked across the bed, in no rush to get moving. His business required that he carry secrets, other people's and his own. When he'd begin to feel remorse over Luis and Javier he envisioned Luis Baste saying, "...then we're going after that whore girlfriend of yours." Fuck them. That was enough. They deserved to die.

Johnson was not a brave man, though he knew that in his business the possibility of violent death always lurked at the fringes of life. Dead be quick, soon. People he'd known died because of their business. Shorty-Fat took a bullet to the head during a street corner drug deal. Harvey Singer disappeared. New York mobsters drowned Harry Warren in his own bathtub when he wouldn't cut them in on his night club. Monkey Muertobia died because he thought he was smarter than the Colombian suppliers. Johnson added Javier and Luis Baste to the list. Johnson didn't care that he'd led those two men to their deaths, but he couldn't ignore the trembling that shook his body when he realized how close he'd come to his own. Dead be quick, soon.

Someone knocked on the door.

"Yes," Johnson said.

"Spiro," said the voice.

Johnson wrapped a towel around his waist and opened the door a crack. "My girlfriend's here," he said.

"I know," Spiro said. "The IRA just bombed Canary Wharf."

"What does that mean?"

"Turn on your television, you'll find out." Spiro nodded. "The Irish know how important their enemies are. Know how important it is to hate. Really hate. You should admire that."

"I do," Johnson said, and closed the door. Johnson reached across the bed and grabbed the remote control. The television screen brightened.

An unsteady camera panned a large cream-colored building. Each glass-less window said to Johnson, "A bomb's been here." Dead be quick, soon. In the screen's lower righthand corner a digital clock marked the passage of time in seconds. 'BBC London' floated just below the clock in white letters. Police, their uniforms wrapped in flak jackets, directed people toward small vans. Disaster Response Crews carried things about.

"What's that?" Al asked.

A male voice with an Irish accent said, "I don't think it's premature to say that the cease fire has ended. The government knew the..."

Johnson saw blood on a man's arm, his shirt ripped and torn. "A bomb. Somewhere in London." Jesus Christ.

Another man spoke. "We have just received confirmation of at least two deaths and, of course, many many people injured. Please remember, these are preliminary reports."

Al crossed the room and took the remote control from Johnson. Without looking at the screen, she turned off the television.

"What are you doing?" Johnson asked, on edge for the next word -- the next picture.

"I'm not watching it," she said. "I'm not getting caught up in this, this tragedy."

"I don't think you can avoid it, Al. We're in London. A bomb just went off. You're already caught up."

"I'm not. It happened on television. Not where I am."

"Shut up," Johnson said. "The bomb happened here, Al. You

know, boom. There could be others."

"I don't care. It's our last day in London. That stuff has nothing to do with us."

"Right," Johnson said.

"You're twice as likely to get killed in Miami than you are in London if a bomb went off here every day."

He couldn't tell her how close they both came. Dead be quick, soon. "Fine," he said. "But I don't want to die here, and if an IRA bomb killed me in London, I'd be an innocent bystander. A tourist. Not part of the discussion. If I got killed in Miami, at least I'd be a part of it."

"Part of what?"

"The discussion. The argument, you know, about who should have what. And who decides. How much can you get for yourself. You know -- that whole Miami thing."

"What are you talking about?"

"I'm talking about not being a part of it here. Let these people kill each other and we'll get back to Miami and give somebody there a chance. At least in Miami, they'd try and get your wallet. Here? Boom. Dead. Nothing. Dead be quick, soon." There he'd said it.

"You're a chicken shit."

"Fine. I'm a chicken shit. But I'm not going out any place where someone might plant a bomb."

"Bombs can be anywhere."

"I know. So I'm staying in." He loved the sound of the words and needed to repeat them. "I'm staying in. I'll order take-out. Have it delivered. Watch TV. Read the guidebook again. We're getting out of London tomorrow. No bombs. No nothing." Gone, he thought. Done, he thought. He was already packed and on the plane.

"I am not going to let some terrorists ruin my last day here."

"Who the fuck are you? Ronald Reagan?" Johnson said. "Don't think of it as terrorists. Think of it like the weather. The weather's lousy. There's a seventy percent chance of a bombing, with high opportunity for maiming and injury. The death factor

is 20 degrees below zero. It's just a good day to stay indoors."
Dead be quick, soon.

"You're very funny," she said, crossing her arms over her
breasts. She turned her head to the darkened TV screen.

Johnson could hear her thinking.

"How about a park?" she asked. "We could walk to a park.
Wander around. Would that be okay?"

"I'd rather stay in."

"Okay," Al said. "You stay in. I'm going to a park."

"Show me again," he said.

"Here, it's simple."

Johnson looked over Al's shoulder at their Map of London.

"See." She traced a route with her finger. "It's easy."

Johnson followed her finger across the map, reading the
street names: Kensington Church, Palace Gardens, Bayswater
Road. Bayswater was rendered as a thick gray band -- a busy
street.

"There," she said. "No busy streets. Well, one, Bayswater, but
once we cross it, we're in Kensington Gardens."

"So where's Canary Wharf?" Johnson asked, scanning the
map.

"It's down over here," she said, waving at a space off the map's
lower right-hand corner. "It's farther out than the map goes."

Johnson nodded. Bombs. Canary Wharfs. What the hell did
that mean anyway, Canary Wharfs? Where the fuck did they get
canaries in London? What the fuck did they do with them? Why
would anybody want to blow them up? He didn't have to go out.
He could stay in. She could go.

"You don't have to go," Al said.

"I'm going, damn it," he said, putting on his cap, wrapping a
scarf around his neck and pulling his coat from the closet.

He followed Al down the hall, past open doors where maids
ran vacuum cleaners and swabbed out bathtubs. The sweet
chemical aroma of their cleaning fluids comforted to Johnson.

He slid the key across the front desk and followed Al out the door. He said, "Boom," under his breath.

"You say something?"

"No," he said.

The houses up and down the street looked pale as bone in the thin gray light. Johnson saw his breath and looked up, wondering if it would rain.

Pembroke Court was quiet except for the scrape of their shoes against the sidewalk. Johnson knew each of the tiny British cars parked against the curb could hold a bomb. How did you live in a city with bombs? He wondered. Were he and Al the only ones dumb enough to go out? A car approached them from behind. Johnson turned his head. A small delivery truck. Carrying a bomb? No. Jesus. He couldn't let himself think that way. He took a deep breath and smelled the damp sulphured London air. What was that smell? Car exhaust, diesel, what else? What else?

"See, this isn't so bad," Al said.

"Right," Johnson said. Boom, he thought. You won't even know it. BOOM. Dead. Traffic rushed madly through the intersection at Bayswater Road. There's still life here, he thought. At the street corner, waiting for traffic to stop, he tapped his foot and noticed Al tapping hers. "Nervous?" he asked.

"No," she said.

"Then why are you tapping your foot?"

"Am I? I hadn't noticed."

"We could go back."

"Go back," she said. "I don't care."

"What, and have you think I'm a chicken shit?"

"I already think that."

"Fuck you."

"Yeah, right," she said, stepping off the curb.

Traffic had stopped. Johnson walked quickly to catch her and was at her side as they passed through green iron gates into Kensington Gardens. The trees were leafless and the grass had a weary yellow pallor. Across a broad meadow he saw another person. A woman, he guessed. She walked a small dog on a long tether.

"There's a lot to see here," Al said.

"I don't want to see anything," Johnson said. "I've seen enough. Who gives a shit?"

"Johnson, I don't think there's a bomb here."

"Who said anything about a bomb? I'm just kind of sick of all the old crap in London. Oh, we're in London. We gotta see this. We gotta see that. I don't want to see any more. I'm over it. The park is nice. Trees. That person walking a dog. It's nice. I don't need anything else."

"It has nothing to do with a bomb?"

"Would you please stop talking about a fucking bomb? Please?"

"Fine," Al said.

Johnson stayed in the center of a broad walkway that meandered through the park. He avoided trash barrels, monuments and drinking fountains. The walkway rolled down a gentle slope. Near its end a gravel path ran off to the left. Tall hedges, over eight feet, separated the path from a busy street he didn't remember from the map. Johnson heard car engines and horns on the hedge's far side. Green benches lined the path. He didn't like it. He imagined trip wires and booby traps.

"Let's go back," he said. "I'm getting tired."

"Go ahead," Al said. "I'll see you at the hotel."

Sweat rolled from Johnson's armpits. Goddamn. Goddamn. Al always has to do stuff her way, he thought.

Al started away from him down the path. She was walking toward something colorful on a bench.

Johnson saw a small doll propped up on the bench. A RAG DOLL! What better place to hide a bomb than A RAG DOLL. Goddamn. He was going to die because of A RAG DOLL. His tongue swelled in his mouth. His hands shook.

"Look, Johnson," Al said, bending toward the bench. "A Raggedy Ann."

Johnson ran down the path. He lunged at her, grabbed her shoulders, and spun her to the ground. He hit the ground hard, knocking the breath from his lungs.

"Are you fucking nuts?" Al shouted. "Are you absolutely fucking nuts?"

"Bomb," Johnson gasped. "Maybe bomb."

"Bomb my ass. You're fucking paranoid," Al shouted. She rolled away from him and snatched up the doll. "It's a goddamn doll," she said shaking it in his face. "A fucking doll." Al threw the doll down and stalked down the pathway.

Johnson listened to the gravel crunching beneath her feet. He lowered his head to the path, feeling the tiny stones cold and damp against his cheek. Maybe I am paranoid. But this is not my town. This is different. The only people with bombs in Miami were the Cubans and they just killed each other. But in London? How could I know? Dead be quick, soon.

Johnson pushed himself up. He could feel his left knee skinned beneath his jeans. He put his weight on the knee and winced at the pain. Jesus.

Al sat on a bench forty feet further down the path. She had her arms folded across her chest and her head down. Johnson bent for the doll. It had black Xs for eyes, red yarn hair and a crooked red smile. Johnson smoothed its yarn hair and hobbled down the track. If he'd hurt himself, he must have hurt her. He could have just shouted, 'don't touch it.' Jesus.

Ten feet from the bench, Johnson increased the limp and winced audibly. "Al, I feel so damned stupid," he said.

Al looked up at him, then down to the doll and stared for a moment. She lifted it from his hands and smoothed its hair. "There. There," she said. "No need to cry. Everything will be fine if you let it. Everything." She sat the doll on the bench and looked up to Johnson. "Let's get out of here," she said. "This place is creeping me out. And, you. Jesus, Johnson what happened to you?"

Dead be quick, soon, he thought. "Nothing," he said. "Thank god."

As he and Al cut back through Kensington Gardens. The woman walking the dog was gone. They had the park to themselves.

They passed through the gates at Bayswater Road and stepped to the traffic's edge.

A red double bus decker passed.

Johnson jumped back. "Jesus," he said.

"Do you want a drink?" Al asked.

"Yes," he said. "That's it. Yes."

Dead be quick, soon. It was how insects lived and died, beneath your foot. One minute you're there, and the next... Johnson snapped his fingers. Gone.

The bartender turned toward him. "Another, mate?'

The man startled Johnson from his thoughts. He glanced at the pint sitting on the bar. His third; still three quarters full. "Not yet," he said.

Al sat beside him staring up at the television screen, watching the emergency crews live from Canary Wharf.

How easy it is to watch TV, Johnson thought. Al and he hadn't spoken since they entered the bar. They sat next to each other and drank slowly and solemnly. They drank as if it were medicine. After his fourth pint, Johnson asked the bartender if he sold cigarettes.

"You bet, mate," he answered. "Marlboro?"

Johnson nodded.

The bartender slid the pack across the bar. Took coins from the stack in front of Johnson.

Al turned to him. "I thought you quit."

"I've decided to unquit."

She nodded and turned back to the TV. "We'll be back in Miami tomorrow night, Johnson. Maybe you could quit again."

"You folks from Miami, is it?" the bartender asked. "I've been to Florida. Disney, Epcot, MGM. Never Miami though, it's too dangerous."

Johnson nodded his head and tore open the pack of cigarettes. The sweet smell of the tobacco reminded of bubble gum. Bubble gum and candy. "You know, I've lived in Florida most of my life, and I've never gone to Disney."

"Oh you should, mate. It's heaven on earth; I swear. Clean, safe. Educational. Heaven," the man said. "Absolutely."

Johnson stuck a cigarette between his teeth.

The bartender flourished a lighter.

Johnson leaned to the flame and sucked the smoke deep into his lungs. He blew it out -- a steady plume at the television. "Disney is shit," Johnson said.

"Don't curse at the bar, mate," the bartender said.

"I didn't."

"You most certainly did," he said.

"What are you talking about?"

He leaned closer to Johnson. "You said, 'shit'."

"Shit," Johnson said. "Are you kidding? Shit is not cursing."

"Yes it is."

"No, it's not."

The man crossed his arms over his chest and nodded his head. "Yes, mate, it is."

"Listen, buddy" Johnson said. "In my country, the United States, everything is shit. You have your shit and I have mine." He grabbed Al's beer. "See this. This is her shit. In America, where I'm from, we eat shit, could give a shit, talk shit, we're shit on, up shit creek, and we get out of the way when the shit hits the fan. Sometimes I smoke a little shit and sometimes, like now, I'm shit faced. And, you know what you're giving me right now -- that's right -- SHIT. In America shit is not cursing, shit is everything."

Johnson turned to Al. She stared at him.

"Yeah?" he said.

She shook her head. "Nothing."

"Disney?" Johnson shook his head. "Maybe you're right," he said. "Maybe Disney is not shit. Because for something to be shit it needs to be real. And Disney is not real."

"Are your dreams real, mate?" The man's voice changed, he challenged more than asked.

Johnson thought for a moment about his dreams. He only had the one dream about sex in space, and he wasn't going to share it with this guy. "I don't have dreams," he said.

"Then don't go to Disney," the bartender spat. "It's only for people with dreams." He turned and started toward the bar's far end.

"Hold on," Johnson said. "What do I owe you?"

"Two pound ten."

Johnson put a five-pound note on the bar. "Disney is not for people with dreams. Disney is for people without dreams. They manufacture dreams there, the same way you build a car in Detroit or make a computer in Japan. You don't get your own dreams, buddy. You get Disney's version." Then he said, "Al, let's get the fuck out of here."

"You're wrong, mate," the bartender shouted. "You're wrong."

"I don't care," Johnson said.

Johnson put on his sunglasses as he stepped out the door. He looked up into the sky and a blotch of rain fell on one of the lenses. Then another and another. He turned to Al. "Hey, it's raining." He grinned. "I'm in London and it's raining."

Rain soaked Johnson's hair and collar on the walk back to the Pembroke House. He and Al tried to huddle together as they walked, but they staggered into each other. The rain soaked into Johnson's bones and his limbs grew stiff. He felt like the Tin Man from the Wizard of Oz, and nearly squeaked out the words, "Oil can," but he didn't think Al would get the joke, so he kept it to himself. When Johnson opened the hotel's doors, the heat flowed out at him in an easy breath. Dry, dry, dry. No cats rushed the door. Sheila stood behind the desk, writing in a logbook. She smiled at Al and grimaced at Johnson as she slid their key across the counter.

"Have a nice stroll?" she asked.

"It rained," Johnson cried. "And we found a little rag doll," Johnson said. "The cutest little doll." Tears welled in his eyes and words thickened in his throat. "The cutest doll. Left all alone on a bench in the park." Johnson choked on the words.

Al patted his shoulder. "We stopped in a pub."

Sheila nodded.

"We stopped in a pub," Johnson said, his sadness suddenly gone somewhere else. "The bartender was a fool." He leaned into the counter and pointed a finger at Sheila. "Have you ever been to Disney? Have you ever seen the Rat?"

"No," she said. "I haven't."

"Do you want to?" Johnson snapped.

Sheila leaned back from the counter and looked from Johnson to Al. "No, I don't. I'm sorry."

Johnson nodded his head. "You have nice tits and you're smart -- I like you. I don't even give a shit about those cats. If you're ever in Miami, come by the house. Al and me will show you a good time."

"Thank you," Sheila said, smiling.

"Oh yeah," Johnson remembered, "Tell Spiro I said, shut up."

Sheila nodded. "I'll do that."

Al put a hand on Johnson's shoulder. "We have an eight o'clock flight out of Gatwick tomorrow. Could we have a five o'clock wakeup call and a car here at six?"

"Of course," Sheila said, writing in her book. "Anything else?"

"Yeah," Johnson said, but he couldn't remember what it was. "Forget it," he snapped. "Just forget it."

"C'mon, Johnson," Al said, "I need to go lie down."

"I bet you do," he replied. "I warned you not to try and keep up with me, and now you're drunk."

"Right," she said. "Right."

Johnson turned and started toward the Dunkirk. A wet man, staggering, eyes squinting toward him, made Johnson stop for a moment and rest both hands on his hips. "Fuck you," he said. When he realized it was his reflection, he said, "Yeah, fuck you, too."

CHAPTER 22

Johnson's eyes opened in a dark room. He stared at the ceiling for a moment and the day came slowly back to him. Canary Wharf, the doll, the bartender and after that not much was clear. His head hurt, his mouth was dry and he needed to piss. He leaned to the left and listened to the small snoring sound Al made as she slept. She was deep asleep. He flipped the covers from his legs and dropped his feet to the floor. His stomach rolled with the quick move and he had to brace himself against the bed before he could stand. He knew he had to piss; he hoped he wouldn't throw up.

He walked carefully through the darkened room and tripped over something stacked on the floor. Suitcases? Packed. He didn't remember packing, but then again he didn't remember much after leaving the bar. Maybe he'd helped pack. Maybe not? It didn't matter he supposed. If Al packed for him, it was just something he didn't have to worry about.

He finished in the toilet, thanked god he didn't have to puke and crawled back into bed with Al. He would be in Miami this time tomorrow, he thought. He would wait a day before calling the Fat Man. Then he would do the business. Then he would....

The plane banked over the Gulf Stream and Miami came into view. Johnson craned his neck to see where they were. He saw the clock tower on Lincoln Road. It read 6:47 and 81. Six forty-seven and eighty-one degrees. Eighty-one, God I love this town. They flew over the beach and the bay, getting closer to the ground, until finally they had flown past the entire city and out over the Everglades. The pilot swung the plane through an arc and headed into the airport.

The message light on his answering machine blinked angrily when Johnson and Al walked back into the house. Johnson ignored it. He wasn't home yet, or he wasn't home for business yet. They'd just gotten off a plane. Couldn't they give him a break? Everyone wanted a piece of him. Never a break, never a rest. He lugged his suitcase into the bedroom and dropped it on the floor beside the bed.

Al trailed in behind him. She said, "Your machine's blinking."

"I'm not listening to it until tomorrow. We just got home. I want to be back without having to put up with any bullshit until I'm ready."

"Suit yourself," she said, throwing her suitcase on the bed and pulling back the zippers.

"What's that supposed to mean?"

"Nothing," Al said. "If you don't want to pick up your messages, I don't think you should."

"Okay," Johnson said. Jesus. Everything's rush rush rush. What if he just wanted to go out and sit in the yard for a while? Get warm on a Florida night? He heard Al mumble something under her breath. "You say something?"

"No," she said.

"I thought I heard you say something."

"No, I was just talking to myself."

He nodded and looked at the suitcase on the floor. What the fuck? He hauled it up onto the bed and began lifting his clothes out. They were cold and smelled like travel in the bottom of the plane. Al said something and Johnson heard her this time. He heard the word, important. She had said the word important. "You were talking again," he said.

"Just to myself."

"Well, what the hell is so important that you say the word important to yourself?"

"Just work stuff."

"You think I should listen to my messages, don't you?"

"No, Johnson. I think you should do whatever you think you should do."

"Right," he said. "Listen, just because you do things when you're supposed to, doesn't mean I should."

"I'm not saying anything."

"Yeah," Johnson said. "Exactly. You're thinking it because you know when you say it I'll only get pissed off."

"Unlike now."

"I'm not pissed," he shouted. "I just hate being told what to do. Okay?"

Al nodded her head and smiled at him. "I understand."

Johnson looked into her eyes. Son of a bitch. All I wanted was a few more moments in that other place. Where people don't know where you are. Where maybe you don't know where you are. Johnson, he's in London. Or someplace. Jesus. He looked over his shoulder toward the machine. The light blinked on and off. Could be important. Could be business. "All right, goddamn it, Al. You win."

Johnson crossed the room and pushed the play button. The machine rewound, taking longer than Johnson ever remembered. It continued backwards, playing his life over again. It stopped, clicked and the tape hissed forward and beeped.

"Buddy, it's mother. I was wondering if you'd come to dinner this Friday. You can bring your little friend if you like..." The machine beeped.

Al said, "Am I your little friend, Johnson?" Johnson turned to her and shrugged.

The machine beeped. "Johnson, it's Frank. Do you know anybody who'd have a use for some Cuban rum? I got forty-three fucking cases of high-end Cuban rum. It's not moving like cigars. Call me." The machine beeped.

"Listen fucker, I know you're there. Pick up asshole. Pick up. Okay. Fuck you if you're there. Call me." The machine beeped.

"Who's that?" Al asked.

"Pepe, the bartender at the Ocean Wreck."

"Oh," she said.

"London. A beautiful city. The Romans. The Normans. The Brits themselves, all of them created something that you can't find in any old deli, I can tell you that. It's your good friend. I know you would call me the moment you got in. But I just wanted to welcome you back. After a long journey, it's good to hear the voices of your friends. Don't you think? I certainly do. I look forward to your call and the story of your trip. Hello, to your lovely girlfriend. You told me her name, something odd. Henry was it? Hank? Jerry? Oh, it doesn't matter. Just know that your old friend awaits your call." The machine beeped.

"Johnson, here's the deal. I got two cars going to Detroit, empty. You want one? Call by Thursday." The machine beeped.

"Buddy, it's mother. Don't worry about the doctor's report, it's really nothing." She sighed heavily. "Not to worry, but please call." The machine beeped.

"Friends. We judge men by the number and power of their friends. Some people have many friends and no power, others have few that can be counted among the most powerful in the kingdom. Where do you fall against that measure, Johnson? Remember your friends, Johnson. Remember your friends." The machine clanked loudly, hissed as it rewound and squealed as it neared the end.

"The squeaky voice?" Al said.

Johnson nodded and picked up the phone. He dialed the Fat Man's number. He answered after the third ring.

"Need a friend?" he shrieked.

"It's Johnson, sir."

"Johnson, my friend. When did you return?"

"Just now, sir."

"Just now? And you called me. That's the sign of a true friend. Have you unpacked yet?"

"No, sir," Johnson said. "I called you first thing."

The Fat Man squealed. "Oh, you do honor me, Johnson. You do."

"Yes, sir."

"Tell me of London. Tell me of the theater. The Thames. I

love the people. Was the Queen in residence? The weather. Oh there is so much to tell. But enough of this. Any news for our friend?"

Johnson nodded his head. "Yes," he said. "I have a letter."

"Have you read it?" The Fat man asked, conspiracy in his tone.

"No, it's in a sealed envelope."

"When can you bring it here?"

"Well, I just got in, sir. I am kind of tired."

"I imagine so, Johnson. Is eight too soon?"

Johnson looked at his watch. Six-thirty. "No, sir. I can make it at eight."

"Then eight it is, Johnson."

"Right, sir."

"Say hello to your friend for me. Her name's... don't tell me..."

"Al," Johnson said.

"That's it, Al. Say hello to your friend Al for me."

"I will, sir."

"Eight, Johnson."

"Yes, sir." The phone went dead. Johnson dropped it back into its cradle. He looked to Al. "I'm going out," he said.

"The Fat Man?"

"Yeah. He said to tell you hello."

"You told him about me?"

"Well, I said we were going to London. He asked for your name. I don't know. The guy's a little strange."

"I'm assuming you, of course, are speaking from the height of supreme normalcy."

"Is that a shot?"

"Depends on how much stake you have in being normal."

"Well I'm normal for me," Johnson said. "Right now that's all that matters."

"Exactly," Al said.

The Crown Vic smelled of cat urine and mildew. Johnson wasn't sure how a cat could have gotten into the car, but it smelled like one had. The weather -- no rain -- allowed him to ride with his windows open. He'd showered. Al had started to do laundry. She was walking back and forth between the bedroom and the laundry naked when he left. He loved that.

As he rode over the Miami River Bridge he surveyed Miami and knew that it would never be another London. It was just a small town beyond the Disney Empire that wanted to be the Main Street Parade and Epcot's version of South America but never would. Even the skyline pretended to be real. From one angle it looked as grand as a future Manhattan and from another it was the gap-toothed mouth of a homeless wino. Johnson didn't care. He was happy to be home. He knew Miami.

Johnson drove across the causeway and loved everything he saw. The cruise ships, the fuel lighters, a seaplane landing off Watson Island. The homeless shacks along the water. Johnson decided he loved Miami because it was the anti-Disney. Everything about it was real. Real enough to taste. And it tasted good to Johnson.

He pulled onto Teitelbaum's island and stopped at the gate. A thin Latin guy leaned out of the guard house.

"I'm a friend of Stephen Teitelbaum's," Johnson said.

"Of course, sir," the man replied. The gate swung up.

Mondongo's car sat in the driveway. The Fat Man's '62 Lincoln sat near the garage. Johnson pulled the Crown Vic to the curb and shut off the engine. He grabbed the letter for Mondongo and walked up to the door. He pushed the bell and the door swung open. Mondongo and the Fat Man stood just inside the door.

"Johnson," the Fat Man shrieked, "home safely from across the pond are you?"

"Yes, sir."

"So good to see you. I understand there was some nasty business with bombs while you were there. My heart sank to think that you could have somehow been injured."

"No, sir," Johnson said. "I was nowhere near any bombs."

"Good. Good."

Johnson looked to his left. Mondongo stared wide-eyed, rolling his hands as if he cradled a ball.

"You remember *Señor* Mondongo, don't you Johnson?" The

Fat Man asked.

"Yeah," Johnson said. "How are you, sir?" Johnson stuck out his hand.

"*Señor* Teitelbaum says you have an answer for me."

"Yes, I do." Johnson handed the envelope to the man. Mondongo tore it open. Inside it another smaller envelope. Johnson could see good paper. Nice stock. Mondongo tore open that envelope and held up a tiny piece of paper. There wasn't much written on it.

Mondongo's eyes glowed; his body shook. He crumpled the paper, threw it on the ground. "I am sorry. I must go, now," he said. He clicked his heels together and bowed slightly, before walking out the door."

The Fat Man said, "It would appear our friend Mondongo didn't receive the answer he wanted."

"Don't you care?" Johnson asked.

"What's to care? I got my end. You got yours. We did what he wanted. It's obvious to me he didn't think through the strategy."

"I think the guy who got Mondongo's letter, Antonio Gomez, is dead."

"People die all the time, Johnson. The world is a dangerous place."

"I know, sir. I think they killed him."

"I'm sure it doesn't matter, in the final result, who or what kills you, Johnson. You're dead."

"That's true, sir."

Johnson picked up the response to Mondongo from the floor. It was a small note-sized piece of paper. He smoothed it against his thigh. *Palacio de Presidente, Havana, Cuba* was written in black type across the top. Beneath it a strong hand in blue ink had written: *No me jodas* and beneath that, *Fidel Castro-Ruiz*. Johnson grinned when read it. He handed it to the Fat Man.

"Interesting," Teitelbaum said. "It appears Mondongo's message got all the way to the top."

"Yeah, I'd say he did."

"What's this no me jodas?"

"*No me jodas,*" Johnson corrected. "Don't fuck with me."

Teitelbaum shrieked with laughter. "Mondongo sure put the fear of god in Fidel, didn't he?"

"His name's not Mondongo," Johnson said. "I learned in London, Mondongo means tripe."

"And you know Johnson, I'd love to hear about your London adventures, but I have so many things to do. It's so good to see you, my friend. So good. I believe you know your way out." The Fat Man turned and walked back toward the living room.

Yeah, Johnson thought. I know my way out. He pulled the door shut behind him. Well, it was done. The London trip. The letter. He tried to add up what he netted on the job, but fuck, he was ahead. It didn't matter. Driving home he wondered if Al would be interested in going out for a late dinner and a visit to Heaven's Gate.

CHAPTER 23

Four months after Johnson's return, Cuban MiGs shot down two airplanes flown by Miami Cubans. On the island they called them terrorists, violating Cuban air space. In Miami they called them patriots and claimed they were over international waters. Johnson knew it was Mondongo and Fidel poking at each other. It would never end.

Johnson's memory of the London trip had become like a good movie, to be cherished when recalled and dredged up when he wanted to sound worldly to his friends. He hinted there was more to the trip than race tracks and beer, but other than telling Eddie hello from his cousin in London, he never mentioned Javier, Luis, Spiro or the delivery in either direction.

June arrived in Miami, hot, humid -- the sun at eight a.m. was already bright enough to make him squint. Dressed in paisley pajama bottoms and a white t-shirt, Johnson stepped out onto his front porch to fetch *The Miami Herald*. He didn't think he was hung over, but he had a stabbing pain over his left eye. As Johnson bent to grab the paper, a Yellow Cab creaked to a stop in front of the house. The rear door opened and a voice vaguely familiar called his name.

"Johnson."

Johnson looked up to see Spiro climbing out of the cab, black briefcase in hand. "Johnson," he repeated. "It's Spiro. Remember? The porter."

Johnson did. He looked left and right, trying to decide whether to run or not.

"I've come to America to seek my fortune," Spiro shouted. "I will be rich."

That was the last thing Johnson needed in front of his house. Some crazy spy shouting how he was going to get rich in America. "Spiro, good to see you. Come in. Come in."

"I can't stay," he said. "But I've brought you something." Spiro turned back to the cab. "Ten minutes. I'll be out in ten minutes."

Johnson led Spiro into the house. He took him to the kitchen and gestured for him to sit. "Coffee?" Johnson asked.

"No. I really can't stay. But I want to thank you, Johnson."

"For what?"

"Well, I saw the way you handled yourself. Not the cowardly demonstration of your bankrupt society, but the way you looked out for yourself. I admired that, so I put out some feelers."

"And?"

"I have an agent. I've met with the Turner organization, and they're interested. Some people in Los Angeles are interested."

"Interested?" Johnson said. "Interested in what?"

"My archive," Spiro said. "My films. Everybody knows J. Edgar Hoover wore dresses, but I'm the only one with film. Spiro Agnew spanking a young hooker? Heads of state barking like dogs. Generals dressed in French maids' outfits. Ambassadors..." Spiro waved his hand. "My agent tells me, I've got what people want. I'm selling it to the highest bidder."

"What about the Russians?"

"What about them? They've got bigger things to worry about than me. I've got film. Some people have bombs."

Johnson nodded. Maybe if he'd have played his cards right he could have gotten a piece of that deal. But he hadn't. "Well, good luck to you, Spiro. And thanks for stopping by."

"No. No, Johnson. I brought you something." Spiro opened the black briefcase and slid a videocassette across the table to him. "When I cataloged the collection, my agent asked who you were. I said no one. She said they didn't want that tape. You're only porn, there's no key to power there."

Johnson looked at the tape. "That's me?"

"You, your girlfriend. That Cuban girl. Nice production

values, but no real market."

Johnson nodded. "No market, huh?" He wasn't sure why he felt bad, but he did.

"I'm sorry," Spiro said.

"Don't be."

Johnson waited for him to say something else, but Spiro said nothing.

"Coffee?" Johnson asked. "Beer?"

"No. No, I've got to go," Spiro said. "I'm catching another flight in an hour."

"West coast?"

"Not yet," Spiro said, grinning. "I'm going to Disney World."

Johnson laughed. "Disney? Well, that should be fun," he said. "That should be a lot of fun."

Spiro nodded. "One last thing, Johnson." He stopped smiling and lifted an envelope from the inside pocket of his jacket. "I switched letters," he said. He placed it on the table.

"You did what?" he asked.

"I switched the letter from the Cubans."

Johnson stared at the envelope and the tape, then looked back up to Spiro. "Right," he said. "You switched the letters?"

"Yes, I did."

"Spiro, you've changed history."

"You are still such a fool. I changed an event, not history. An event that history will never know of." Spiro waved his hands, as if clearing something from the air. "I'd stay longer if I could," he said. Then he smiled. "No, I wouldn't. We're done here."

"Yeah," Johnson said. "We're done."

Johnson walked Spiro out onto his front porch. "Good luck with the tapes," he said.

Spiro nodded.

They shook hands and he was gone.

Back in his kitchen, Johnson held the envelope out at arm's length. What the fuck could he do? It was over. Johnson opened the silverware drawer, slid out a knife. He sliced the envelope open and snapped out the letter.

Mi padre, it began in Spanish. My father... *Muchas cosas han sucedido para hacer nuestra vida diferentes.* Much has happened to make our lives different... Johnson read no further. He folded up the letter and pushed it back into its envelope. Sometime in the future, he might give it to someone. He wasn't sure who. In the meantime, he stuck it in a covered roasting pan and slid the pan back into the drawer beneath his oven.

Johnson planned to meet the Fat Man on the beach at eleven-thirty and drive him to a meeting in Lauderdale. Still only eight-twenty, he had a couple hours to kill. He slid Spiro's tape into Al's VCR and hit play. The interior of The Dunkirk room appeared on the Sony Trinitron. He saw Al, Helena, then himself. The light was good, the picture clear. Helena and Al touched each other's nipples.

Johnson's cock got hard.

###

ABOUT THE AUTHOR

Timothy Schmand

Timothy Schmand fled upstate New York's oppressive winters and settled in South Florida in 1982. He has spent the ensuing decades immersed in the human experiment known as "Miami." Schmand's award winning fiction has appeared in literary journals, popular magazines and anthologies, regionally and internationally.

Schmand's novel Just Johnson: The London Delivery was published by Jitney Books, a micro-publisher celebrating the best of Miami's literary talent. He holds an MFA from Vermont College.